# illegitimi

# illegitimi

## Light up the night

*Tyler Scott Ward*

Illegitimi by Tyler Ward

## Contents

## 1 Scott

As I walk into the public restroom, I noticed a large disheveled old man tagging along closely behind me. I will always remember that face. It was not the normal face of a passing bystander. I looked back and his eyes met mine. Mine were blue and his were black. They locked onto mine as his lips remained straight and his eyebrows furrowed. It was the face of a man that had a plan and this plan included me as the star. As I walked into the bathroom, I noticed that there were no other people in the restroom. I was hoping for someone else to be there as I began walking toward the urinal. It was just him and I walking in line with one another. I could hear his footsteps coming closer to me. I realized that I needed a "plan b" so I improvised. I increased my pace to a brisk walk and headed for the stall instead of the urinal. My plan was to enter, lock it, and figure out my next move.

I entered the stall, closed the door, and tried the lock. It would not latch completely closed so I tried again. I tried with all of my force and remembered the sharp metal edges nearly cutting my fingers as I heard his footsteps grow closer. I could now hear the scuffling of his dirty sneakers nearing closer and closer. The seconds turned into minutes, and it felt like time stood still. I see his sneakers stopped in front of the stall and I tried one last time to lock the door. No dice.

The door opens as I push with both hands. My feet slide backward as the door presses me back. It is now him and I in the same stall. A six-year-old boy and a grown man. Little did I know that I would have to fight for my life. Shit was about to get real.

I try the more "political" option and offer to let him use the stall first. I was sly even back then. He looked down at me and said, no I'll just watch you go first. His hands hit my neck and clamp down with more force than I have ever felt in my entire life. I can feel my blood pressure rising in my face and I know that I do not have much time. His other hand goes to the back of my pants as he tries to pull them off. I yell as loud as I can because I know that he will have to cover my mouth. I know that he is going to release my neck and cover my mouth or else his plan is foiled. It worked.

By this time, my pants are halfway off my legs. Only one shoe and my underwear and shirt remain. His hand is over my mouth as he is struggling to remove my pants still. Fuck this, I am biting down. I feel my teeth crunch into his hand as he lets out a gasp. I look into his eyes as they turn red with rage. At this point, he knew that he picked a kid that was willing to fight for his life. I saw his face, tasted the skin on his hand, looked into his eyes, and would forever hold a vivid image of him. The battle was won but my war was not over.

I feel his hand take the back of my shirt and the other on the back of my head. He grips my hair and I feel him pushing down. I am now facing the bowl of a public restroom toilet.

Deep breath, start counting. 1, 2, 3, 4, 5. I remembered when my father would tell me stories about bears and what someone should do when attacked by a bear. At six years old, this was the closest strategy that I could think of, and it would have to suffice. This was an attack by an animal, and I needed an exit. I hit twenty-three seconds. The longest twenty-three seconds of my life. I relaxed my shoulders, dropped my arms on the sides of the toilet and let my knees hit the ground. I was dead until further notice.

He releases his hand from the back of my head. As I slump out of the public restroom toilet, I keep my eyes closed and fall to the floor. I remember my skull crashing against the white dingy tile floor and the pain that came over me. I had to win an Oscar for this one or else I may not get out of there. I open my eyes just enough to see his feet walking out of the stall. I have water in my eyes as I see the stained discount store sneakers scuffling out of the stall. I knew that I had to stay quiet.

This is not how a normal childhood begins for a young man in the early 1990s, but it was mine. Random selection, luck of the draw, fate. The single action that mapped the course for the rest of my life.

**Perry:** "Scott, it's 0600 hours. Time to move, right now. The squad leader is about to take roll call before we head out again. We have to get to the ammo tent and pick up before 0630 and meet at the rendezvous point by 0700. It's a 1.5-mile ruck up to the ammo tent so let's move."

**Scott:** "Did anyone say where we are going?"

**Perry:** "You know the deal. We will find out on the way."

Perry was my best friend. We joined the air force together, went to basic training, and went through cyber training. Now we are together in Afghanistan. Situated somewhere along the mountains was a nice little outpost that never existed. Right before this deployment, we went to combat skills training somewhere in New Jersey and we did not understand why until three days ago. Air Force guys rarely see combat unless they accidentally get lost on a convoy or volunteer for air force special operations. We were neither. We were selected to go on special missions as cybersecurity experts.

Before this, we were comfortable behind keyboards at the Pentagon and were hacking our way into foreign adversary networks around the world. Any army that stood up to Uncle Sam has likely met my team on the glorious internet in some way or another. Our mission was simple to us as we both grew up in the typical fashion that most hackers begin: playing world of warcraft in our parents' basements until we were forced out. Joining the military seemed like the best option for us. Free school, cool technology, top secret missions, and rules… Lots of rules. I was never very good at following the rules. I guess that is what makes me an effective hacker. I live to bend the rules. Computers are simple. It is either a one or a zero. There are no in-betweens. Whether in hexadecimal, binary, or decimal, everything has an intended purpose, even when it does not belong. People were the only variables.

As we loaded up our M-4 rifles, extra ammunition, laptops, satellites, and radios, we heard someone shouting for us to change clothes. We were wearing our standard summer-weight desert camouflage, but this mission was different. We both dropped our bags, reached into them and pulled out a mini drawstring backpack. These were issued to us from the military and contained one pair of sand-colored cargo pants, socks, lightweight desert boots, and a long-sleeved sand t-shirt. We knew that when we were suiting up in civilian clothes that this was a black mission.

We waited for thirty minutes until three identical Toyota trucks pulled up with a driver in each. Eight of us split into each one of the trucks and were given a trifold mission briefing. This one was special. We were heading into the city to a safe house on the western edge. 5 days ago, Perry and I were finally able to locate a Taliban safehouse on the western edge of the city. We were working on this case for months, 118 days to be exact. Our target was different from the rest of the missions that we worked on. This one hit close to home.

Our target was the leader of a particularly savage group that specialized in kidnappings and ransoms. Since late 2001, the mission of the United States in Afghanistan had changed, and we became deeply invested in the security of this awful place. Since this group was causing such headaches for the political regime, they called in some special favors and my team was activated. The group had recently kidnapped the daughter of a well-known political figure and we were getting close. We had been following him online for months now and had managed to narrow our search down to an 8x8 block stretch of the western edge of Kabul.

See, my team didn't use any military-grade technology to put crosshairs on our targets. We stuck to what we were used to. About a month before this car ride through the desert, my team had located the head of this group online. We had managed to locate a forum on the dark web that was run by his group. The forum was used as a place where people could buy and sell basically anything illegal. Whether that be drugs, guns, hitmen, kidnappings, child pornography, body parts, you name it; you could find it there. We became accustomed to finding these types of forums as many of our targets operated on these channels. Some smarter than others but we had a one hundred percent success rate in mapping the physical locations of our targets.

This one was actually quite easy. Once we learned of the group operating on this particular forum, we had Dari, Farsi, and Pashtu linguists that initiated conversations online with them. We coached our linguists through exactly what should be said to them so as not to raise suspicions. We began to negotiate a business deal with them to become a new supplier of encrypted handheld radios. They loved that stuff. See, all of these jokers wanted to be like American spies. Deep inside each and every one of them was this longing desire to be important. When it comes to hacking humans, the ego is the best vulnerability and exploiting that is as simple as women picking up a guy at a bar. Step 1: Stroke the ego. Step 2: Gain trust. Step 3: Go dark and make them wait.

In the time that we "went dark" from the conversations online, our propaganda machine was creating a fake underground news story that was running through the dark web. This one was a story about a successful smuggle and trade operation that ultimately resulted in Turkish authorities seizing a truckload of encrypted radios. We had resources everywhere and we could write the truth. We had signature marks on all of our gear so that when we re-appeared online, our story would be fool proof.

Step 4: Re-engage the scumbags. We popped up online to initiate chats with them. We had several dark and angry messages from their group while we were away playing. We fed them the bullshit story about having to go dark because our shipment was seized in Turkey. Since they had already found out about that, the story seemed legitimate. It was not mainstream news so how they had found out was another story. We learned two things that day. We had gained more trust and there was a rat in the Turkish forces that was involved with underground crime in Afghanistan. Two birds and one load of camel shit. Bingo.

We did not care about the Turks. We wanted these guys, badly. We talked with them for days and days, leading them into our spider web until their curiosity grew and their egos exploded. They requested photos of our encrypted radios and we obliged. We knew that the group would not likely open a program and execute it for us, so we had to be a bit craftier than that. We wanted control of their computer or at least a grab at the information on their system. So, we used a little thing called steganography or otherwise known as "stego." You can actually embed malicious code within an image such as a JPEG, GIF, or another common image file format and actually hack into someone's computer without them ever executing or installing a program. What a time to be alive.

That is exactly what we did. We had a legitimate JPEG of a handheld encrypted radio from the Russian military. If we showed them one from the US, that may raise some suspicion. We marked the radio with the same logo that was on the seized radio shipment in Turkey and began working on the malicious code that would tag along for the ride. We loaded some simple code into the picture and formatted it to exploit the web browser of the victim. We knew that the image would only remain on the system for a few seconds, maybe a minute, so we needed to get the information quickly. We also figured that the group was anonymizing their location with some sort of a VPN before they even entered into the dark web. We knew exactly what information we needed from them. It would be difficult, but where there was a will, there was a way.

Malware packaged into the image, sent to target, target opened. At this point, we were sweating bullets just waiting for them to go off-line. However, we see a download on our server, and it is a 300KB file. We knew that we had something. The target responded back to us and put in an order for 1,200 handheld radios at full price. We told them that we would get the order ready and let them set the meeting place.

As we looked back to the file on our command-and-control server, we looked through the data that had been downloaded. We found out that they were anonymizing their IP address using a private VPN located in the

Netherlands. The system that they were running was only running in memory, which meant that it was basically a disposable system that was erased every time it was turned off. We sifted through logs, application data, browser history and nothing.

As I turned to my partner and said to him "check the network interface configuration," he looked at me and smiled. He knew exactly what I was looking for. You remember when I said that even the best criminals make mistakes? Here it was. We had the name of the wireless router that the computer was connected to. It was not a generic Wi-Fi SSID. It was actually quite unique and flavorful. ManchesterUnited1999. Apparently, these guys enjoyed watching soccer as much as anyone else. Manchester United won the European championship in 1999. Those details didn't really matter to us at all. However, the fact that we could go and find that Wi-Fi name was absolutely perfect.

About six hours later, we received the meeting point from them. Western edge of the city, leave the truck in front of the market. This is how they did things. No meeting, just a general location. However, they would almost always set up these "drop offs" within a 5-mile radius of their locations.

Going back to our mission now. We were heading out to the western edge of the city nearly 5 hours earlier than our planned meeting. We were going to a safe house about 500 meters away from the meeting point at the market. As we got closer to the safe house, Perry and I started to talk about what we would need to find them. The special operations guys in the car looked at us like we were crazy. They were an amazing group of guys. Three of them had been in more combat than they could remember. They were legitimate bad asses, and we were a couple of nerds riding shotgun with gaming computers and foggy glasses. Nevertheless, we had an important job to do.

As we got into the zone where the safehouse was, two of the trucks split off and we took the lead. We stopped in the back alley of the safehouse and grabbed our gear. Perry, our driver, and I ran into the backroom of the safehouse. It was eerily quiet inside and smelled like stale coffee beans. Very odd. I found out later that it used to be a warehouse for storing imported goods. This was probably a pretty active place given the central location. Now it was falling apart and riddled with bomb blast marks and infested with rats.

Our driver led us up a narrow stairwell in the back corner of the building. The stairs shook as the three of us lugged our gear behind us. I remember how loud the stairs were and thinking that if anyone were in here, we were definitely going to be shot. We made it to the third floor and were told to set up our gear. Perry and I knew that we had to be on the rooftop to get the best signal. The special operator with us told us that the area was an active Taliban stronghold and snipers were all over the place. Roof-top was out of the question. I knew that the heavy concrete walls were going to be a problem if we wanted to scan the area for wireless signals. We would get scattered results at best and if they were out of range, we could wrap this mission up in a few minutes.

We managed to convince the operator that we needed to set up our Wi-Fi scanning antenna on the roof. We did not have to be up there but needed to have the antenna there. He chatted on the radio and called for surveillance drone support to scan the nearby rooftops for activity. We waited over an hour for the all clear. We had a window of ten minutes to get to the rooftop, set up the antenna, and drop back down to the third floor. There was a hatch in the ceiling of the third floor that led to the roof. Perry went up, set up the antenna, and dropped the cable back down the hatch. I plugged it into my laptop and gave him a thumbs-up. He came back down and nearly broke his ankles jumping down. Remember, Perry and I were not combat operators. We were geeks in uniforms and body armor.

Here we go. We turned on our laptops and loaded up Kali Linux. The special operator was watching us as we powered up our laptops and he saw Perry's background as a dragon and mine was Inigo Montoya from the Princess Bride movie. He was rolling his eyes at the stereotypical nerds in the room. We didn't give a shit. These laptops were about to find some bad guys so he and the other trained killers could move in. We loaded up 2 programs, one was named Fluxion and the other was called AirCrack-ng. They were both designed to scan, locate, and hack into wireless networks. They were two of our favorites.

As I scanned the area, I told Perry to move the antenna to the east, then to the west, then north, then south. We had nearly 500 wireless networks within range of our location and were looking down the list. They had different names, some generic and some unique. Each wireless network that we picked up showed the strength of the wireless signal next to the name of the network or SSID. Some of the networks had very weak signals while others were extremely strong as if they were in the same building. We did this for about 10 or 15 minutes until I saw it: **ManchesterUnited1999**. Our antenna had a maximum range of 1.5 km, so this meant that our soccer buddies were southwest of our location within that 1.5 km range. There were signals weaker than theirs as their network had a medium-strength signal. They were close, very close.

Truck number 2 of our convoy was equipped with a mobile wireless network with a control name of Liverpool FC. It was a bit of a sick joke. We had to find the humor wherever we could. We were in hell over here and latched onto any form of comedy that we could. We instructed truck 2 (a.k.a. Liverpool FC) to head to the southwest corridor and stop exactly 1.5 km from our location. We saw their wireless signal come up on our screen. As they drove back and forth to and from our location, we began to track their wireless signal and their actual location. After almost two hours of doing this, we had this down to a relative science. We did this until Liverpool FC's signal matched the exact strength of ManChesterUnited1999. There was about to be a soccer match and we had front row seats.

We were about to make our next move. Perry began to jam the targets wireless network with Fluxion. We were doing something that we had done hundreds of times before. As we jammed their wireless signal, it kicked all of their connections off-line. When their computers automatically reconnected, the wireless password was transmitted, and we could capture it. We jammed their wireless signal over 10 times, waiting for someone to reconnect. Finally, it worked! We had the wireless password and could now log into the wireless network ourselves.

Once we were logged into the wireless network, we began to scan the systems on the network and set up a traffic listener called Wireshark. We were sniffing network traffic while simultaneously scanning internal computers for potential vulnerabilities. We found a relatively large list of servers and workstations attached to the network. In fact, we had over 20 servers and fingerprinted them as a variety of Windows and Linux systems. Someone had a lot of floorspace and tech running in this network. We finally found a system that had a suitable vulnerability, and it was ripe for exploitation. It was a Unix-based camera system server. We navigated over to the server in our web browser and were met with a default login page for a security camera system. I was thinking in my head, "please God let them be as dumb as our other targets." I tried the first combination of usernames and passwords:

1. Username: Administrator
2. Password: Password

No dice.

3. Username: Admin
4. Password: Admin

**In. like. Flint.**

We were now looking at the internal and external security cameras for the target facility. This could not get any better. We saw the outside landscape. In front of the building was a red jingle truck and a vendor selling some foods. In the back of the building, we saw an empty alley littered with plastic bags, trash, and a dog that was sleeping in the shade under a rusty metal awning. Inside, we saw seven military aged males. 2 of them appeared to be guards and were sitting in the front entrance atop a carpet on the floor. They were drinking tea or some sort of brown liquid. They were chatting and seemed to be completely unaware that we were about to destroy them. We heard the radio chatter calling for a quick reaction force to move into the block that we had pinpointed. Within a matter of twenty minutes, nearly 25 special operations personnel were closing in on the location.

We heard the commanding officer give the green light. Team one was positioned in the back entrance of the building, team two was covering the two side exits, and team three was approaching the front of the building.

Team three threw a flashbang grenade into the front door and the camera feed dropped. We were watching the camera on the second floor and saw the other 5 men taking up defensive positions inside. The operator with us informed teams 1 and 2 to enter the building while team three made it into the stairwell leading up to the second floor. It was like watching a beautifully choreographed performance as the three teams moved throughout the building. The two men at the front of the building were dead before they could even drop their teacups and pick up their AK-47's. The other men in the building were about to feel the wrath of professionally trained super soldiers, compliments of Perry and I and our knack for pounding on keyboards.

At the end of the day, two of the men inside survived. The other 5 were dropped like sacks of potatoes as we watched. The teams grabbed everything. Servers, hard drives, laptops, cell phones, SIM cards, maps, books, pictures, DVD's, USB drives. The two survivors received zip ties and bags over their heads as they made their way to their new homes on the other side of the mountains in an interrogation facility. All Perry and I cared about were the systems that had been seized. Those systems held the keys to potentially find kidnapping victims all around the country and save the lives of innocent men, women, and children that were caught up in this violent circle of evil.

## 2: Zone F

Anyone who stepped foot in the interrogation facility had heard of Zone F. It was something of folklore that was reserved for the worst of the worst. I mean, these guys were so bad that even the most seasoned terrorists wanted them dead. They were cruel, dark, and shadowy creatures that lived in the overcast of the most volatile countries in the world. This place was one in which, if you were placed there, you had less than a 0 percent chance of seeing the light of day again. There was an international agreement that these people were worth more alive than they were dead, but they deserved to be locked in solitary confinement for the rest of their natural-born lives. Among them were the most despicable people on the face of the Earth. They had caused so much damage to society that their mere presence was unacceptable. The criteria to be placed into Zone F was more difficult than most things in this world. Even if you were a mass murderer, you did not win an automatic ticket to Zone F.

There were stipulations that the person must have committed heinous crimes against children, and they had to have started loyal followings. These were the types of people in Zone F. Beyond rapists and murderers, the true evil of the planet that were located within 10 meters of my team. A hallmark for Zone F captives was something out of the ordinary, even for high security detainment facilities. When you are brought to Zone F, the public was made to believe that you were deceased. The reasons that this was a requirement ranged from many different perspectives, but the point was that as long as your followers believed that you were alive, your living presence was too dangerous to allow. There were many elaborate, and sometimes boring, stories of these prisoners being killed in military strikes, suicides and martyrdoms. However, we all watched presidential briefings and news stories all while knowing that they were locked in 5x5 foot cells to our left and right. It was almost comical to see the mass media stories about how these people were taken out. Some of them were actually quite creative and left me wondering if the person was actually dead or alive. It did not matter after all. They would never see the light of day again. When I say that, it's true. These scumbags were locked twenty feet underground in cells that had absolutely no lights, soundproof walls, and no chance of hearing the voices, screams, or cries of fellow inmates. They were spread fifty yards or more apart so that no sounds or light could travel to their cells while they sat there for the rest of their lives.

They were brought into the facility in the middle of the night, every single time without fail. We knew when they were coming in. Not because someone told us preemptively but because we could hear the rotors turning on a very special sort of helicopter. This helicopter was so distinctly quiet that you could only hear it when it was within about 100 yards of the landing zone. The landing zone was very close to our working offices so when they came in, we knew that it was one of the doomed. We called them the doomed because that is just what they were. Their life choices had brought them into the clutches of the beast, and they would never have even a remote chance of being free again. When they were brought into the landing zone, they were always accompanied by at least 4-8 professional and trained killers. These were not US Special Forces though. The first time that I saw them, I noticed that the men that jumped out of the helicopter never stepped foot in our facilities. They never wore military uniforms and were always dressed in civilian clothes. They never showed their skin and always wore long sleeves and gloves. Usually, they wore jeans and work boots with bulletproof vests on. They all made sure to wear masks that covered their faces and necks underneath their black tactical helmets. It was the strangest thing.

Even the CIA guys that were with us did not know who they were. We called them the demons because they always brought these scumbags to the last place that they would ever see. The demons brought these people in about once every 2 months or so. It was always exciting and frustrating when they did. We wanted to know who they were bringing in, but we never knew unless there were some news story weeks or months later. One night, something different happened and I will never forget it. 0200 as Perry and I sat in our work area playing Xbox, we heard the churning sound of the rotors. We rushed to the heavy brushed steel door and pushed it open. That gave us an unadulterated view of the helicopter landing pad. There was a small dirt road to the west side of the landing pad that was reserved for politicians and military commanders that were visiting the facility. It was always staffed by at least three people that were on guard.

Nobody ever used this entrance at this hour of the night. However, we noticed a small black Mercedes Benz ripping up the dirt road and coming toward the gate. The helicopter was approaching at the same time, and both were at about equal distance to the landing pad. As the car raced up the road, the guards at the gates radioed back into the command center and asked for permission to fire on the vehicle. We could hear the voice of the one-star US Army General, Damian Yost, telling them to stand down immediately and not to engage. General Yost was a nice guy from Kentucky that had made it through the ranks of the army. He had a farmer's handshake and always seemed to be a step ahead of the enemy. I had the chance to sit down with him for lunch at the chow hall and he shared some of his knowledge with me. He actually gave me some sound advice about my career

16

that I had envisioned when I was done with the military. I had a lot of respect for the guy and so did all of us. When the guards at the gate asked him to repeat his command, he said, "open the gate and do not check them." Perry and I both looked at each other with a bit of confusion. It was not standard protocol to let anyone into the facility without first checking them. We were in one of the most secretive and secure facilities in the entire Middle East and that was not something that had ever happened during our tenure there. Those gates opened up and the car came skidding across the sand and dirt courtyard as the helicopter hovered about twenty meters above the earth.

The car parked itself directly on top of the helicopter landing pad so that the pilot had to take the chopper down beside it. We knew there was something definitely not fucking normal about this situation. As the helicopter touched down, the car doors of the Mercedes opened up. Three men got out of the car quickly. One from the driver's seat, one riding shotgun, and one in the back. The driver opened up the backseat driver's side door and a woman stepped out. She had on a black burka, and you could just tell that she was somebody important. She looked at the helicopter and put her hand up. It appeared as though she was signaling them to stop and to not get out. Perry and I were looking around and waiting for General Yost to come out with his entourage of soldiers. It was literally Perry, me, the black Mercedes crew, and a chopper full of demons and God knows what kind of character they had onboard. Perry and I began to worry when the three men from the Mercedes pulled submachine guns out of the car and slung them across their chests. They raised their weapons at the helicopter as the woman began to walk toward it. One of the men on the helicopter jumped out. I had seen him before. He always wore cowboy boots and a big Texas longhorn belt buckle. He waved at us once when they were dropping off another scumbag. I thought that was pretty cool. I never saw his face but the chance of having another cowboy on a secret helicopter in the middle of the night was pretty rare. As he exited the helicopter, he turned around and signaled one of his crew members to get out.

The second guy began to exit the chopper behind an unknown man with one of the black cloth bags over his head. The cowboy demon and his second in command began to walk toward our facility with their captive. However, the three men from the Mercedes ran behind them and grabbed the captured man by the chain around his waist and began to pull him away from the demons. Within a matter of seconds, the courtyard erupted in shouting from both groups. Even the pilot of the helicopter jumped out and got into the middle of this. There were guns pointed in every direction by both of these groups. Perry and I were always armed but we were out of our comfort zone with this one. We got behind the steel door and left just enough space for us to see through while this shitshow unfolded. We watched the entire thing and I wish we never had. There was a lot of yelling in Arabic. This was not normal because most of the locals in the region spoke in Dari or Pashtu. This was the most common language that we heard among the people of Afghanistan. We heard the helicopter crew yelling in English and the Mercedes gang yelling back in both Arabic and English. The woman spoke perfect English without even a hint of an Arabic accent. That threw Perry and I off and we both looked at each other and said silently, "what the fuck is going on"? After about 3-5 minutes of intense yelling and arguing, the woman said to the helicopter crew that the man that they had captured was going to leave with them.

The cowboy began to cuss them out and pointed his rifle directly into the woman's face. I thought that shit was going to hit the fan. Perry and I had been calling for anyone via our radio but heard absolutely no response. We even yelled back into the hallway of our work center, but it was completely empty. It was like the place had been fucking abandoned. Even if people started shooting, who were we going to attack? We didn't even know who the people on the helicopter worked for, much less the assholes in the Mercedes. The woman leaned into the ear of the cowboy and whispered something to him. After a couple of seconds, he looked at his partner that had the captured man and signaled him to let him loose. You could tell by their body language that nobody from the helicopter crew was happy to do this. Cowboy's second in command yelled out, "fuck no! I ain't letting this sick bastard go. This mother fucker ate two years of my life looking for him and we're just going to let him go!? Chris died for us to catch this mother fucker, hell no man!" Cowboy looked at him and told him again, "Cut him loose man, we will get him again. This order is from the top man, let him loose!"

Cowboy's guy took the chains off from around his waist and pushed him toward the woman. She grabbed his hand and led him to the back of the car. They put him into the middle backseat of the car and took off his mask just as the back door was closing. We caught a glimpse of his face and the woman met eyes with us. We hit the deck quickly and could hear the rest of the car doors closing. We heard the car starting up and they hit the gas, kicking up rocks and dirt behind them as they sped to the gate. The demon crew began to squabble among themselves as we listened. We heard Cowboy shouting to them that they would get him again. It was a surreal moment and Perry, and I had no conception of how important this was. Cowboy told his crew to "mount up" and pointed to the helicopter. As they were walking back to the helicopter, we heard people running down the halls behind us. As I looked over my shoulder, I saw General Yost walking down the dark hallway with a group of officers and enlisted soldiers. They yelled at us to get back inside and stay put. We obliged and two of their group members were ordered to escort us back to our work area.

As we were being escorted back, we saw General Yost walking outside and talking with Cowboy. It looked like Cowboy was unhappy to see the general as he spat at the boots of him when he approached. That was the last that we saw of the situation outside as we were quickly brought back to our work area. The two men that brought us back inside stayed with us for about ten minutes or so until General Yost and the rest of his entourage came in. They shut the door behind them as we could hear the helicopter rotors winding up and taking off. We listened to the sound of the helicopter fade into the distance as the general pulled up a chair to Perry and me. When the sound of the chopped desisted, he ordered all but one of his men to leave the area. Now, it was General Yost, Perry, me, and a young army major named Pickens. I had seen Major Pickens around the camp before, but we never spoke. He was about six feet tall with a bald head and looked like the army created him in a lab. He had sunken eyes and seemed to be full of piss and vinegar. For some reason, I didn't trust this guy. He barely blinked but never took his eyes off me. General Yost was a nice guy and had a way of putting people to ease. He said to me, "son, I want you to tell me exactly what you saw. Start from the beginning." I looked at Perry and gave him a wide-eyed stare. I was trying to communicate with him without speaking.

I was reluctant to tell General Yost and his pit bull the truth because I had no idea what this all meant. All I knew was that a bad guy had just stolen from Mr. Cowboy and his crew, and this was ordered from the top. Before I could speak, Perry started talking a bit. He said that he saw the entire situation unfold and was there from the beginning. He told them that I came in right at the end after he called yelling for me to come out to the door. For some reason,

Perry was trying to keep me protected and I knew it. We saw something that we shouldn't have seen. The entire situation was fucked. We saw this evil person's face and the people who set him free. They were not Americans or any ally that we could decipher. Perry told them the entire situation. How they arrived, how many people, type of car, languages spoken, actions taken, types of firearms. He told them nearly everything. General Yost sat there and nodded his head as Perry explained, occasionally looking at me for validation. My reaction to Perry's explanation was surprise as I was not there, supposedly. This creep show, Major Pickens didn't take his eyes off me. He looked like he wanted to kill me the entire time that Perry and the general spoke. He didn't trust me, and I didn't trust him.

At the end of Perry's story, the general turned his chair to me and asked me if I had anything to add to the story. I told him that I came in at the last minute and only saw a car exiting the landing area and people walking to the helicopter. That was the extent of my excitement in this one. He asked me some general questions about where I was from, how old I was, and what my job was. He was just making small talk as I think that he realized that Major Pickens was putting me on-edge. After about twenty minutes of conversation, General Yost and Major Pickens looked at each other and the general got up and put his chair back to the desk that he retrieved it from. General Yost said to us that whatever we saw never happened. He told us that there was a mistake which led to the wrong person being captured and that he was set free before more confusion could ensue. Of course, I didn't believe this bullshit. The look on the faces of the helicopter crew said it all. They knew exactly who that man was, and they knew who those people were in the Mercedes.

This was no mix up; it was more than that and Perry and I were lucky enough to be in the middle of this soup

21

sandwich. General Yost proceeded to tell us that we were not authorized to speak about this event to anyone and if we had any questions about it to forget it because they would never be answered. Major Pickens didn't say a single word throughout the entire conversation. He just stared at me like a fucking robot killer. I swear that I was waiting for him to pull out his service pistol and shoot me. This guy had a screw loose and didn't think too fondly of me. The general thanked us for our time and explanation of the event and told us to have a good day. Just like that, they were gone. As they walked out of our work area, Major Pickens looked back with a stare that will forever be burned into my mind. However, he was not staring at me. He was looking at Perry with even more of a sinister look than he looked at me. The door to our work area slammed shut and Perry and I turned to each other with a confused and worried look. What the fuck just happened and what did this all mean?

## 3: Zulu

Perry and I were always together. We were close as two men could be without marrying each other. We worked together, studied together, trained together; shit we even lived together out there. After our shift, we left the facility and walked back to our quarters to call it a night. We worked night shift, so we departed the facility at 0800 hours to head back for some sleep. However, who could sleep after a night like that? We had questions but could ask anyone. On the walk back, we talked a bit about some other meaningless things. What we wanted to eat that day, how we wanted to go home, and what we were thinking about doing that morning. Neither of us said much about that night's events but I had to ask him something. I looked at him and asked him why he said that I wasn't there. He paused for a few moments and just said, "I don't know. It was the only thing that I could think of at the time." I knew that was bullshit and called him out for it. I asked him why he wanted to put himself in that position and leave me out of it. He calmly told me that it was better that way, and he did it because he cared about me. I understood but still couldn't grasp it. We skipped breakfast that morning and walked straight back to our tent.

We stayed in tents out there the entire time. They slept about ten people but ours was empty except for us. We had the whole place to ourselves which was pretty cool. It was dark inside so we could sleep during the daytime. He had his place set up on one side of the tent and mine was on the other side. We created a makeshift common area in the middle of the tent that we used for playing cards, working out, and relaxing. It was a shitty little mini apartment that smelled like a musty basement. We both got into the tent and went to our own sides. I began to unpack all of my pockets and take off my uniform. I took my magazine out of my rifle just to make sure there wasn't too much sand in it. I brushed it off and snapped it back into the rifle before leaning it against my locker. I could hear Perry opening his locker as I pulled back the covers on my bed, getting ready to call it a day. I was mentally exhausted and really needed some quality sleep.

It took me about an hour or so to get my mind cooled down enough to fall asleep but eventually I did. I woke up around 1500 hours and remember that I was extremely thirsty. I could taste the dust in the air as always when living in an area that closely resembled Mars. I got up and grabbed my shower gear and slid on my flip flops. I had planned to take a quick shower before grabbing some food and making a phone call back home. I walked to the other side of the tent to wake up Perry. I always had to wake him up. The guy slept like a rock. He would sleep through rocket and mortar attacks on a regular basis which made me envious of him. I always had trouble falling and staying asleep. As I approached his area, I noticed that his makeshift partition was taken down. It was a sheet that he had put up for sort of a privacy barrier, but it was gone. I walked into his area and noticed that he wasn't there. His bunk was made up, his sheet was tucked in, and all of his belongings were gone.

What the fuck man? There was nothing left. I walked over to his bunk and noticed a small piece of paper on his bed. I picked it up and unfolded it slowly. There were words on the paper. It appeared to be a short note. The note said, "Scott, I got transferred. I am heading to another camp. They have ordered me to support another mission because they are light on guys with our skillsets. I will give you a call when I get a chance. -Perry." I knew Perry. We were like brothers, and I know that he would have let me know if he was leaving. He had no reservations about waking my ass up in the middle of the night to show me some meaningless picture on his phone. This was way off and smelled like shit. It was shit and I knew it. What happened? Where did he go? Who made him go? Why did this happen right after the situation that we witnessed? Why did I get "tasked" to go? All very good questions that I just didn't have the answers to. As I looked at Perry's bunk, I started to look around for anything else that he may have left behind. In Afghanistan, we were not allowed to have any type of pornography. However, I knew where Perry had stashed his USB drive that was absolutely loaded with nearly every porn video that you could imagine.

He had a metal cap over the top of his bunk rail. He used to hide his illicit materials in the bunk rail within a USB drive. Sometimes, he would let friends borrow it for the night. Hey, the days are long out there, and you are prohibited from any sex, so you have to make do with your resources. I pulled out my Gerber knife and popped open the bed rail cap. I took out my flashlight and looked inside. I saw something about a foot down the tube. I looked on the floor for something to fish it out but couldn't find anything. I ran over to my bunk and grabbed a wire hanger from the locker and began to unravel it at the hook. I had an apparatus that could reach down into the tube, finally. I stuck the wire hanger down into the hole and I could feel it. It felt like metal on metal. As I tried to get underneath the object, I heard our tent zipper opening up and boots walking down the hallway of the tent floor. I quickly took the hanger out of the tube and put the cap back on. The footsteps were getting closer and closer very quickly as I put the metal cap back on the tube and threw the metal hanger on the floor and kicked it under Perry's locker. Just when I did that, I looked up and saw a young army sergeant staring at me. I had never seen him before in my life. I said to him, "can I help you?" He responded quickly, "Major Pickens has ordered you to meet him in Zone C in thirty minutes."

I told him that I would be there as soon as I got dressed. He nodded and walked out. I waited for him to leave the tent and peaked through the tent door to make sure that he was gone. I resumed my search for this fucking object in Perry's bed post. Finally, I got under the object and began to lift it out. I could see it. It was a USB drive, no bigger than an inch or two. I got it up to the top of the tube and pinched it between my fingers. I cut my right index finger reaching in for it as the top brim of the tube was sharp and I was in a hurry. I had it. I ran over to my side of the tent and looked out of the door to make sure that I was alone. I popped the USB drive into my laptop and waited for the folder to load up. Finally, it came up on the screen. There was only one folder, and it was labeled, "Zone F." What the fuck was going on? Am I in a movie or something? I didn't even want to open the damn thing but how could I not? I opened it.

What I saw still gives me chills to this day. Hundreds of pictures and videos. Each of them labeled uniquely; Project 1, Project 2, Project 3, etc... I was supposed to meet the major in ten minutes now, so I had to hurry along. Project 1; double click. A video pulled up on the screen.... There was a man. He was sitting on top of the trunk of a car. He looked familiar. He was holding a book but not reading it. He was just looking at the camera like he was waiting for someone to say something. The camera was shaky.

There were tanned rock walls in the background and the sun was shining. From the clothes that the man was wearing, this was definitely in the Middle East somewhere. The ground was covered in sand and dirt, but it was not dry enough to be Afghanistan. At least not the part where I was. Where I lived looked like the surface of Mars. Dead, desolate, and dry. The video went on for about thirty seconds until the man on the back of the car placed his book down on the trunk and got down. He

26

stretched his arms and legs like he was going to get a workout in. He was wearing tan cloth pants and a long green shirt that went down to his knees. He looked at the camera, smiled, and signaled for him to follow him. The camera followed him as he walked across the dirt road and under a rock gate, leading to what appeared to be a home. It was made of mud, rock, and sand just like the ones surrounding us in Afghanistan.

I could hear the camera man breathing while he walked behind him. The camera man had this weird groaning sound as he followed this guy through a small courtyard and into a dark stairwell. They began to walk down some stairs and it was completely dark. I couldn't see shit for about ten seconds until I saw a bit of light to the left of the man in the front. They came around a corner and a dim light illuminated the small room enough to see what was inside. It looked like a medieval underground tunnel with a room. No windows, doors, or any furniture; just a dirty floor and a small portable light on the ground. The camera panned to the left and the right and then finally zoomed into the man in front of him.

The man in front reached down at the ground at a metal handle. He grabbed it and began to pull upward. When he pulled the handle up, a small hidden hatch opened up. I could hear someone crying from within the room. It sounded like a child. It sounded like a young girl. She was saying something in another language that sounded like Arabic. The man leaned over and began to speak into the hatch as well. They talked for a few seconds. The camera man walked to the corner of the room and placed the camera on some kind of a stand and positioned it to the center of the room. I saw the camera man walk to the middle of the room and put his backpack on the ground. He opened it and pulled out a blanket and some kind of a dirty plastic box. The other man reached slowly down into the floor hatch and grabbed onto something. You could

27

see his back strain as he tried to lift something out of the hatch. Eventually, I saw hands, then arms, and then finally; a small boy being lifted out of the hole.

He was only wearing his underwear as the man pulled him out and placed him onto the blanket. The camera man opened his dirty plastic box, and I closed my laptop. I couldn't watch it. I knew what this was. This was the evil that I knew existed. Many questions began to flood my mind. I was angry. My heart was beating so fast that I thought my chest was going to explode. I was sweating profusely and wanted to jump into the video to help this young boy. I was confused. Why did Perry have this video? Why did he leave this here? Was he into some sick shit or was this a message to me? The situation was FUBAR--fucked up beyond all recognition.

Holy shit, Major Pickens! I was late. I had to go. I threw my uniform on my body and ran out of the tent. Wait! I forgot the computer and USB drive. What if someone found it? I ran back to the tent and grabbed the USB drive. I didn't want to leave it there, so I put it inside of my sock and tucked my pants back into my boot. I ran out of the tent and sprinted a couple hundred yards to the first Zone F entrance. This was the same entrance where the guards from last night were ordered to let the Mercedes in. I knew them so I knew that they would let me right in without checking my ID card. I got up to the gate, but I didn't recognize these guys. They were new. "Where are the other guys?" I spoke. They told me that they were shipped out early this morning for another mission. Naturally these guys had to check my ID and call into Zone F for authorization to let me in. It took them a good 5 minutes to do so. I was about ten minutes late for my meeting with Major Pickens.

I was not in a good place and was rushing these guys to hurry up. I heard Major Pickens voice come over the radio and tell them to let me in. I ran through the gates and into Zone F. When I arrived at the big steel door, it opened before I could touch the handle. Major Pickens was right there. He had eyes that were so dark that they looked black even when the Afghanistan sun was shining on his face. He told me that I was late, and I nodded and apologized. I told him that I lost track of time trying to find my dog tags that I take off every night to go to sleep. I didn't expect him to believe me. He responded, "follow me. I want to have a chat with you." We began to walk down the concrete floored corridor leading to the south wing of Zone F. The south wing was where the medics were stationed and was reserved for treating inmates for various injuries and illnesses. I had been down there a couple of times in my tenure here but not much.

We walked past the cell blocks and medical units. As we approached a stairwell, I looked behind me and couldn't see anyone within earshot or screaming distance for that matter. I followed Major Pickens into a stairwell and walked into a small office. It was made of corrugated metal and had a single desk, computer setup, chair, and a small bookshelf with some pictures on it. Major Pickens pulled out his chair and dusted off the seat. He sat down as I stood in front of his desk. He was twirling a pencil in his fingers and told me to relax. I asked him if he had something specific, he wanted to talk to me about. He paused and took a deep inhale before looking at the ceiling very quickly and looking back at me. His eyes widened like he was trying to signal something to me. I knew every camera within this facility and knew that there was one directly above my head. I also knew that there were not any microphones on the cameras in the medical wing of Zone F. He looked back up one more time before beginning to talk to me. His first words were, "I am going to ask you a series of questions and I want you to respond to me honestly. I want you to look at me and only me the entire time while you tell me your answers." I knew what he was trying to say. He didn't want the cameras to pick up my mouth movements and he was trying to tell me that we were being watched. Should I trust him? Why should I trust this man? He still looked like he wanted to scalp me and wear my skin. This guy fit the bill for a complete sociopath.

What the fuck should I do? His first question: I want you to tell me everything that you know about the men in the helicopter last night. He put his pencil down on the table and made a circle with the eraser while looking right at me. I said, "well, I was working on compiling intelligence for the previous mission that Perry and I went on. As normal, we heard the helicopter rotors coming in closer to the landing zone. Perry got up and ran to the door. I was so immersed in my intel file that I didn't get up this time." Before I could get out another word, he looked at me and said, "try again. This time, tell me the truth. Start over." I knew that he knew. He knew that I saw the entire situation unfold. How much did he really know though? Should I tell him everything? I didn't know what happened to Perry or the guards from the gate. How could I be certain that this guy wouldn't make me disappear as well? I started again from the top. It was me that went first to the sounds of the helicopter blades turning. I opened the door and Perry followed. I was the one that saw everything unfold as it happened. I told him everything that I saw that night. He continued to nod while tapping his pencil on his desk. I was sweating inside of my body as I unveiled what I saw. I still had no earthy idea of what actually happened. All I knew was that some people showed up and took this prisoner away from the men on the chopper. It was not pretty, and it looked like neither of them were too fond of each other. He asked some more questions, and I told him my account of the events.

The last question that he asked was about Perry. He asked me if Perry had said anything to me before he left.

I told him no and then he left a short note explaining that he was being repositioned for another tasking. That was it and it was the truth. I left out the details of the USB drive that I found. I still had no idea if that had anything to do with this or if my best friend was into some really sick shit. He responded, "is that it?" I said, "yes sir. That is all that I can remember at the moment." He looked at me and told me that I was dismissed. I stood there in disbelief as I was sure that I was going to get a black bag over the top of my head. I turned and walked toward the door leading to the stairwell. Major Perry said, "one more thing. I am going for a run around the base tonight. I heard that you are a solid runner. Aren't you training for a marathon, son?" I confirmed that I was a runner and was indeed training for a marathon back home in the states. He said, "good. Meet me at 2100. We will run together tonight." I nodded and walked down the stairs. I felt like someone was watching me, like it was a game, and my time was soon coming. I couldn't make sense of any of this, but I knew that something wasn't right. I was right in the middle of something serious, something big. I stepped into a lion's den, and I couldn't see any way of getting out.

## 4: Bright Lights

All of the events that have transpired over the last day are making my head race. It's as if I have been awake for a week. The headache in the back of my eyes radiates to my shoulders. I had some Percocet stashed in my locker from when I blew out my shoulder. I was in a Humvee rollover a while back in training and it bothers me every so often. The military docs are great. Percocet for anything above a pain level of seven. Since you cannot measure pain, I was always a solid eight. Anything under a pain level 7 is treated with Motrin and/or antibiotics. In my military career, I took more antibiotics than ten humans should consume in a lifetime. I digress.

I pop three pain pills into my mouth and drop them back with a warm water bottle on the floor beside my bed. As I stripped my uniform for some running gear, I wanted to find a place to carry a knife on me. When you're wearing running shorts and a tight tee shirt, there are no clear places to conceal a deadly weapon. I had actually become fairly proficient in Brazilian Jiu Jitsu during my time back at home station, so I wasn't all too worried. If something were to happen, it would involve the type of people that could make me disappear; regardless of if I had a knife, gun, or even a grenade. If I was fucked, I was fucked.

I walked toward the edge of my tent and lifted the door flap. It was cooling off at night and the red hue of the desert lit up the nights. It was actually quite peaceful when the bombs and mortars weren't dropping. As I walked toward the spot that Major Pickens had set up, I wanted to run in the other direction as fast as I could. Where was I going to go through? The entire area was surrounded by malicious insurgents and other Taliban forces. I would be labeled as a deserter and thrown in Leavenworth even if they did find me. If the Taliban found me, I would have my dick cut off and shoved into my mouth with a black flag behind me. The last thing that I would see would be a machete swinging toward my neck before I went headless horseman. The options were shit and I knew it. I didn't have a helicopter exfil coming to get me this time. I was on my own and I had nobody. I had the overwhelming feeling that I was walking back into that bathroom stall. A predator was lurking, and I had a fight coming. I just knew it. I put my shoulders back and walked forward. Head up.

I approached Major Pickens and saw him standing there talking on a satellite phone. I was about fifty meters or so away from him when he saw me and ended his call. He had a small backpack on and put the sat phone back into the front pouch. I couldn't tell what else he had in that pack, but it was certainly large enough for a pistol. No doubt. I walked up to him and nodded. He had the same killer look on his face that he always did. His eyes had some serious shit going on behind them. It was like his brain was screaming but his face always remained static and unwavering. He looked at me and said, "I didn't think you were going to come out tonight. When you left my office, you looked like you were planning on commandeering a vehicle to get out of here. You wouldn't do that though…"

My face said everything. I was always bad at hiding my rage. I wanted to take this guy out and make a run for it. We started walking away from the base. As I looked behind us, I could see us going further and further away from the camp. I didn't want to drift too far away. Maybe one of the troops at the camp could hear me if I needed to call for help. Nevertheless, we picked up a jogging pace and went forward. In front of us, I could only see desert for the next 5-7 kilometers and then mountains. The Hindu Kush mountains had a certain appeal to them. You couldn't mistake them for any other mountain in the world. They were grand, red, and went on as far as you could see. Major Pickens started to run faster as I ran alongside him. We ran without speaking for nearly 15 minutes before he said, "we are going to pick up the pace a bit." We were in an all-out sprint. I looked behind us and could barely see the camp anymore. Just the front gate station. We sprinted for 3-5 minutes and then Major Pickens brought it down to a walk. He said, "you can run boy. Are you getting winded at all?" I wasn't even close. I had been preparing for a marathon for months now. I could run a full sprint for twenty minutes without slowing down. I had some legs on me. I always felt like I was running toward something, not away from it. My whole life, I ran toward things of danger, not in reverse. But I never really wanted to be in danger. I was fucked up.

Major Pickens stopped suddenly and so did I. He looked back at the camp and squinted. He pulled out a pair of tactical binoculars and peered back at the camp's location. Then, he panned across the desert with the binoculars and over toward the southeast mountain range before putting them back into his pack. He looked at me and said, "can we trust each other for a minute here"? I was nervous and said "of course, sir." He proceeded to ask me again if Perry had left anything behind. "Anything at all"? I dropped my shoulders back and repeated myself. "Sir, I told you already. He left nothing. What more do you want me to say, respectfully"? He let out a sigh and told me that Perry had information that was very sensitive. He said that he and Perry had been working on a "side project" and he entrusted Perry with certain information that was on a small digital device. He needed to have that "small digital device" out of everyone's safety. I looked at him with a confused gaze and told him that I would check again, but I had no fucking idea what he was talking about. I had to get emotional here. What if he already knew? I said, "sir, did you bring me all of the way out here to ask me that? If so, I am out of here. I need some sleep." He said, "No, I did not. Walk with me. I want to show you something."

He pulled out his binoculars again and panned across the desert. Then, he gazed toward the camp again. He looked up in the sky as if he were looking for drones or something. The Taliban didn't have fucking drones. I was confused to say the least. He pulled out the satellite phone, punched in an 11-digit number and handed it to me. He had not pressed the dial button yet. I looked at the small and dimly lit green digital screen and read the numbers back to myself in my mind.

- 7: Country code for Russia
- 89: The year my little brother was born
- 12: My best friend's birthday month
- 1945: The year WW2 ended
- 7: Great movie
- 3: My lucky number

I was good at remembering numbers if I broke them down like this. Major Perry said, "dial the number son." I pressed the white dial button. It was slightly illuminated as it was getting a bit dark out now. I pressed the phone to my ear, and it buzzed with a foreign ring signal. Definitely not US A Russian robot voice said something as if it were connecting my call. I had listened to enough Russian in my tenure that I could pick up a little bit.

The ringing stopped and I heard some static.

"Hello?"

I knew this voice.

**Me**: "Perry?! Is that you man?"

**Perry**: Yes, it's me. I am ok man. I am good. I'm with some good people here. Is General Yost with you?

**Me**: No, I am with Major Pickens.

**Perry:** Ok.

**Me:** Where the fuck did you go man? You scared the shit out of me. You must have left in a hurry?

**Perry:** There's no time for that man. I need you to follow Major Pickens. It's not safe there. I don't know if I will be safe here for long either. They might be moving me again.

**Me:** Moving you where? What the fuck are you talking about man? What is going on? Give me something!

**Perry:** Listen man, don't trust anyone other than Major Pickens. Nobody! Not even the fucking contractors cleaning the latrines there. This shit is deep man. We saw too much, and they know it.

**Me:** Holy shit man. What is this?

**Perry:** I can't tell you much more man. All I can say is that I am safe right now. I don't know where I am going. They won't tell me. I need you to do me a favor. Can you promise me something man?

**Me:** Anything. Of course.

**Perry:** Silence

That's all he said. Silence? What the fuck is going on? The phone line went dead. The last thing he said was "silence"?! As I handed the phone back to Major Perry, I read the screen again. I had to remember the number.

- 7: Country code for Russia
- 89: The year my little brother was born
- 12: My best friend's birthday month
- 1945: The year WW2 ended
- 7: Great movie
- 3: My lucky number

He asked me what Perry said. I told him that all he said was that I should trust you and you only. Nobody else. Major Perry nodded with a look of approval. I was not going to tell him what the last word he said to me was. "Silence"….What does he mean? What if he was talking about the files that he stashed? If he told me to trust Major Pickens, why wouldn't I tell him? I wasn't about to tell Major Pickens what I found. Not yet. This could be a setup. I could be dead. They could have just killed Perry and I wouldn't know anything. I read the numbers back in my head again.

- 7: Russia
- 89: Little brother
- 12: Best friend
- 1945: WW2
- 7: Movie
- 3: Lucky

I repeated it in my head five more times and found a phrase to remember the number. I can't write it down, so I have to retain this information. I was good at learning this way. I am good with numbers and sequences if I can map them to words.

"Russia stole my little brother and best friend. WW2 made many movies and three is my lucky number"

7-89-121-9573

Major Pickens then turned to me and told me that Perry had been a part of a 2-year investigation into some high-ranking political members from Afghanistan. He didn't mention much more than that before I asked him how this has anything to do with me. He firmly grabbed me by the back of my head, looked me dead in my eyes and told me that I had witnessed one of the high-ranking politicians being extracted from the helicopter. Remember the cowboy and how furious he was to have to release that man? Well, that man was obviously extremely important to whatever the fuck was going on. I asked Major Perry what the investigation was about. "Was it regarding chemical weapons or counter insurgency operations, like usual?," I said.

Major Pickens: "This is not the usual op that you have been working on this tour. This is bigger, broader, and involves the most sinister characters in the Middle East. We don't give a flying fuck about chemical weapons, nukes, missiles, or insurgents here. This mission cuts to the core of humanity. We are the last line before this plague sweeps across Europe, Asia, and eventually the United States in a way that we have never seen before."

Me: "Major, is this about drugs and the heroin cartels in Afghanistan?" I have worked some counter ops for this mission, and it is very intricate. The players in the heroin space in Afghanistan are absolutely ruthless. They supply more money to the insurgency, Taliban, Al-Qaida and Al-Shabab than all gun running ops combined. Stop the drugs, stop the money. Stop the money, make the bastards show their faces. Show their faces; meet the might of the US Department of Defense.

Major Pickens: "No son, this is bigger and more sinister, as I said. This is not a common mission and unfortunately it runs through the highest ranks of government in the Middle East and globally. It is a

38

problem even for the US" This is about children. The children of the world, not just the Middle East, not just Afghanistan. This is about the children. They are alone and we are their only hope…

Me: "Children, sir?"

I thought he was fucking joking. I mean, I know that there are millions of missing kids in the Middle East, but third world countries seem to all have that same problem.

Major Pickens: "We have been tracking the sources of the largest and most prolific child extortion and prostitution rings in the world for the last two years. This is an ongoing operation that involves only a handful of people. Our agents are not CIA, they are not uniformed military, nor any other US agency that exists. We are ghosts.

I thought to myself: Perry was involved in this shit? For how long? Does this make any sense? I mean, my best friend involved in a ghost operation for two years? We are practically brothers. I would have known. I don't trust this at all. What if Major Pickens knows about the videos and pictures that Perry left behind and is just trying to pull something out of me? What the fuck did Perry have on that drive? Holy shit, I am so fucked. They're going to kill me. I know it.

Major Pickens then went on to tell me more details. He said that I couldn't trust anyone anymore. Absolutely nobody. He said that the depths of this operation and who may be involved is currently unknown. They had been working on a particular political figure from Afghanistan, the guy in chains from the helicopter, when everything went south. Major Pickens said that he had suspicions of high-ranking US military officials and Department of Defense civilians that were likely top dogs in this sick fucked up chain and he was working some sources to bring them close. Major Pickens told me that a certain US general on the camp is involved, and he was assigned as a mole to bring him down. However, this "certain US general" is getting his orders from higher. This means that this situation is above the general.

Me: "Major...Above the general means..."

Major Pickens: "The Pentagon or the White House. Correct, son. That's correct."

Jesus Christ. What did I fall into? I wanted to run. I wanted to run anywhere but where I was. My heart was beating so fast that my chest felt like it was going to explode. My face got hot, and I was dizzy. I squatted down and stared at the ground for a minute, not saying a word. If this is all true, even a little bit of it then I am a man on borrowed time. So would be Major Pickens, as well as my best friend. As we started to walk back to the camp, we were both quite silent. What more was there to say? We were going to be hunted. I saw something that day with Perry on the helicopter pad and someone knew it. If they rushed Perry out, when would I be exfiltrated? Or would I be exfiltrated in a box?

As we approached the fence line of the camp, Major Pickens said to me, "You can only trust me. If you say a word of this to anyone else, they will come for you. If anyone asks you about this, what we talked about; tell them that we are training together for a marathon, and you are showing an old guy how it's done. Be fucking natural and act cool. The walls have fucking ears in this place and if you want to make it home on two feet, keep your mouth fucking shut. Even if they torture you, your mouth stays fucking closed. If anyone tries to take you anywhere other than your normal work zone, find a way out. Find an excuse and come get me, ok?"

Me: I nodded

Major Pickens: "Do you fucking get it?!"

Me: Yes, sir. I understand.

We walked through the gate, and he waved at the two guards standing duty. They saluted him as he walked through the gates, and he threw a fast salute back to the two guards. They knew him to be an officer. Everyone knew this guy. As I said, he had a presence about him that people feared or respected. We split our different ways. He split off toward the officer's quarters and I went toward the enlisted tent areas. I was in row 4, tent B-1. It was about ¼ mile from the gate and fence area. They put the enlisted guys at the front of the base and the officers in the middle so that if shit hit the fan, we would be the first hit. God bless the US military.

## 5: Beyond the Wire

That night, I laid in my bunk thinking. A million things ran through my mind. I went back to my childhood and remembered how I felt that day in the bathroom. It was similar to what I felt right now. Stuck. I felt stuck. None of my options were good options. I couldn't fight back, or at least I didn't see a way to fight back. I couldn't play dead. I couldn't run. Where would I go? If I called for help, I would give up my position. I couldn't fully trust anyone at this point. I even had my doubts in trusting Perry. He had known about this for a long time and never uttered a word to me. What kind of friend does that? Then, I thought about it a little more. Perry didn't want me to get involved in this. Maybe he got involved in a similar way as I did. Maybe he made a mistake or saw something that he shouldn't have seen. Maybe that's how he got wrapped up into this spider's web. Who knows? I don't know if I will even ever see him again anyway so what the fuck does it matter?

I sat up in my bed and turned my flashlight on, pointed to the floor so that I wouldn't draw any attention to myself. "Russia stole my little brother and best friend. WW2 made many movies and three is my lucky number" 7-89-121-9573. I wrote down in my notebook this phrase. I didn't write down the number as if someone found it, they wouldn't be able to decode my message. My pen struck the top of the page, "Russia stole my little brother and best friend. WW2 made many movies and three is my lucky number." Damn, I have to get ahold of him, I thought. I don't have a sat phone with me and even if I did, how do I know someone isn't listening? I couldn't call him. No fucking way. I didn't even know if he was under duress or even being tortured when I talked to him. He could be hanging from a ceiling in some meat locker right now while they are peeling his skin off. These people were sick fuckers over here. You couldn't trust a single one of them.

I remembered back in the interrogation facility when a few of the Afghanistan National Army guards were actually undercover Taliban. They managed to throw a handful of grenades into the mess hall one afternoon and blew up about eight soldiers in broad daylight. When I said that you couldn't trust anyone, now I really understood what that meant. I thought about General Yost. He was always on my radar. For some reason, ever since I was a 6-year-old boy, I could just smell bad people. It was like I had a radar that sounded an alarm whenever a malicious actor was near me. General Yost gave me that feeling before. However, so did Major Pickens. Maybe I was wrong about Major Pickens though. I had no idea. My mind was wandering like a lost camel in the desert sand. For a minute, I actually thought about leaving the wire at night and going AWOL. Maybe if I went AWOL, the military would find me, bring me straight to Leavenworth, lock me up and I would be back in the USA where I could reach out to a lawyer and get some protection. However, if this was as deep as I thought it was, it wouldn't take long for someone to choke me in my cell with a wet bedsheet. They would say it was suicide. The prison cell cameras would conveniently go dark, or the guards would be distracted. I know how this works and have seen corruption in other countries. They can reach out and touch anyone, at any time, however they like. The news wouldn't even hit CNN. I'd be dead and cremated by the time anyone even uttered foul play. AWOL was out of the fucking question for me. No way.

I turned my flashlight to my left boot. I had stowed away the USB drive in there. My mind was running again. I needed to know what Perry saw. I needed to see through his eyes. I knew that this would drive me deeper into a place that I couldn't return from so easily. When I was a late teenager, I had stalked the man that stole my soul that day in the bathroom. I knew that this subject of children was one that was near to me. If I flipped that switch on, turning it off wasn't an option. What if I could help someone? What if I could help even one of those kids or at least help Perry? I thought about it for a few minutes before making a move. I reached for the boot, put my hand inside, lifted up the sole, and felt the cold plastic of the USB drive in my fingers. I pulled it out and set it on my lap. My stomach turned at the thought of what evil lurked on this fucking thing. I grabbed my computer from under my bed and placed it beside me on the cardboard box that I used as a nightstand. Placed it into my computer, pressed the power button and my screen lit up. I knew it would change my life forever. I couldn't turn away.

Video after video of the most sadistic, ruthless, and horrible footage that I have ever seen. There were thousands of videos and pictures of this. Brutal killings of children, violent rapes, horrible mutilations, and worse. There were adult women involved, grown men from ages 20-75 or so, and so much fear in the eyes of these children. They were helpless and I was watching the last moments of some of their lives. I cried for hours sifting through the footage. Tears streamed down my face as I had overwhelming feelings of anger. One of the videos was so horrendous that I had to turn it off. It was twenty-four full minutes involving a three-year-old girl. The look on her face was not of any fear that I had ever seen. She would try to smile at these mother fuckers in order to make them stop. It was too much, and I was in a dark place. I had discovered an evil that I never knew the depth of...

That video was the last one that I was able to watch before running outside of the tent and violently vomiting for nearly 20 minutes. I vomited until I couldn't breathe. I rolled over in the sand and rock and whimpered like one of the children in these horrible videos. I remembered my little brother. I remember lying on the bathroom floor when I was six years old. How could there be such evil in this world? How could something like this be happening in the dark corners of humanity?

I laid there silently looking up at the night sky. It was a beautiful night as I lay there. The wind was cooling across the desert sand, but not too strong as to kick up dust. The sky was perfectly clear that night and all of the stars were bright and glimmering. No bombs bursting in the distance. No chirps of AK-47 fire coming from the mountains. Everything was still. As I laid there in peace, I wondered if some of the children were still alive. I prayed to God that someone was helping them. Those poor babies in the hands of monsters. I felt guilty simply being alive at that moment. It was not a feeling of suicide, just guilt for me being safe. I wanted to take the place of that 3-year-old girl. Her smile was her only defense mechanism, and she had no idea that it was all in vain. A smile was her final effort to save herself. The purity of children made me cry again and again that night as I lay there in the rock and sand. I was lost, the children were lost, our world was burning. Hell was not a biblical place of mythology, and it wasn't a place that bad people went when they died. It was right fucking here, and human beings were the devil.

I rolled off the sand after nearly two hours there and crawled back in through the door flap of the tent and immediately closed the lid of my computer. I simply couldn't carry on any further and watch this. There were hundreds more that I didn't look through. I couldn't do it. I cleaned my face up with wet wipes as I was covered in dried sand and dirt from the tears and laying on the ground outside. I kneeled down at my bedside and pulled out the Saint Christopher medal that my mother had given me before I left for this awful place and prayed. I prayed not for myself but for the children. I prayed for them hard and then I prayed for their salvation. However, I knew that

45

it was too late for most of them. I had watched their last moments and it was eating me alive.

That night, I was in and out of sleep. I would close my eyes and go to sleep only for a few minutes before I woke up with a feeling as if I were free falling. I sat up in my bed with my pistol and flashlight nearly every hour until morning came. From 0430 to about 0700, I managed to get a bit of sleep. Although, when I woke up, I was exhausted. I was mentally checked out and my brain was foggy. It was time for me to report to my post. I got up and cleaned my entire body with water from the plastic bottles that were sitting on a wooden pallet outside. I used some paper towels to wipe the dust residue from my face and neck. Maybe if I cleaned myself off, I would feel a little better. It did give me a bit of relief. However, the pain was still ever-present in my heart and soul.

I donned my uniform, put on my bulletproof vest, and grabbed my helmet. For some reason, I felt compelled to load up that morning as I readied myself. Maybe my mind was in a state of trauma, and I was just on-edge. I stacked up 4 extra magazines for my rifle that morning and two extra magazines for my pistol. I carried an Italian-made Beretta 9mm. Not my favorite pistol but it did the job. Italians are much better at food, art, and culture than weaponry, in my opinion. I was a fan of Glocks. They were made right, and I was a fanboy of Austrian weapons. My rifle was the classic M-4. I liked the size of the rifle as opposed to the M-16 A2 that many of the other guys carried. The M-4 was lightweight, and it was great for urban areas that are riddled with maze-like walls, spanning building to building. I wasn't a combat guy, per se, but you just never knew. We would get called out on patrols from time to time and we had to play a part in the bigger picture of the war.

I walked across the tent areas and onto the thin dirt road leading to the complex that I worked in. It was already above 100 degrees outside, and it was still early in the morning. It was going to be fucking brutally hot today. The intense heat sometimes made the mental stress go away. All you could focus on was the heat, nothing else. Every day, I was soaked in sweat. There weren't many areas that actually had air conditioning but when I found one, I tried to always stay away from them. See, when you are living in a climate like this, going to an air-conditioned area for an extended period of time just makes the heat feel even worse. As I approached the side doors of my work area, I looked off into the troop staging area and noticed three Humvees and an MRAP (Mine Resistant Ambush Protected) vehicle. The MRAPs were pretty badass rides. If you had to go across the desert, those were exactly where you wanted to be. I found them safer than most vehicles as the bottom hull of the MRAP was V-shaped. The V-shaped hull was designed to deflect the blasts of improvised explosive devices (IED) if you were to run one of them over. The blast would radiate outward and away from the vehicle rather than concentrating inward. The Humvees were literal death traps. They were small inside, cramped, and in the shape of a fucking refrigerator. I mean, it was almost like the DoD wanted people getting blown forty feet into the air if they ran an IED over.

As I looked around the side of the MRAP, I saw one of the small dune buggies as well. Those belonged to the British special forces or SAS. Those guys were absolute lunatics. They preferred dune buggies. Two men up front. One driving, other riding shotgun. Two men would stand on the back rails of the buggy so that if they hit an IED, the two guys would either jump off or get blown into the air. They said that they had a better chance of surviving than riding in a Humvee. They were insane but I really enjoyed going outside of the wire with them.

I stepped into the door and walked down the hallway. It was about a one hundred yard walk down a narrow corridor before reaching the center atrium of the facility. As I approached the atrium, I heard the whirling of helicopter blades revving up. A chopper was taking off. I know the sound of a Blackhawk, but this sounded like a Chinook. Chinooks were used to carry large amounts of troops. Usually 15-30 men. I came into my work zone and noticed Major Pickens talking to a group of younger officers and a handful of enlisted guys. There was a female analyst there as well. I knew her as I had worked on an operation with her a few weeks back. She was a counterintelligence analyst, and she was fluent in at least five languages that I knew of. Most of the languages were Middle Eastern but she knew Russian and Chinese well enough to work counterintelligence operations with the CIA that were at the black site. She was holding a manila folder that was opened. I wasn't close enough to catch a look at it but as I walked past the group, on my way to my station, Major Pickens signaled me over to him with a head gesture. He looked concerned. His eyebrows were furrowed as he glanced my way. The whole walk over to him, we were deadlocked at the eyes. It was like he was trying to tell me something. I couldn't tell what it was. Maybe he was saying, "keep cool" or "run." Who the fuck knew what he wanted to say? He was an enigma anyway. Maybe he had bad coffee this morning.

As I walked up, the group looked at me and nodded. I didn't know any of them. Not that I could remember anyway. Except for the female analyst. Her name was Jones. Well, her last name was Jones. I didn't know her first name as we were not close. But I had remembered her from the past operation that we were involved in. She was cool and laid back. Super fucking intelligent and she knew it too. Everyone listened to her, even though she was a young, enlisted army solider, maybe around 21-23 years old. She knew her shit when it came to intelligence, counterintelligence, and linguistics. I was fluent in Brazilian Portuguese. That was my second language. Kind of useless in the middle of Afghanistan but I learned when I was in junior high and into high school. My mother and father started a business operation in Brazil when I was young. They setup a health supplement production factory in Brazil and brought the family with them. I had been to Brazil 7-8 times before I had graduated from high school and learned the language pretty quickly. I kept practicing nearly every day, even out there in the desert. I kept a notebook in my right cargo pocket of my pants and learned new words and phrases each day to keep me sharp. I really enjoyed the Latin-based languages and the culture of Brazil. Peaceful place, yet dangerous and deadly. It had some alure to it for sure.

The group was talking about a mission. Some kind of operation outside of the wire. They were looking at a digital map on a tablet computer that one of the other soldiers was holding as Major Pickens pointed to the device. I spoke up when there was a break. "Sir, did you need me for something?"

**Major Pickens:** "Scott, glad you could join us today. Orders came down from the top. We are heading out this morning at 0800 hours. We have a quick pick-up mission as the top believes that a confidential informant (CI) has information on one of the top Taliban leaders in Easter Afghanistan. Our job is to go and pick him up. He and his family live about 100 km from here and it's a quiet zone. No need to bring a shitload of supplies on this one guys. We should be back here within four hours and home time for chow."

**Me:** "Sir, with all due respect, I am behind on some reports that I have to get to. Is there a specific need for me to come along on this one?"

**Major Pickens:** "You've been tasked from the top as well. They need a cyber guy to do a data dump on any hard drives that are in the building. They believe that there may be valuable intelligence within the facility."

Major Pickens looked to the group and said, "remember guys, this is a pickup of a friendly informant. No kicking in doors today, you hear me"? Yes, sir, the group said in unison.

I thought about it for a second while the group continued to listen to Jones's rundown on the area and subject. Maybe the major just wanted to keep me close because he was afraid that something could happen to me if I wasn't close to him. I'd like to think that was the case anyway. I caught myself daydreaming when Jones was asking me a question. It must have been a good 5-10 seconds of me staring into space before I came to again. I had a constant ringing in my ears that happened when I would become deep in thought sometimes.

**Jones:** Scott, did you hear me?

**Me:** Sorry Jones, could you repeat that?

**Jones:** The whole thing? Damn, did you sleep last night?

I shrugged and cracked a smile. She smiled back. She was cool.

**Jones:** We need you to bring your gear with you. Encrypted radio, Toughbook laptop, wireless range finder and antenna; the works. Bring whatever you need to gather as much area intel as possible.

**Me:** Are you coming along?

**Jones:** Negative, I'm hanging back in the TOC (Tactical Operations Center) to help guide you guys if you need me. I'll be on the comms with my crew back here.

She worked for a colonel that was directly under General Yost. I don't remember his name as we had never spoken before, but he seemed to be an ok guy from what I had heard around.

**Major Pickens:** Ok, everyone let's move out in fifteen minutes. We want to get a head start just in case we get some fucking freak sandstorm. This is Afghan-land, so you never know. Our weather guys are telling me that we are clear until at least 1500 hours but they don't know shit really. So, let's get a move on, roger?

I went to my area and grabbed my gear. I opened my pack and started to load in some stuff that I may need. Laptop, antenna, two radios, three extra hard drives, and a bunch of miscellaneous items. I packed a few protein bars, four extra bottles of water and a small medical kit. I was already loaded up on ammo though. It was like I had willed this mission upon myself when I loaded up on ammunition in my tent that morning. I just had a feeling that today was different. I closed up my pack and looked around to see if there was anything else I needed. I had a feeling that I was missing something. A satellite phone. I went to the back metal shelf and grabbed a satellite phone and an extra battery pack. I wasn't supposed to take these but after all of the shit that has been happening, fuck it.

We all met up at the staging area where the vehicles were parked. Major Pickens started to point people into their vehicles.

**Major Pickens:** "Scott, you're riding with me. Any shit goes down, I need my comms guy with me."

**Me:** "Yes sir."

He motioned me over to the middle Humvee. I asked him who would be riding in the MRAP. He said, "nobody son. That's not for us today. There is another convoy going out at 1100 hours and they need the MRAP for a mission going into Kabul city. We're heading toward the foot of the mountains. No IED's along those routes. We're traveling light today as to not spook anyone."

Major Pickens and I got into the middle Humvee, and he radioed the lead Humvee to roll out. As we approached the gates, the guards had already opened them up and we drove right past. Major Pickens threw a salute to the gate guards as we moved past their position. We were heading toward the Hindu Kush mountains. I just knew that there was something wrong with this situation. Why would I be going out on a mission with major Pickens after all this time? We had never gone out on a mission together before and right after all this bullshit, we were heading out.

As we ripped through the desert sand, I looked in the rearview mirror and couldn't see anything behind us. There was at least one Humvee behind us, but the sand was so thick in the wind that I couldn't see it. Major Pickens and I talked a little bit on the ride over about what happened the day before. He didn't ask any questions this time, we just talked about who to stay away from. He told me the truth about our mission outside of the wire finally. it wasn't meant to be a pickup mission. It was meant to be an exfiltration mission, our exfiltration mission! Major Pickens told me that things had gone south overnight and that some very powerful people knew that he and I had seen too much. He told me I was in great danger, and he needed to find a way to get us both out of here.

The plan was to go and see his CI, a trusted partner in the area who knew of a way to get us out. He told me that the man's name was Mohammed Al-Shivar. At least that was his name that he had known him by for quite some time. Mohammed was to take us into an underground tunnel that leads outside of the city. The tunnel stretched for about 300 yards apparently and once we reached the end, we would be picked up in a truck to take us to Pakistan. From there we were on our own, no more tunnels, no more trucks.

The vehicle in front of us slowed down to about thirty miles an hour. It was common knowledge that you kept up a speed of at least sixty while going through the desert. Slow vehicles were sitting ducks for RPG and small arms fire. Major Pickens called over the radio to the lead vehicle and asked them why they were slowing down. The driver responded that there were vehicles parked across the road ahead. Major Pickens told him to pick up speed and go around them. As we picked up speed and went around the roadblock, I saw 4 Afghan National Army soldiers standing outside of their vehicles as they waved us by them. We drove another 5-6 miles before we entered a small village. It was desolate. Nobody outside at all. It was like the people in the town had vanished.

Major Pickens radioed over to the lead vehicle and commanded him to hold position. The major stepped out of the Humvee and looked around with his rifle hanging off his chest, pointing to the ground. He motioned me to get out. He said, "follow me, Perry. Stay close and watch my six." As I stepped out of the vehicle, I heard the loud crack of a rifle in the distance. I was used to hearing enemy AK-47 fire as they would shoot wildly from the mountains and never really hit anything. They were generally terrible marksmen for the most part. I came around the front of the Humvee and saw Major Pickens with his knees on the ground and his face on the desert sand, looking at me with his eyes wide open. He was hit in the neck by an enemy sniper. The personnel in the other vehicles cranked their engines and began to back out of the area. I was signaling them for help and cover, but they were already pulling away from the rounded opening where we had parked.

I quickly returned fire to a small opening in between two buildings, leading to a nearby mountain about 350 yards to the east. If there was a sniper, that is where I would be. I ducked down and grabbed the major by his Kevlar vest shoulder and dragged him 10-15 yards across the dirt to the side of a clay hut structure. I could hear the distant cracking of sniper fire just before the rounds hit the side of a nearby building, and then our Humvee. The other vehicles had stopped one hundred yards back down the incoming road and the soldiers had exited their vehicles and formed a suppressing fire point. They were laying down fire on the same mountain that I was before. I used my radio to call back to the TOC for air support or backup. No response. Fuck! Tried again and nothing. My radio was working because I could hear the others in the vehicles calling over to me. I told them to keep suppressing fire on the mountain.

Major Pickens was in bad shape now. His neck wound was so deep, and he was losing a lot of blood. I could already see his face begin to pale. He didn't have much time. I tried to field dress the wound by packing it with Quick-Clot, a blood coagulant that could stop blood loss on gunshot wounds. However, the shot had ripped across the side of his neck and a quarter inch wide gash running from the back of his neck to the front, near his throat was visible. This was too much to field dress. "Son of a bitch! Sir, hang on man. We're going to get you out of here!"

The major leaned into my shoulder with his forearm and pulled me closer into him. He was trying to speak. He

54

said, "pocket, my pocket," as he pointed to his left breast pocket on his vest. He said it again, "pocket!" I could hear him choking on his blood as he tried to instruct me. I opened his pocket and there was a folded piece of paper in there. I grabbed it and unfolded it. It was a small hand-drawn map of the area with a red circle around one of the buildings to the west. I could see the building from where we were. It was only about one hundred yards or so from my position. Major Pickens pulled me in close to him and said, "Mohammed Al-Shivar. Go to him. Tell him."

**Me:** Tell him what sir!? What do I do?

**Major Pickens:** "tell him....You know about program southern front. Tell him.. You are with me"

I was panicking. Should I go to the other soldiers in our small convoy or make a line to the building and go to some fucking guy named Mohammed that I never met, nor trusted, nonetheless?

**Me:** "Major, I am going to get you help and make it back to the convoy. They can help you. We can help you!"

**Major:** "Don't trust anyone! Only Mohammed Al-Shivar. Only Mohammed! Go!"

From the looks of it, Major Pickens had minutes, maybe even seconds before he was going into shock and dying. I had to make a move. Convoy or this random man. I closed my eyes and breathed in deeply. I looked over to the route to the convoy. It was wide open space. This sniper was damn good, and I knew that I would be next if I went that route. I gazed at the building to the west and looked at the map. I took one last look at Major Pickens and said, "yes sir, I got it! I'm going!" I braced my hand on my knee, picked up my pack and rifle and made a run for it. I was heading toward the building to the west as I

55

looked back at the other soldiers. They looked confused as I ran away from them. My heart was racing, and my breath was getting short as I ran in an all-out sprint toward the building. I finally arrived at the side door of the house and without knocking, I opened it and panned my rifle across the room. There was a man standing in the other room as I shouted for him to get his hands up. He placed his hands above his head as I shouted "Mohammed Al-Shivar?! Mohammed Al-Shivar? It's you? Mohammed Al-Shivar?"

He replied, "Yes, that is me. Where is Major Pickens?'

**Me:** He's gone. He told me to find you. What the fuck is going on?!!? I know about p*rogram southern front*!"

**Mohammed:** "We need to get you out of here. Quickly, come with me. No time. Come with me now!"

We entered into a dark room toward the back of the house. It was a small kitchen that was dimly lit with a small table lamp. He began to push the kitchen oven away from the wall. Behind the oven was a 3x3 foot hole in a mud and cement wall that led downward into the ground. He told me to get inside. I said, no you go first! Fuck that, as I pointed my rifle at him. He said, "ok, ok. Calm now, calm." He turned on a flashlight and went inside. I followed him into the hole as he grabbed the back panel of the oven and told me to help pull it back to the wall to conceal our position. I helped pull this fucking oven back against the wall until it was pitch black inside of the hole. He pulled on my vest as we walked down a narrow stairwell before he turned on a small LED flashlight. I looked in front of me and could see a dark tunnel going as far as the light would shine. We began to walk down the tunnel as I followed closely behind him. I was off the grid in the most hostile country in the world, deep in a tunnel with a potential terrorist and the only person that I trusted was likely dead.

## 6: The Landing

Two years later... The sound of motorcycle engines fills the air as I sit in a small one-bedroom apartment in the northeastern city of Brazil of Fortaleza. I used to visit here when I was a kid but haven't been back in years. I live here now, away from my previous life. My small apartment was located off the grid in a nearby favela. This place was packed with people living on top of each other. Homes were stacked on top of one another and anywhere from 15 to 100 people lived in a straight line of houses they went from ground to mountain top. It was a dangerous place, no doubt, if you didn't know how to get around. If you were too flashy or didn't know the Portuguese language and local dialect, you wouldn't make it here. Luckily for me I have been studying, speaking, and writing in Portuguese for years since I was a kid. Sometimes your passion projects become your life preserver, and in my case, it was cultural immersion and language.

I have been here for two years now and had a steady girlfriend. She was beautiful and pure. We had met about three months after I arrived at a small restaurant a couple of miles from where I was now living. She thought that I was a cryptocurrency investor expat that made a lot of money in Bitcoin that came down here to live a cheaper life away from it all. She had no idea who I was before or who I was now. A lot had changed from Afghanistan until now. I was a different person. I didn't have the same innocence as before. I didn't have the fear anymore. It was like someone had hit the reset button on my life. However, I felt like I was on borrowed time. It's hard to start a new life and support yourself in a different country with no friends, no family, and no job. Before I got here, I hadn't saved any money whatsoever. I was a young man who spent all of his money on useless shit. I had just enough money to last me a couple of months when I arrived. Mohammed had given me about $10,000 to get me started. His connections created a new identity for me as a Brazilian citizen. Passport, driver's license, a Brazilian CPF card, and even a credit history. It was enough to get me on my feet. After Muhammad brought me into that tunnel, he told me the real story of with him and major Pickens were fighting against. It was deeper than I had seen before, and it was enough to get Major Pickens killed.

The people that day in the black Mercedes that met the helicopter were at the top. However, they had significant influence into corrupt personnel from the highest tiers of government, to include the United States. Mohammed showed me just how far the corruption went and there was enough reason for me to disappear for the rest of my life. Mohammed introduced me to a few people in his crew once we reached the other side of the tunnel. They smuggled me out of the country in a box truck to Pakistan. From there, we traveled via car all the way to Turkey. I spent nearly a month in Istanbul waiting for directions. Mohammed sent a courier to give me my new identity while I was in Istanbul. It was a tiny little apartment then I couldn't wait to get out, but I had no idea what was in store for me. Mohammed had given me the choice of where I wanted to go who I wanted to be. I chose Brazil as I knew the culture and was confident that I could hide there among the people forever. Once I had my new identity, I got on a plane that took me from Istanbul to Rio de Janeiro where I was greeted by one of the others in the resistance. His name was Carlos, and he took me by car all the way to where I am now. It was nearly a 16-hour drive Carlos filled me in the whole way through. He gave me more information about the fraternity that I was now a member of. It didn't have a name, it didn't have a leader, it didn't have a face, it simply did not exist. We were all contributors to a noble mission. Most of us did not choose to be in this fraternity but nevertheless were a part of it. There were many others like were many others like me That had stumbled upon the snakes in the grass. They were from around the world and were placed in locations that spanned the globe. I perceived that Carlos had a personal mission. I could see the fire in his eyes when he talked about the cause almost as if it was his entire being. Toward the end of our drive, I asked Carlos why he did this. He told me that he had a son once. He did not go beyond that comment, But I knew exactly what he had went through. Like me, his young son was also struck by the hand of the devil and Carlos made it his life mission to fight back.

As I got my feet planted in Brazil, I knew that the $10,000 was going to run out soon. If I had to live on the mean streets of Brazil, I wouldn't last a week. I had been a part of some online forums before I joined the military. They were not the type of forums that a military member could be a part of, so I lost contact a long time ago. I was involved in early channels like 4Chan, a forum for early-day hackers, and some other pretty dark places on the Internet where kids could make money for hacking. I had to drop contact when I joined the military as it could have wound up getting me into a lot of trouble.

So, I went to a small electronics store via bus in the first week that I was in my new apartment in Brazil. I bought a laptop and a couple of extra hard drives. Later that night, I opened the computer and I started to tap into some of the old channels that I had previously been a contributing member of. It was very different and saturated with bullshit. I downloaded a Tor browser so that I could enter into the dark web without being tracked. I was using the Wi-Fi signal of a nearby business. They had a default password associated with their wireless access points. I did that so that any traffic coming from my computer could not be traced to me as it was all coming from the business around the corner. Surprisingly, they actually had a pretty strong Wi-Fi signal which is rare for the favelas in Brazil. A Tor browser is used to access a different part of the Internet through onion routing. This was not the traditional Internet that normal people were used to. When I first purchased this laptop, it was loaded with Microsoft Windows. However, I used a flash drive that was loaded with Kali Linux so that if I needed to destroy my trace, all I had to do was pull out the flash drive from my computer. That would remove the traces of my activities and leave nothing under the local computer hard drive or RAM.

You see, I knew that the type of people who wanted me dead were not the type to lose track of me or to forget about me. I knew that someday they would likely come for me. I was just prolonging the inevitable by hiding in the shadows. However, I was always proficient at hiding in the dark spaces. That is where my mind always lived, always had. Maybe a week, a year five years, who knows when they would come for me, but I knew that they would someday. All I knew was that in order to stay alive I needed money. The only thing that I needed to make money was a computer and an Internet connection. Now that I had both of those things, I could get to work on what I do best. I started with small stuff, just getting back involved with the community. I was a member of a small group of hackers called "Redgate." Redgate was committed to the single purpose of doing good for the world. We focused mainly and tyrannical governments around the world that were abusing their people. However, from time to time we went after the real scum bags of the Earth; child predators . . .

After about a year of working with Redgate, I had saved enough money in Bitcoin and other cryptocurrencies to not really ever have to work again. Our group was well respected among the hacker communities and feared by tyrannical governments around the world. We had grown to over 20 core members that actively contributed to our projects. Again, like the resistance we had no leader , no central authority, and our mission was pure. We had a code of honor that we abided by which was to never take anything from someone who didn't deserve it. Before each one of our operations, it had to be a unanimous vote on the target that we were going after. If the vote was not unanimous, the operation was called off. We were mainly funded by various rebel and resistance groups in oppressed nations. However, we always took a little extra from the mother fuckers that deserved it. We would hit them hard, fast, and swiftly with various cyberattacks such as ransomware, leaking of sensitive information, and exposing their greed and corruption. We were hated by so many around the world because they knew that we were watching. Our tentacles began to reach places that we never thought possible, and we developed a name for ourselves among law enforcement authorities around the world such as Interpol, the FBI, even the CIA knew who we were. The funny thing was they never touched us, and they damn well could have if they really wanted to.

About six months ago, my partners within Redgate place their crosshairs on a large financial institution within Indonesia. The motive for this hit wasn't any different from any of the others. The big bank had some members on the executive team that were making themselves rich with money that they were stealing from their customers. The customers didn't know that this was going on, but the bank was simply placing fake bank balances into peoples' accounts without really putting money in there or allocating anything of value behind it. Big banks have so much power that they can show you one thing on a computer screen or an ATM receipt, but in actuality you have nothing more than digits on a worthless LED or computer screen. We found out about this little circus many times and had previously identified a large number of banks around the world that were doing this. So, we formed a game plan. We would hack into their bank using their newly developed mobile application. We used some common tools such as burp suite and various tools on Kali Linux to proxy the traffic from their mobile application to our devices. It was a mere three days before we had access to their systems. First, we wanted to validate that our convictions were true by looking into the accounting systems and watching the flow of the money. We noted large scale discrepancies. In short, more money was shown to be available accumulatively to their customers than what they actually had. Our suspicions were indeed confirmed. We worked our way through their network in the shadows for nearly a month before we pinpointed the CEO on his right-hand man. They were at the top and we knew who they were. I was given the task to take on the CEO as I had the most experience in social engineering. I did a lot of digging on this guy; personal bank accounts, email accounts, physical home address, addresses of his vacation homes, information on his family, what he liked to eat, where he liked to go; I even knew this guy's blood type by the time I was done with him. He seemed normal, that's what was so strange. For a man who's stealing millions of dollars he was rather normal, not much out of the ordinary.

Everything changed when I hacked into his cell phone. The cell phone providers in Indonesia don't have the best security practices. I found his phone number, called his cell provider, and socially engineered them to believe that I was him. By giving them all of his personal information, they were able to clone his phone SIM card on to my new device. Once I had his cell phone in my hand, or rather a mirrored version of it, I started to see some different things that we're not on the beaten trail. He had an encrypted messenger application that seemed to be receiving quite a few messages. This would explain why his personal and business email traffic was relatively clear and free of corruption. I dove in headfirst into the encrypted messenger application as I noticed that the bank fraud may not be his worst fault or sins. it appeared as though he was not only a member, but a leader in a very prevalent and active sex trafficking ring. I scoured the messages for days, and I watched his conversations for weeks just to understand the full spectrum of what he was involved in. He was funding operations all across Asia in a well-developed ring of international child exploitation artists and traffickers. This fucker was in deep, had the bankroll, and was connected to the top of his circle of evil. He was responsible for brokering trafficking deals of children under the age of nine from Indonesia to Europe and other parts of Asia.

Once I understood the full spectrum of this man's secret life, I took it back to Redgate. Our group Did not typically dabble in this specific area. However, I put the message out on to some other communications boards that did deal with this sort of thing. You see, in the deep recesses of the Internet there's a place for everything, even this. I had run into some people in the past on the dark web that went after these scumbags. So, I put a generic message out "high-profile financier in Indonesia involved in child extorsion and sex ring." Within a matter of hours, I had a hit. I was contacted by a person with the online moniker of "gamble." I knew my way around these forums pretty well as most of my days were spent inside of my small apartment staring at a screen. However, I don't think that I ever ran into Gamble before; at least not that I remember. He contacted me in a private encrypted chat and began to ask me very direct questions about the target. I gave some details but not enough to identify the man. Gamble had asked me how much it would cost for his identity. I paused for a few minutes to think about that question. It didn't seem right for me to take money, not for this one. "This one's on the house," I said. I saw the ellipses dots on the screen as Gamble typed and then erased his text before sending. He finally responded and asked what I wanted in return for this information. I told him that I didn't want anything and that this was a subject that I would never take money for. I didn't need money at this point in time as I had enough in cryptocurrency to last me 5 lifetimes in Brazil. I had no need for this person's money, nor did I want one cent that was in any way connected to this piece of shit. Gamble and I talked for an hour or so while I filled him in on all of the details about this person. I couldn't bring myself to say goodbye to gamble, it was like I wanted to see what would happen to this man. I wanted to be a firsthand witness to his downfall. I had a choice at that moment; to say goodbye knowing that I did the right thing or to contribute. I hung on to that question for quite a while before making my decision. I was under the radar now and I needed to stay under the radar if I wanted to live. But living in quiet desperation behind the thin veil of an untrue identity was not sitting right with me. the truth is, I had always enjoyed the hunt.

Gamble told me that he knew me or at least knew of me from some of my more notable work in the Redgate group. Gamble was a smart person, I could tell that he was detail oriented, meticulous, and patient. He gave me an opening and offered an opportunity for me to contribute. He said that since I had already taken it this far and I had invested this much time, then it must mean that I was along for the ride. Gamble and I talked all night about different things, nothing personal obviously. We were both ghosts in a digital world. I didn't know where he was or if he was a girl, I didn't know where he lived or where he was from, and I didn't want to know. The next morning, I awoke extremely early to these sounds of my computer notification chiming. I had new messages from somebody. I opened up my laptop in saw that it was Gamble again. We planned our next move against the Indonesian.

Since I already had access to all of his personal devices, we had set a foothold already. For the next few days, we collected evidence of his extracurricular affairs. Email chains, private messages, pictures, and videos; all implicating this man it's not only financial fraud to the tune of millions per month But, also some serious crimes against humanity. One particular set of videos was labeled "Black Book.." we watched hours of footage. It seemed as though this man was a broker between the higher authorities in the child sexploitation community. After a few days of collecting the intelligence that we needed, we sent an anonymous folder digitally to Interpol. Then we waited...

I remember that we sent the information to Interpol on Tuesday afternoon. It was so hot that day, I'll never forget it. The small fan in my apartment had been making a loud noise for some time now and that day it had quit on me. It must have been 115 degrees that week. Gamble and I waited until Friday before we reconnected. We both had wondered what was going on with the apprehension of this man, or lack thereof. Gamble and I talked a little bit more about life in general and it seemed as though we both had similar views on the world. It was weird, Gamble was so well educated. He knew about everything; law enforcement, world politics, cyber security, international laws; he was even well versed in geography. I wondered how gamble had so much time on his hands to spend with me on the dark web chatting. I guess it was normal, I didn't think much about it after that.

I remember on Saturday night, I was laying in my bed and listening to the buzzing of motorcycles outside of my apartment window and the shouting of vendors in the street selling food. I was getting hungry, so I decided to go out for a little walk. As I came outside and took a left to go up the block, I noticed a TV inside of a small open-air restaurant. It was the Evening News and it had English subtitles. I don't know why but I stopped and watched for a few minutes, just to see what was going on outside of my cave that I lived in. I saw a man's face come up on the news. It was a photo, a professional corporate photo of a man in a suit and tie. I stepped inside of the restaurant as the host asked me if I needed a table. I said yes please, just for one person. As I sat down at the table, I got a better look of the man on a TV screen. I knew this face and I knew it well... it was none other than, our Indonesian friend. The headline read, "Indonesian business mogul commits suicide by way of hanging." I was shocked. I stayed for a few more minutes to hear the whole news story but there wasn't much to go on. The man had killed himself, or at least that is what the world saw.

I had a beer and then headed straight back home. As I opened the creaky door to my dimly lit apartment, I had that feeling in the pit of my stomach like somebody was watching me. I opened up my laptop and fired up my operating system, went directly to my messages and noticed a few missed messages from Gamble. He had asked me if I was watching the news. Then, it appeared as though he was frantically asking me where I went. I replied back to him and within less than a second, and I could see that he was replying back to me as well. I told him that I saw the news and that our Indonesian friend had played his last game. Gamble was rather quiet that night. It was unlike him as he was usually the one talking, and I was the one listening to him. He always had something interesting to say.

A few days went by until I spoke with Gamble again, but when I did, I just had to ask him what was really on my mind. "Who are you?" Up until this point, I thought I knew who he was, but something was different, and I didn't believe for a second that the Indonesian had actually taken his own life. It took a little while before Gamble started to tell me exactly who he was. He never told me his real name, but he confirmed that we never sent the information to Interpol. It appeared as though Gamble was part of a larger initiative, concentrated on cleaning up the dark underbelly of the beast. Gamble confirmed that he was in the United States and was a member of the National Security Agency. It took me quite a while to process this new information. I had been running from the clutches of the government for so long now. I didn't know if I could trust him. However, gamble was just as guilty as I was at this point. I couldn't confirm that Gamble had this man executed, but I knew that the selfish motherfucker definitely did not kill himself, I knew that for a fact. Gamble told me that he wasn't like the others in the NSA. He used his resources do not bring these men to justice, but to wipe them out completely. No court of law, no due process, no defense attorneys; just vengeance.

Gamble told me about the process and why it was so. He told me that the process of bringing these people to justice was unjust in itself and riddled with flaws and corruption. As I knew from my past experiences, the arms of this monster touched the highest places in government, and they had enough resources to take out anyone and anything in their way. Gamble was a broken person inside from being a firsthand witness to this systemic corruption and filth and so was I. We were on in the same. The only difference was that Gamble was deeply entrenched in the government from which I was hiding.

## 7: Black Book

I have learned some tradecraft over the years. Running and concealing yourself from some of the most ruthless people on the planet will do that to a person. My skills in hiding archived data were impeccable by this time. Throughout most of my hacking targets, I always cleaned up behind me and never took away anything from the job that could call problems my way. Files, videos, and any other traces of my activities were burn-after-use materials and I was good at sanitizing my digital footprint. However, I did keep a few high-capacity USB drives stashed at various locations around northeastern Brazil. There was a small *Pastelaria* a few miles from my apartment. Pastelaria's in Brazil are cheap and have great food if you're looking for something quick and home-made. I didn't go there for the food all that much though. They had no cameras, light traffic in the area, and were in business for over 40 years. Their storefront hadn't changed in decades, and they prided themselves on that motto of, "old traditions." It was the perfect place to hide some materials when I needed to. If I ever had to get out of my hole in the wall apartment in a hurry, I could come back to the Pastelaria when I needed to pick up my critical items.

In the back of the store, there was a metal shelf that had assorted breads, pre-packed sweets, and other small market items. No liquids within ten feet or so, no magnetic interference from any machinery, and it was raised above the floor; just in case there were ever a flood. Northeastern Brazil was dry anyway so there wasn't a huge concern on humidity eating up digital drives. That small shelf was out of view from the cashier and the front door. There was a small camera on an adjacent wall and my shelf was in its blind spot. On the bottom far right side of that shelf, there was a small opening between the shelf's wall and a 2 ½ inch metal lip that extended below. It was the perfect concealment location for a small USB drive. I had a couple of other places around town like that and was always looking for more. I kept lots of important stuff there, mostly money in the form of digital currency wallets. However, in my favorite Pastelaria, I kept many of my *get out of jail free cards*. I had dirt on some major players and kept those aces in my back pocket if anything were to ever happen to me. I had befriended a nice reporter for a metropolitan journal in Fortaleza within the past five months. His name was Cristiano, and he was a down-to-earth kind of guy and specialized in scandal news. Talk about the most dangerous and busy job in Brazil; that was it. There was more corruption in that country than 1,000 people could write news stories and exposés for a lifetime.

I had set up a system, to where if I were ever to be in serious trouble, I could send all of the locations of these drives to Cristiano, along with some instructions on what they were and what to do with them. I found that journalists are more trustworthy than the authorities when dealing with subjects of great secrecy. Guilty people were more afraid of journalists and reporters than cops and other governmental authorities. Afterall, once a hungry journalist had a story in their hands; the lights came on and that story was hitting the press by close of business that day. My girlfriend had a letter that was addressed to Cristiano, and she was instructed to send it to him if anything were to ever happen to me. It didn't have much information in it, just the address and location of the first parcel at the Pastelaria. Once Cristiano found that digital drive, it would lead him to the rest of them and he would have news stories for the rest of his career. The people that I had dirt on were located around the world. Mostly high-profile business leaders around the world that were stealing money. However, there were a few key players in there that were involved in some seriously nefarious business. Brazilian politicians that had been scamming the taxpayers for years, high-profile defense attorneys that were paid-off by the cartels in Bolivia, and officials at the US embassies that enjoyed young girls on the weekends. I probably had nearly 100 people that would spend an average of fifty years a piece in federal prisons if these stories were ever published. Their secrets were safe with me, for now.

I was apprehensive with Gamble still since I knew who he worked for. It was too close to home for me, so I had gone off the grid for a few weeks after the Indonesian job. I thought it would be good to lay low for a bit. I wasn't sure of Gamble's intentions. When money isn't involved, you always have to wonder about someone's motivations. As I thought more about it, I remembered my childhood and what was taken from me at a young age. I wasn't alone and there were thousands of children in dire situations. Maybe I could help them. I began to become angry with myself for hiding all of this time. I was so afraid of what would happen to me that I had overlooked what was happening around me to the kids. I felt compelled to make a move; to come out of the dark. I had been a ghost for years now and it wasn't sitting well with me. There was a level of power in my hands that I held. I could hide for the rest of my life under my assumed identity. Or I could emerge from the shadows to meet evil, eye to eye. I wrestled with these personal convictions. I was plagued by many sleepless nights, bouts of depression, anger, and pure hatred for what my life had become. They had taken everything from me, from the time that I was six years old until now. I was still hiding from them. I was thirty-three years old at this point in my life and I suddenly felt lucky. The images and videos that I had seen in Afghanistan and within the hands of the Indonesian showed what the other side of luck really looked like. I was alive, strong, healthy, and had the resources in my hands to make a difference. The children were afraid, lost, hopeless.

**3:15 a.m.:** I am still awake, glaring at the top of my closed laptop. I hadn't opened my computer in nearly a month at this point. I plugged in the power cable to the adapter and put the prongs in the wall outlet, opened the lid, and pressed the power button. The deep blue screen of my Kali Linux desktop fired up as my stomach tipped upside down again. The logo of the dragon in the computer's background looked fierce and fearless. The dragon appeared motivated, yet not predatory. It seemed as though the dragon was apprehensive to strike, but something had backed him into a corner, and he was about to release a holy fucking shitstorm of fire on his enemies. I felt the same and took it as a sign. I loaded up my Tor browser and entered the onion site that I used to chat with Gamble. He wasn't online but I pinged him anyway and just said, "hey stranger..."

I waited...15 minutes went by, and I laid back against the stucco wall with a small pillow behind my head. I was browsing some recent news articles from the United States, just catching up on what was going on in the world. I heard the faint sound of a message chime. I opened up the messenger tab and saw that it was Gamble. He sent me a sword emoji and a smile. It made me crack a slight grin when I saw it. He knew that I was in for the next job, and it felt good to be back.

We talked for a while before I asked him what the next move was. He said, "our Indonesian friend has more to offer. Shall we?" I knew that he was talking about his black book. I didn't have the stomach to sift through any more horrible videos that night, so I asked him what he had in-mind. We gave the Indonesian a nickname of "Titanic" as Gamble said, "he would take the whole fucking ship down." Gamble explained that Titanic had left his own version of an insurance policy as well. I guess those sorts of things are common in the cockroach community. The Indonesian had left compelling and gruesome evidence that he was no more than a middleman, just working for his bosses. The difference with this guy was that he left enough information on his bosses for us to start making moves. He left the names of some of his co-conspirators and the person that he worked for.

His boss's name was *Saad Ali Ayad*. Gamble and I split the work. He would dig into the colleagues of Titanic, and I would start to track down Saad Ali Ayad. From the name, I already knew that he was Arabic. I had been around Arabic culture for some time in my military career and knew where he was from, just by his name. I dug into his online persona. He was a military officer in the Saudi Arabian Royal Air Force. He was high up as well and held the rank of *Liwa*, the equivalent to a major general (two-star) in the US military. Not bad, eh? Like I said, this shit runs deep and through all parts of society; even the most prestigious. I found his entire military career and studied it. He was revered as a hero in Saudi Arabia, a political diplomat, and had significant family connections in Saudi culture. He was tall, around 6 ½ feet and was an avid basketball player. I located pictures of him with some famous European and American basketball stars. He went to Syracuse University in New York and studied law before coming back and joining the Saudi military. He was one of those guys that always hid his real persona through his life. Well educated, tall, dark, and handsome. What a perfect ruse for someone that specializes in exploiting people globally. I did some more research on General Saad and found that he was a on the board at a charitable foundation out of Qatar, aimed at combating global poverty with oil funds donations. It was well-established and had been running for nearly 30 years at this point. We all knew how these "charities" worked and they were nothing more than brick and mortar laundry machines for billionaire oil tycoons to hide their money. Swiss bank accounts were too hot so these guys usually funneled money through charities and real estate development projects. This one had both, it was building homes for the poor around the world so that they could have a place to live, instead of on the streets.

I had managed to get General Saad's personal email address through some reconnaissance and a tool called *The Harvester*. This was one of my favorites as you could find lots of juicy information on targets. I coupled this with another social engineering platform named *Maltego* to start charting my course. My first move was to send a generic phishing email to General Saad, just to see how susceptible he really was. It was nothing more than a fake "you have a new digital voicemail" email that I sent him first. It was supposed to lead him out to an online portal that captured his login credentials. Simple, yet effective. I sent it and waited a few hours. I could see that he had opened the email from the tracking beacon that I had on the fake website. However, he wasn't falling for it. Didn't take the bait that time; I had to get more creative...

I thought about it for a while before realizing what the next move was. I did some more research on the charitable organization and took notes. He had recently given a keynote speech at a live event in Qatar to an audience of around 500 people or so. This was only a few weeks back. I watched the entire live speech on YouTube and studied the man's movements, tone of voice, and general demeanor. He was calm, cool, and collected. He had a certain energy to him that was great for convincing people to buy into the cause he was pushing. He reminded me of one of those Ponzi schemes guys that you see trying to get people to do drop-shipping on Amazon. After reading through some of the organization's materials, I realized that the way to this man's heart was through media exposure. He was a glutton for the spotlight and his ego needed puffing every so often. It's weird; I found that most bad people love the spotlight. Those were the easy targets. The ones that rested in the shadows were the tough fish to catch as they made it a point to stay away from the limelight. Not General Saad, though. He was a slut for the bright lights of Broadway. I assumed the online identity of "Mack Wallace," a reporter for a national news outlet in Ireland. I created a social media presence, LinkedIn, Facebook account, Instagram, and had a legitimate email account. It was a good cover as I spent some time on this one. General Saad would need some assurance that I was who I said I was.

The cover was solid and tight. I sent him the first email message. The subject line read: *Keynote Speaking Opportunity in Dubai.* In the body of the email, I introduced myself and the news outlet that I was with. Then, I went on to show him evidence that we were putting on an event in Dubai that would include international stars, political figures, and multi-billionaires. It wasn't too long of a message, just long enough to stroke his ego and get him interested. I put a rush on the message as well, letting him know that our previously selected keynote speaker had become ill and wouldn't be able to attend. We needed confirmation of his interest within the next couple of days or else we would have to procure another. I told him that he was selected for his humanitarian contributions and military career history. I also learned that he was fluent in several languages and threw a nugget in the email that we needed someone who could answer questions from an international audience.

Within ten minutes, he replied back with interest in the event. He said that I could "count him in." The greedy bastard also asked what the payment was for the keynote speaker. I replied back that it was $150,000, with a 30 percent bonus based on event turnout. If event turnout was 100 percent, he would get 20 percent. If the turnout of attendees was over 120 percent, he would get an extra 30 percent. He was hooked in. I told him that I would be sending along a form that I would need him to fill out at his earliest convenience so that we could get him registered. I had set up an actual website for the event and everything. It looked legitimate and needed to be. The form that I was sending him wasn't a normal document though. I had loaded it with a malicious script that went out to a web server that served remote access trojan malware. It was my nice little command and control server that I had built. Once he downloaded the document in the email, it would reach out to my server and download the malware in the background of his system. The malware was well-written, and I had spent a pretty penny on it from the dark web marketplace. It was written in Python, and they used a program called *Veil* to perform antivirus evasion techniques. You could find anything on the dark web. When I say anything, I mean it. From drugs, guns for hire, body parts; shit, someone could buy a human being on there. However, most of the nasty shit was right in front of people's faces on the regular internet and hidden in plain sight. When you see the other side, it's easy to see the signs but to everyday people, internet browsing was innocent and built for a noble purpose.

I sent the email to him and waited. I had done this before and knew that if things took too long, the target was unlikely to fall prey. Every hour that the victim did not open the package, the likelihood decreased exponentially. However, within no more than fifteen minutes, my target had opened it and the malware was present and running on his system. I logged into my command and control server and saw the beacon chiming back to me through a reverse proxy connection. A reverse proxy connection is a backdoor route or covert tunnel that we use to communicate to and from malware present on victim systems. By using this reverse proxy connection and the malware on his system, I could do a number of things to the victims' computer. Turn on the webcam, record audio from the microphone, log keystrokes, deploy other software, record screen captures; you name it. Once you've made it around the thin veil of defenses on a system, the world was yours. I took all of the military training in hacking that I had received and applied it to my other life. Thanks, Uncle Sam.

I set up some hooks in the victim's computer to ensure that his antivirus program did not flag any of my activities. The fastest way to work around antimalware programs is to simply disable the program and silence the alerts or create exemptions in the program to allow my activities, while still running. I usually set exemptions because I was worried about other malware being present on the system. With this type of crowd, their organizations would often infect their computers to spy on them just in case they got froggy and wanted to talk to the authorities. Criminal enterprises spy on their people without their knowledge so that they can get ahead of any surprises. Therefore, I wanted to ensure that I was the only hacker on the system.

I watched his internet activities through browser hooks. Anything that he typed on the screen, I had sent to a log file. He went to his social media accounts, email, and bank's website that evening. I had the passwords to all of them since I was logging his keystrokes. He had a nice bank account. I actually thought about siphoning off the money in there for a second before I snapped back to the mission. I focused on this one. Everything seemed rather normal that evening. Nothing out of the ordinary that I could see. Scrolling on Facebook, liking pictures of Mercedes Benz's, re-tweeting celebrity gossip on Twitter; normal shit. There was one thing that stood out to me though. He went back to Facebook using a private browser. When he loaded it up, I saw that he was using a program called "Brave." This is a privacy-built web browser that leaves you anonymous when browsing the internet, relatively. Not uncommon for people to use it as nobody wants to be spied on. However, he loaded up an eBay account and signed in. He was an eBay seller? A guy with this type of prestige, performing keynote speeches for nearly a quarter of a million dollars selling widgets on eBay? Not likely, but hey; everyone has a hobby or passion project.

He wasn't on eBay all too long. Just enough time to check some messages and recent sales while he was away that day. He logged out rather hastily and the connection to his system went dark. Shit, he must have closed the laptop. It was late so maybe he was tired and heading to sleep. I waited a few minutes to see if my connection resumed but it did not. Looks like I was off-air for the evening. I laid back in my small twin bed. The mattress was only about four inches thick with a wooden board underneath. No box spring here. I don't know why box springs aren't a thing in Brazil but that was definitely one thing that I missed. I laid there with my hands behind my head, listening to some Samba music coming from the street down below my apartment. There was always music on in July in Fortaleza as it was a month of celebration. Brazilians love to party. I looked at my phone and saw some missed messages from my girlfriend. She was asking if I was all right. I hadn't talked to her in almost two days. I texted her back and told her that I hadn't been feeling well and was catching up on some sleep. She sent me a smile emoji and a kiss. She was cool and relaxed. We didn't need to talk for hours a day as she was independent and knew that I needed space from time to time.

I decided to dig a bit further that night. I wasn't interested in the bank accounts or social media of General Saad. The eBay thing was rubbing me the wrong way for some reason, so I got back into the ether. I signed into his account using the same browser that he was using, just in case he checked his last logins. I made sure to proxy my IP address to his area as well so that he would assume it was him if he checked. I logged in and started to look at the recent history. He wasn't a buyer of any products and I found that odd. He only sold. They weren't large items though. Small stuff really. It looked like his main products were bicycles. They were boring bicycles really. Simple blue bikes or red bikes. They weren't adult bicycles though; they were children's bicycles only that he had been selling. The list was full as he had sold over one hundred of them in the past ninety days. One thing was wrong though. The prices of the bikes were abnormal. Not one of them was under $15,000 and most of them were between $18,000 to the highest at nearly $75,000. Who the fuck is buying shitty blue and red children's bikes for $75,000? Then, it hit me. The feeling came into my stomach like a wave. He was moving people, not bikes. This was his code for an online marketplace that he used to sell human fucking beings. He had bidding wars on his sales as well. All of the sales ended within twenty-four hours of posting.

I knew that I had my hooks into evil again. If I found this within a day of digging; what was this guy doing behind the scenes? He was pushing human beings on a public website, run by a legitimate company, in front of the whole world. I mean, who the fuck searches for children's bicycles for $75,000? Nobody searches for this, even law enforcement. When I said that most of the most insidious shit happens on the normal internet, this is a prime example of just that. I contacted Gamble that night and showed him what I had stumbled upon. He wasn't surprised whatsoever and appeared as though he had seen this type of thing before. He said, "Good job. We got ourselves a top tier seller." I asked him what our next move was. He told me that the next move was nothing. Nothing?! What the fuck Gamble? We could take this motherfucker out right now and expose him to the world. Gamble told me to calm down. "When I said nothing, I didn't really mean nothing," said Gamble. He meant that we were going to follow the breadcrumbs. This guy didn't have humans in some kind of a room in his home that he was pushing via eBay. He was working for someone, and they had access to these people. We needed to figure out where the rabbit hole would lead us. Patience, persistence, and tradecraft were needed, not brute force.

## 8: The Cut

It was a holiday in Brazil; Corpus Christi to be exact. The entire country was off work and the streets were filled with vendors, music playing, and a general party atmosphere. It wasn't carnaval, but it was close enough. Holidays in Brazil were my favorite part since I was young. My girlfriend called me that morning. She was soft-spoken and sweet. Rayssa is her name. The antique translation of that name meant "Rose;" I believe. The origins of her name were Hebrew, Yiddish, or Jewish. I thought that it suited her well. Beautiful, but thorns wrapped her stem. If you held on too tightly, you were sure to draw blood. She called me on my second cell phone. The one that I gave the number to very few, if any, people. She wanted to meet and go out for a bite to eat that day. However, I was head down in a couple of different projects with Gamble. We were running through the Indonesian's black book, and I was still working on exfiltrating information from General Saad. I had two solid leads that were bearing fruit at every turn.

I needed to fucking get out of the apartment though. I had been holed-up here for nearly a week and hadn't seen the light of day for some time. If I let my South American tan go away for too long, I stood out like a sore thumb. So, I decided to oblige Rayssa and meet her at a small restaurant down the street from my place. It was immensely hot that day, but a bit of clouds covered the city. Just enough to block the sun but not rain. It was my favorite time of year for sure. Every time that I walked out of my apartment, I had my routine. It was simple, yet enough to spot the obvious. My checklist was as follows:

1.  Cut connection with any internet on my computers or cell phones.

2. Unplug USB drives and wipe everything completely.

3. Hide any evidence that I was an American. Notes in English, shirts with US branding, even my coffee cup that had an American flag logo on it.

4. Check camera feeds from nearby traffic lights and adjacent businesses. I had "hacked" into the camera systems a while ago. The camera operators used the default vendor usernames and passwords so there wasn't much of a challenge in getting access there. If I spotted anyone on the cameras that didn't belong, I waited. If not, I proceeded to the next step.

5. Toss something over toward the door to the apartment, so that it makes a decent noise when hitting the floor. If anyone were awaiting me to stand by the door and fill me up with silenced rounds, they would be shooting into the air while I climbed out a window to the next building. No noise, in the hallway; no shooting. Good to go.

6. Proceed to door and check the peep hole. All clear.

7. On the inside of the apartment door handle, I placed a coin on the lever when I closed it behind me. If someone opened the door while I was away, I would not hear the coin hit the floor when I opened the door on my return. If the coin hit the floor, there was a good chance that I didn't have any visitors.

8. I always carried a gun with me in Brazil. Made of hardened plastic and printed with a 3D printer setup, a ghost gun. Easy to find on the black market here. It held seventeen rounds and one in the chamber. As reliable and accurate as a Glock nineteen. Looked like it too.

Metal detectors were invalid for this kind of setup, and it fit in right in my waistband.

9.   Make my way down the narrow stairwell into the atrium of the apartment. There was a window right before the base floor. I looked out and panned 180 degrees to see if any new sightings were present from when I checked the camera systems. One new car; a black Fiat. A woman in the driver's seat on the phone. Not malicious, all clear there too.

10. Exit the apartment's atrium and say "tchau" to the guy sitting in the chair in the atrium. He was supposed to be "security." However, no gun and he was about one hundred kilos overweight. Any legitimate threat would run through him in no time. He was a nice guy though. I enjoyed some conversations with him. He was usually sleeping with his feet up. There was this brown street cat that always hung out near him. He gave the cat treats once in a while, so the cat never left his side. "Good kitty." Ok, I'm walking out.

I always wore an inconspicuous outfit. Something that fits in. I had a hat on and dark cheap sunglasses that covered my eyes. Ice blue eyes in Brazil were a dead giveaway that I wasn't from here. Rayssa texted my phone and changed our meeting location. She said that the other restaurant was full. I texted her back and told her that it was ok, and we could wait there for a table to open up. I hated changing plans as it introduced complexity and unknowns. I didn't like unknowns. Unknowns could get a person killed. However, she was adamant that we go to a restaurant that was a few blocks in the other direction. I wasn't going to argue with her, so I obliged. I was almost at the original restaurant when I turned around to go to the new meeting place. Out of the corner of my eye, I saw a silver truck parked to the north of the restaurant. Windows were tinted jet black. I couldn't see inside. Even the windshield was tinted enough to conceal the occupants. I found that to be odd. The area was so poor that a truck of that type was rare to see. Expensive cars and trucks had no place in the Brazilian slums as they were frequently robbed. It was weird but I didn't think much more of it. I carried on to our meeting place.

As I approached the restaurant, I saw Rayssa waiting at one of the back tables with her hand up. She was calling the waiter over for something. She was always so cool and relaxed. I envied that of her. I was sure that she perceived my nervousness, but she never asked questions about it. I walked into the restaurant and sat down by her side. We both seemed to like facing the exits of the restaurant. It was a Brazilian thing that they liked to see what was going on outside. It was a dangerous place. We kissed as I sat down. Her smile lit up my day and took away all of the bullshit that encompassed my life. Every bad moment that had passed in my life, and the current turmoil went out of the window. She always held my hand; even when we were sitting down. I really enjoyed that about her. Her warmth was comforting and made me feel normal again. My life was not fucking normal, so this was the one piece that made me feel all right.

We began to talk about things a bit. Normal chatting about the holiday that was upon us, her family, her work, and other things that were happening in her life. I was always a bit more reserved. Again, she thought that I made a lot of money from trading crypto. She probably thought I was lazy as hell and retired. We talked about when we first met. It was a story that I would never forget. I am not a big believer in fate, but this was one circumstance that I believed was bigger than me. When I first arrived in Brazil, I was alone. When I say alone, I mean it. After I was removed from Afghanistan, I made my way to Brazil through a network of couriers. I passed through nearly 20 different countries making my way to Brazil. The last continental hop in the trip was Venezuela. When I was crossing through the Venezuelan border, I was stopped by the federal authorities and questioned for over an hour. I didn't speak much Spanish so they brought in a translator so that they could understand my Portuguese. I was posing as a Brazilian citizen. I had the passport and other documents to prove it. I waited for over an hour in some little interrogation room while they gathered a translator. The guy that came in spoke absolutely terrible fucking Portuguese.

He tried but I couldn't understand a word that he was saying. It was just Spanish that he tossed a French accent onto. I told him that I still didn't understand, and I waited some more. 3 hours passed by, and they finally gave me a fucking phone with a true Brazilian translator on the line. It was Rayssa. They put her on speakerphone that was on the desk as I told her what I was doing, where I was coming from, and other items on my cover story. She translated excellently and after only twenty minutes, they gave the green light through the border. Before I got off the phone with her, she passed along her office phone number so that if I had any problems, just call her. That was the warmest thing that anyone had done for me in months. Through all of the border crossings and pieces of shit that I had encountered, that was the best thing I had.

After I got through the border, I took a flight from Caracas to Sao Paulo, and then a short flight to Fortaleza. The entire time throughout the flights, I couldn't keep my mind from wondering who she was, why she helped me, or how she was able to convince them so quickly. I didn't know her, but she was on my mind. Like I said, the past few weeks before that phone call had been hell for me. I was surrounded by people that wanted to either get rid of me as quickly as possible or people that were trying to make me disappear. Neither of which are the most welcoming that you could imagine. It was the first time that I had something bright in my life in quite some time. When I arrived in Fortaleza, I knew that she must have been from the Brazilian consulate or embassy here in the city. My last courier had given me the keys to the apartment where I would be staying, along with a phone number if I ever needed to get out quickly. He told me that if I called the number, they would come and get me wherever I was. However, if I called too early or was suspicious, the number would be deactivated, and I wouldn't have any rescue line waiting for me. I guess it was protocol so that if I was compromised, they could go dark as well. Just the type of amenity that one could expect, given the circumstances.

After I unpacked some of my things, I did a quick search for the nearest consulate or embassy in the area and found that it was only about a mile away. A mile in crowded Brazilian cities could take an hour to get through when busy, so it's not that close. But I wondered if she was there. I mustered up the courage and finally called her. I remember her answering the phone and sounding surprised to hear from me. I thought that she didn't remember me. I had immediate regret when she told me that she did remember me. I regretted calling her because of the situation that I was in. I wasn't thinking and was letting my heart guide me when I called her. What if she wants to see me? Would I be putting her in danger? I had questions and more reservations. I told her that I wanted to thank her for helping me out, nothing more. She told me that if I wanted to, we could grab some lunch sometime. I told her where I was staying, and she told me that her work wasn't too far from where I was staying. So, we made plans for the next day.

It was funny when we met. She knew that I wasn't a native Brazilian. It was either my accent, or the fact that I looked more Swedish than Brazilian. Either way, she didn't even question it. I gave her my cover story about being independently successful in the cryptocurrency trading market and she didn't ask anything else beyond that. She was cool and laid back and didn't focus on the petty stuff. Our relationship developed from there and we became close, but not too close. I knew about her family but hadn't met them. She knew my cover story but didn't go beyond that. We were interested in each other, not the peripheral nature of our separate lives.

Back to today now. As we talked in the restaurant, I wasn't really focused on what we were talking about. I could only think about General Saad and the situation with the Indonesian. I couldn't wait to get back to the apartment to dig further. I received a message on my burner phone's encrypted messenger application. It was from Gamble, and it read, "got em...Ping me when you are able..."

I cut our lunch short and told her that I had to go and pick up a package from the shipping company before they closed early today. We embraced for a moment before parting ways. She gave me a big smile, as always as we went in different directions down the sidewalk. I picked up a good pace on the way back to the apartment, looking down at my phone and waiting for any other message from Gamble. I rushed into the apartment and locked the door behind me. I opened up the laptop, fired it up, and saw that Gamble had sent a headshot of an American woman. I could tell that she was American because of the American flag behind her in the photo. I thought that I knew the woman's face but couldn't put a name to it. I sent a message back to Gamble asking him who this was and what it meant. He responded, "it's General Saad's boss." I went back to the picture and zoomed in. "What the fuck, I know this person from somewhere." It was puzzling me. I tipped the front legs of my chair back and thought about it for a while. I couldn't put my finger on it, so I went back to the messages and started talking with Gamble more.

I asked him how he knew that this was General Saad's boss. He had done some digging into General Saad and was fully entrenched in his other mobile devices. Gamble had been monitoring communications on General Saad's devices for a while now. He said that General Saad had contacted this woman via email this morning and gave her some kind of cryptic message. General Saad sent her an email from a different email address. The email address looked like it would be from someone that would land in your junk or spam folder. It was *h09023r2r3rkfok@protonmail.com*; totally fucking spammy. General Saad sent her a link to one of the eBay "items" that he had for sale. However, this one was priced higher than all of the rest of them at USD $200,000. Gamble thought that was odd. Why would General Saad use a scammer-esque email address, with a message that was sure to end up in someone's spam or junk folder? It didn't make sense, so he followed the lead. He tracked the recipient's email back to a legitimate employee's email address at the United States Department of Justice (DOJ). Now, at first, I thought that an officer in the Saudi Air Force sending an email to a member of the DOJ wasn't all that strange. However, the link that General Saad sent over to this person was anything but normal.

The woman's name was Helena Clark, and she was the civilian equivalent of a 2-star general in the United States military. She was high up, connected, and had something to do with General Saad and the ring of fire that he was involved in. We weren't sure what exactly her role was, but we knew that she was more than a cog in the wheel. The reason that we knew that she was important was because Gamble had monitored General Saad's activity before, during, and after communicating with her. Gamble was covertly watching him through his laptop's web camera and General Saad was acting extremely nervous. He would type out a message and delete. Then, he would type again and then delete. General Saad spent more time on a one-line email than most people do with philosophical essays. Then, General Saad made a phone call to a colleague and asked him if he was sure that Helena would approve of him sending her a message directly, as he had never done so before. It was a true mark of hierarchy, and she appeared to be near the top.

The conversation with Gamble took a strange turn at this point. As Gamble dug deeper into the identity of Helena Clark, he became a bit evasive in our conversations. It almost felt like when you were doing something dangerous, like jumping off a water reservoir with some friends, but then one friend is encouraging you to do a backflip. It was that type of fear or apprehension that I sensed in Gamble. I had done my own research on her as well and found that she was a figurehead at the DOJ Her official position title was, "Intelligence Director-- Middle East and Northern Africa Division." That type of position came with power and a long history of climbing the ranks of that agency. She was fluent in six languages and was born in Tunisia, before immigrating to the United States at the age of sixteen. She had an undergraduate degree from George Mason University, a master's degree from Yale, and a doctorate in political science from Cornell. Distinguished, educated, and powerful.

I kept gazing at her photos. I looked back through her career to determine whether I had seen a picture or video of her at some point in time. Her eyes were familiar to me. Maybe it was in an article or government publication that I had read in the past. It was inconsequential at that point, so I moved on. The point was that we had a lead to a higher source. We had no idea where the head of the snake was, nor were we directly looking for it. However, we knew that we were not fucking around with low-level pedophiles anymore.

## 9: Full Circle

5:12 a.m., Saturday. August 12th...

I don't sleep much anyway. Going to sleep at 8 a.m. is normal for me. I sleep better when it's light outside. I'm not scared of the dark, but the light seems to reveal things. The reason that I usually stay awake all night is because I know that the moonlight hours are usually when the evil side comes out to play. I don't stay awake all night because I am afraid someone is coming for me. I knew that could happen at any time, and it didn't have to be at night. I stayed awake thinking about all of the kids that I had seen trapped in these situations. It infuriated me and I thought that if I stayed awake working, that I could be some kind of beacon of light for them. Even if they didn't hear me, I was awake when they were. At their darkest moments, I was awake. I don't know, maybe it was karmic or something, but it was my thing.

This particular morning was different. Gamble had sent me a video a few hours before. It had the title, "full circle." I didn't have the stomach to open it, so I just sat here for hours contemplating what I wanted to do with my life. I was scarred by the new world that I lived in and questioned whether or not I wanted to continue. Even though I was doing some sort of good, I had a moment with myself and thought of leaving it all behind. I had enough money to last me for a long time and knew I could make more in the future, so money wasn't a barrier for me. I couldn't walk away though. Something magnetic drew me closer to the belly of the beast and I wanted more. I wanted vengeance and so I decided to open Gamble's latest video. I just knew that it would be something that would leave a mark on me in a negative way, but I watched it, nevertheless.

I put on my headphones and turned up the volume as loud as they went. Techno-trance music was my thing. I had to blast the sound to keep my mind from wandering during this video. I had to remove myself from what I was about to see. This was business.

I clicked the play button. A blank screen rolled across; the title "full circle" rolled past the screen. Then, it cut to the inside of a dimly lit room. What appeared to be a grown man sat in a wooden chair with a black burlap sack over his head. A caption rolled across the screen that said, "turn the sound on." What was this? This wasn't a child. It was a grown man who was obviously being held against his will. His hands were tied to the arms of the chair with some kind of metal wire. It was wrapped so tightly that I could see the indentations into his arms. He wasn't moving.

I turned off my music and raised the volume on the video. Someone in the room was blasting the song "Closer," by Nine Inch Nails inside of the room. A guy walked in front of the camera with a black ski mask on and gave a lighthearted wave to the camera filming. He walked over to the man in the chair and stood behind him. He put one hand on his head and removed the sack from his head. I paused the video to get a look at his face. Holy shit! It was the same guy from the video that I watched when I was in Afghanistan. The guy from Perry's USB that he left. The same guy that had the little boy in the cellar of that nasty shithole. How the fuck? I pressed play quickly, as I was anxious to see what was happening.

The man with the ski mask on didn't says a word. He picked the guy's legs up off the floor and dragged his chair closer to the camera. The guy had been beaten. I could tell from the marks on his face. The blood was dried, so that meant he had been there for a little while at least. His capture walked over to the stereo and plugged in an iPod.

I was wondering what he was doing until the music stopped. He was playing a constant loop of the sounds of children laughing. It was like they were playing in a park somewhere or something. They were having fun, laughing, running, and playing. The look on that mother fucker's face when he heard that was a type of fear that I had never seen before. His face was white, as if all of the blood went to his feet.

The man walked back over to him and pulled a box from underneath the camera area. He opened it and it was the same box that I had seen in the video before. He started to pull items out of the box. A knife, scalpel, hammer, corkscrew, and blowtorch. There was also some kind of syringe set to the side next to a coiled-up rope. The man's face quivered as he saw what the man was about to do. I saw front of the main's pants become soaked with urine as the man turned the volume up all of the way on the speakers. It was so loud that I had to lower the audio on my headset. I could hear the track shift to children singing a nursery rhyme that I had never heard. It was in Arabic. He started to go to work on him.

He started at the feet. He slowly removed his desert-worn sandals and took a pair of needle-nose pliers to each toenail, ripping them one by one from the muscle. One foot down. The next foot, he took another approach. The hammer. Each one of the toes was placed on a small wooden cube block and smashed. With each toe, the man's screams became louder until the very last one when you could barely hear his voice. It sounded like another man's voice screaming, but it was from his blowing out his vocal cords. The man went back into the box and pulled out the corkscrew. He cut the man's pants off from the feet to the waist on both sides, exposing him completely. He pulled his penis up with the pair of pliers and began to insert the corkscrew into him. With all of the hate that I had for this man, I closed my eyes until the screaming slowed down and I head the man's black boots walking away from the suffering man. I thought that this was the worst. I had no idea what in store for him was.

For the next four and a half hours, I sat there stunned. I couldn't move, I couldn't stop the video playback, I couldn't take a drink of water or go to the bathroom. I had never seen anyone physically suffer like this man. He used every single tool that was in that room, and then some. He even poured some kind of chemical into his eyes as he held them open with a pair of medical prongs. He turned the music onto a repeat of Nine Inch Nails' "Closer" for the last hour of the movie. If one knew the lyrics to that song, you could put together the connection to this scene of carnage.

He hit him with the syringe at least fifty times during this ordeal. Each time, the man would awake screaming and crying. In the last hour, the man was blinded first. I believe this was to show him what it was like to see the darkness. Then, his tongue was clamped, dragged out of his mouth and cut slowly with a box cutter. This was to show him what it was like for the children to not have a voice. I fathomed how this man could still be alive. At this point, it must have been the adrenaline or whatever chemical was being administered to him. He couldn't talk, couldn't see, but he could hear what was happening to him. The sounds that his body made when he was being violated were inexplicable. I couldn't even begin to put them into words.

The last thirty minutes of the video contained a metal rod being slammed into the man's anus, with his chair flipped over frontward so that his face was pressing against a towel on the floor. The man finally flipped the chair back up, untied his arms and legs and dragged him onto the floor, lying him on his back. He brought over a cage. However, this cage had a set of straps around the

93

bottom of it. It looked like a bird cage without a bottom and straps hanging from it. He placed the cage atop the man's abdomen and wrapped the straps around his back and buckled them. I knew what this thing was. It was a medieval torture device that they put rats in, and they would chew through the person to get out. He hit him with another 5 or 6 adrenaline shots before putting three large rats into the cage. They were those huge fucking rats that they had in the Middle East. Not the rats that you see in cities. It was like these things were bred for pulling livestock carriages. They were enormous and running on top of each other frantically. He closed the top of the cage and the man's legs wiggled uncontrollably on the blood-soaked floor. The man took the blow torch and heated up the cage. The rats were exposed to only the bare abdomen of the man as they began to squeal as if they were being tortured themselves. The top of the cage was glowing red, and you could hear the man's skin sizzling as the metal cage became welded to his abdomen. The rats began their escape by gnawing and clawing through the man's stomach. They burrowed into his intestines until you could not see them anymore.

The man was alive the entire time. The video was approximately four hours and forty-three minutes long. Of which, the man was alive, conscious, and aware for nearly 95 percent of it. The other 5 percent that he was passed out were only due to the man filling the large syringe and preparing him for another dose. I didn't throw up watching this video. I didn't feel much of anything at all, as I remembered who the tortured man really was and what he had done in his life. I had only seen a fragment of what evil this man had done before, and I am sure that was not his first time. His captor took the camera off the stand as the man laid there on the floor with the rats completely inside of his body. The camera took a new angle as he panned it into another room, closing the door behind him.

He took out a small LED flashlight as he walked down the dark stone-floor hallway into an opening.

He was in the same room as the video that I had seen before. On the floor, was another grown man completely bound and gagged. I am assuming this was one of the tortured man's accomplices. He was visibly shaking from hearing the commotion in the nearby room. The captor holding the video camera showed a hatch in the floor. He brought me over to the hatch in the floor where I had previously seen the child from the video before and opened it. He extended his hand into the hole in the floor, and I saw a small hand reach out for help. He panned the flashlight inside of the hole and there were three small children inside. A young boy and two girls. They were terrified as he stood there with his hand extended. The boy finally peered out of the hole. The man pointed across the room to the man on the floor, bound and gagged. The boy began to cry tears of joy and raised both of his arms up to the man. The boy called down into the hole to the other girls and they peered out. Their crying stopped as they saw their vicious captor lying on the floor helpless. The man holding the camera brought each one of them out of the hole and panned the camera to the left side of the hallway where another man waited in the hallway. He didn't have a mask on. I paused the video. It was dark but I could see his face a bit.

I stopped the video and captured a snapshot of the man in the hallway who was waiting to court the children to safety. I put his photo into an editor and took it frame by frame, pixel by pixel until the photo was resolved to something manageable. I zoomed in 200 percent, 300 percent, then resolved the photo again. It was still a bit pixelated, so I ran it through Movavi, a photo editor that de-pixelates blurry photos. Cops and law enforcement use it sometimes to clean up shaky security camera footage. The de-pixelating had completed. I opened it and

95

zoomed in 350 percent, right to the man's face. *I gasped,* "Perry"... There was my friend, in the white flames of the fire. Mother...Fucker, I shouted. I stood up out of my chair in complete disbelief. He was alive and he went back to finish what was started.

What did this mean? How did the video get to me? Was I talking with him the whole time? Did he Gamble? Needless to say, I had a lot of fucking questions at this point. I was elated that he was ok on one hand. On the other, I felt guilt that I was on the relatively safe digital end of this nightmare, and he was on the forefront, directly on the fucking battlefield. I wondered who the other man was in the video and where they were now. I started to do some recon on the video to see if I could determine when it was taken, geolocation, and any other information. I was able to pull some information from the video's metadata using a program that I frequented, called Exif-Tool. It was a common tool that we used to decode videos and photos that our targets posted to their Twitter or Facebook accounts. It was helpful in getting information from the metadata and determining varying aspects of the footage.

I was able to extract some info. The video was taken just a few days ago. It was fresh. I wasn't able to determine the exact geolocation coordinates from the video. However, I did get a general longitude and latitude from the video. I checked it three different times as it didn't make any sense. I was expecting Pakistan, Iraq, Afghanistan, or someplace in Northern Africa. It didn't make any sense. The longitude and latitude read out 36.263994, -114.806324. It was northeast of Nellis Air Force Base, Nevada. Suddenly, it made sense to me. The coordinates were within the Nevada desert; a barren landscape that resembled the deserts of Iraq and Afghanistan. The floors were covered with sand residue. The people inside of the building were sweating profusely. Jesus Christ, they were in the United States, not in a distant warzone. This was inside of my home country. The location was a few miles away from a gypsum mining facility in the Nevadan desert, less than thirty miles away from sunny Las Vegas.

## 10: Roll Call

There were only a couple of things in the world that made me feel regret. One was being so distant from my family and the pain that they likely felt in my absence. I wanted to tell them that I was still alive. I couldn't imagine the pain that they felt, knowing that I was dead. The other regret that I had carried was dragging Rayssa into my messy life. I had made a promise to myself that I wouldn't bring anyone else into this hurricane of a life that I led, but I went against my instincts anyway. Things were heating up now and I wanted to shake her so that nothing could come back on her. It's easier said than done when you're completely alone. Getting rid of the only person that you can share thoughts with is not something that comes easily. Perry was alive, I was gunning down targets with Gamble, and someone was going to hit back at some point. It wasn't a matter of "if," but "when." I always had a strong sense of when things were getting hot. I think that was how I had managed to wiggle out of so many dire situations in my brief history on this Earth. Rayssa hadn't contacted me in a day or so and I was happy about that. I thought that maybe we would just drift apart if we let time take its toll.

That day, I went over to the store around the corner to stash another one of the USB drives that I had created. This one had some information for Perry, if he were ever to locate it. I was paranoid at this point and was looking over my shoulder. After I placed the USB drive and was walking out of the store, I noticed a couple of shady characters on a small motorcycle eyeing me from the adjacent street corner. There's a saying in Brazil that if you see two men on a motorcycle wearing flipflops, it's never a good thing. That's how the robberies and murders in Brazil usually happen. The guy on the back is usually the robber or shooter and the driver is the getaway man. They both had helmets on as well, which added even further to the suspicion. Nobody wears helmets in Brazil unless they are concealing their faces. They had shorts on, so at least I knew they didn't have heavy weapons. Maybe a pistol but not anything long-range. I began my walk back to my apartment and picked up the pace when I heard the low rumble of their motorcycle starting up. It was an older bike, definitely not spy-quality. If they were really spies, I'd assume that they would be a bit more adept at concealment tradecraft. However, low-budget hitmen in Brazil didn't have too much training.

I took a hard right down into an alley that was too small for even a motorcycle to go down. It was going downhill at about a 40-degree angle. I walked through the hanging clothes that the residents put out to dry while some people looked down at me from some of the windows in the stacked slums above. The houses were stacked atop one another in an irregular fashion. The residents knew that I didn't live there. Good thing I was dressed in some beat up local attire. If the gangs in the neighborhood smelled a cop, I would be dead in a few minutes. I heard the engine of the motorcycle rev a couple of times before shutting off. I looked back and could see a distant sight of one of the guys getting off the bike. He kept his helmet on as I glanced over my shoulder, looking at him through the lines of hanging clothes. Shit, they were definitely following me. I began to run, jumping from the low concrete porches to the street below. I was in a fucking maze and had no idea where I was going. I looked back occasionally as I sprinted through the slums and could see the guy in the front gaining on me. I cut downside streets and over the top of some houses. The people of the neighborhood were suspiciously watching me as I bolted past them. I entered a long alleyway. Not the best spot to run from someone as they would have a clear line of sight for at least seventy-five meters. As soon as I hit the opening of that long alleyway, I went into an all-out sprint. I saw two adolescent boys standing on top of a house about twenty meters in front of me. The boy in the front whistled to me and signaled me to come up the narrow stairwell. I didn't have much time to think. What if they were with the guys chasing me? If I kept running, the guys from the motorcycle would certainly catch up to me and gun me down in this alleyway. I knew that they were about to turn the corner into the alley behind me.

I made a decision and cut left up the narrow stairwell. I rounded the corner and saw the boys atop one of the roofs. They crouched down and called me over to them, telling me to keep low. I crouched and made my way over to them. They laid down and called me to crawl to the edge of the rooftop with them. We approached the edge of the roof and looked down at the alleyway. The guys from the motorcycle were coming to the spot where I went up the stairs. They stopped in the alley and looked around. They both had pistols and were looking up the alley to the end, scanning for me. One of them grabbed a cell phone out of his pocket and began to type some numbers. Before he could hit the send button, I heard the cracking of what sounded like rifle fire. The guy holding the cellphone dropped as I saw the face shield of his helmet shatter. It was painted with blood inside. The second man drew his gun to the stairwell where I ascended and run up it. I could hear his footsteps clattering up the dusty stairwell. As he made it to the top, I heard another three shots. It sounded like a silenced pistol this time.

One of the boys that aided me whistled loudly as he looked around the rooftop as if he were awaiting someone. I heard the distant sound of another whistle. The two boys stood up and extended a hand to me. I got up as they walked me over to the stairwell where I had made my way up. I saw a group of 5 or 6 men standing there: all armed. Two of them had silenced pistols and one had an AK-47. Three of them had encircled the downed man in the alleyway; the first one hit. They looked down at his lifeless body as two of them grabbed his legs, the other held his arms. They dragged him into a nearby door of one of the slum's homes. The other two men started to drag the man from the stairwell into the alley, eventually leading into the same door. Four of the five men disappeared into the home. However, the one that had the AK-47 emerged and walked toward me. He told the two boys that they could go now and handed them both a handful of cash. I could see how much, but it was likely more money than they had ever seen. The guy told me to come with him as we ascended the stairwell. We passed by the stacked homes as people watched us walking by them. A woman reached out of one of the homes with two bottles of water and handed them to the man. He reached back and handed me one of them as I followed him up the stairs. He eventually led me into a home at the top of the favela. Inside, there were a few guys sitting at a small rusty kitchen table. There was something cooking on the stove as steam was lifting from a pot on the gas burner.

I sat with the group of men at the table as the lead guy told me his name, Joao. I was unsure of why they had just saved my life. I was a gringo in the middle of one of the most notoriously deadly northeastern Brazilian favelas. I shouldn't be alive right now and I knew it. I could hear old school West Coast rap playing in the background. It was a bit different to hear Ice Cube and Eazy-E in the Brazilian slums. However, for these guys to live at the top of this notorious favela, they had to be connected. They ran this place and it showed. These guys were gangsters, and nobody stepped on their territory without permission. Shit, even the cops and military in Brazil knew better. Gangland in the favela was different from gangland in the US. These guys were more heavily armed than the military and knew the streets. The never-ending maze of houses, alleys and rooftops created a perfect urban warfare advantage for them. Once again, I asked Joao why him and his crew had helped me, killed two of my would-be assailants, and made their bodies disappear. This wasn't normal by any means.

Joao responded to me by showing me his phone. I saw a text message from someone saying "they found him, he's heading into the favela now. 2 guys behind him, moto helmets, two handguns." Someone tipped them off. Someone was watching me. I asked Joao why someone would be helping me and who it was. He looked at me and laughed. He said, "You've been living in my area here for a while now. Do you really think that you've just been lucky? Nobody has ever robbed you, assaulted you, or messed with you at all. Do you think that's luck? I guess not, I replied. So, what now?--I said.

**Joao**: Well, you seem to be attracting some attention these days. I would say that it's probably a bad idea for you to go back to your shitty little apartment anytime soon. I will send some of my guys over there tonight to pick up your stuff. You're staying here until we get our instructions.

**Me:** Sure, that's all right with me.

About an hour or so passed before one of Joao's guys came back into the kitchen. He was just getting off a phone call with someone and was looking at me. He leaned over and whispered something to Joao, as Joao looked across the table at me. Joao pushed a 9mm Beretta across the kitchen table. Then, he handed me the small black backpack that was on the floor and gave me a nod. I looked inside and found three extra magazines, a box of fifty extra rounds, a small netbook laptop, and a burner cellphone. In the front pocket of the backpack, I found a Canadian passport, a thick stack of Canadian money, three credit cards, and a driver's license. The passport and driver's license had my picture on them. I had been through this before, so I knew that my time here in Brazil was coming to an abrupt end.

Joao told me that I needed to be relocated and that he didn't know anything other than that. He didn't know who I was, what I had done, or why people were trying to make me disappear. He worked for the money and that was it. Someone on my side had him on the payroll and he was simply a merchant with a lot of resources. He gave me a phone number to contact for my next set of instructions. Joao gave me some advice and told me that the kill squad that came after me would not come back into the favelas. However, they would likely have hitters at the local airports, bus stops, and even marine ports. He told me that I needed to follow the guides that would be set out for me, otherwise I was not going to make it out of here. I looked down at the phone number on the paper card. It was written in permanent marker on a queen of spades card from a standard deck. The guys in the kitchen walked me out of the side door and down the stairs. At the bottom of the stairs, a black 750 cc Suzuki motorcycle awaited. Joao handed me a black shirt. It was a bit battered and worn so that I would blend into the local population. He handed me a helmet with a black tinted facemask as well to conceal my face. The last thing that he told me was the name of an office building complex on the other side of the city. I had remembered passing by it as there was a large sculpture of a man sitting beside it. He told me to go there, go to the third floor, using the back stairwell, head to room B-31, lock the door and call the number on the card. Joao told me not to stop anywhere. No gas stations, no apartment, nothing. Head straight to the mark and make the call.

I got on the bike and thanked them. They didn't care too much about me, I could tell. They were mercenaries who didn't give a shit about what I was into. They just got paid. I put on the helmet and started it up, putting the loaded pistol behind my back into my waistband and tucked my shirt over it. I headed down the alleyway, looking in my rearview mirror and saw them dispersing from the narrow corridor. I hadn't ridden a motorcycle for years now and it felt liberating. I remembered when I was a kid growing up. My father had bought a dirt bike for me, and I used to ride all day during the summer breaks from school. It was like I was a young kid again, wandering into the unknown. I had a strong sentimental moment as I rode out of that alleyway, knowing that I just narrowly escaped certain death. As I rode through the city, I passed police officers, women walking with their children, homeless people begging on the street and selling bottles of water at red lights. It was just getting dark outside at this point and the sun was setting behind me the whole way to the safehouse. I could see the amber hue of the sunset reflecting from my sideview mirrors on the motorcycle. As I approached the safehouse location, I made a lap around the block surrounding the site to ensure that there weren't any suspicious cars or people anticipating my arrival. I was in the government district so there was a significant police presence around the area. That didn't necessarily make me feel comfortable after the corrupt politicians and law enforcement members that I had sniffed out with Gamble over the past few weeks. However, being in a populated area did make me more comfortable than being in a desolate field or favela slum.

I parked the bike on a side street on the southeast side of the office building and made my way across the street and up to the gated entryway. There was a guard present at the gate. I opened up my pack and looked at the name on the Canadian passport; "Michael Jalisto" was printed below my photo. I rang the guard shack's intercom, and they asked my name and office number. I told them my Canadian name and office B-31. The guard buzzed the door open, saying "welcome back, Mr. Jalisto" in Portuguese. I took the stairwell up to the third floor and walked up to the door at the end of the hallway; B-31. There was a keypad to enter the office suite, but I didn't have the code. I tried the phone number on the card that Joao gave to me. Red light and beeping ensued. Wrong code. I tried the birthday on the Canadian ID card, no dice. I pulled out the card with the phone number on it and tried that one as well. Finally, green light and I'm in! I pulled the Beretta 9mm out of my waistband and pulled the backpack off me, propping the door ajar. I crept through the office suite and cleared each room, one by one. It was empty, no company here. I checked the bathroom, the two office suites, the kitchen area, and the communications closet. It was a smaller office suitable for only a couple of people. It looked like a typical small office for a couple of lawyers or something. However, the bookshelves were empty and there was a pull-out couch bed in the main corner office. It had a nice view of the streets below and I could see my motorcycle from the office. I made sure that the doors were locked and rigged a broom against the entry door that I came in so that if anyone opened it up, the broom would hit the floor and give me enough time to get out in front of whomever was in there with me.

I sat on the pull out couch and took out the small laptop and cell phone. Before I made any calls, I wanted to see if anyone was tracking me. I opened the laptop and looked at the outgoing and incoming data packets to determine whether any information was being automatically pushed out before I connected it to the Wi-Fi. There was a sticky note on the desk that had the Wi-Fi name and password. No outbound beacons on the laptop that I could see. I ran a *netstat* command, looked through the running processes, programs, and scheduled tasks. Nothing suspicious, so I connected the laptop to the wireless network. I did some more recon across the local network to see if there were any other computers or devices hooked into the Wi-Fi network. I ran the Nmap program and did a network sweep. I could see the office alarm system, router, and an IP-connected security camera hub. Pretty standard stuff, but no user-based devices.

The next step was to check my phone. With it completely turned off, I grabbed a paperclip and bent it into a straight line. I inserted the paperclip prong into the SIM card slot and opened the tray. I pulled out the SIM card and copied down the IMEI and serial numbers. I went to the manufacturers website and popped in the numbers to see if they matched the manufacturer. They did, so I knew that the SIM card was indeed real and from the hardware vendor. I turned on the phone and setup "Find my Phone" by Google. If the phone were cloned, I would see the phone's SIM card in two different locations. No location came up on the map. That was good since I had airplane mode on. I turned off airplane mode and saw the phone's location beacon on the map. It was the only location, and it was exactly where I was. I knew that the phone was legit, not copied or cloned, and that I didn't have any spies on the newly gifted digital devices. The laptop was clean and cell phone was clear.

I managed to hack my way into the surveillance system and view the cameras outside. I loved it when CCTV and IP camera vendors left the factory default settings for login usernames and passwords. There was a display with a set of eight cameras up on my laptop. Four inside the building and three outside. There was a dead camera not functioning on the Northeast corner of the building that showed a gray screen. At least I could see 80 percent of the building and three out of the four external entry/exits. I had a clear view of my surroundings, one main entry into the office suite, four external entry and exit-ways, and full control over the local network. The place was secure enough for me to make the call. I popped the SIM card back into the phone and watched the upper left corner while the cell service bars propagated to three out of four connectivity bars. I dialed the number on the card that Joao gave to me and listened while it rang. It rang a few steady tones before someone picked it up. They didn't say anything. I responded, "Hello?" I heard a faint voice of a woman say, "don't say any names."

I recognized the voice immediately. It was Rayssa.

It all made sense to me now. It wasn't some twist of fate that we had met. It wasn't coincidence that she helped me make my way into Brazil. It wasn't luck that she changed restaurants. She was watching over me and guiding my trail. I was usually extremely adept at reading people, picking up on patterns, and finding the oddities in life. That is what had kept me alive until this point, but I had overlooked who she was and what her purpose was. She responded back in a tone as if she didn't know who I was and I didn't know her. I imagined that she wanted to protect her identity if someone was listening into our conversation. She told me to open my computer and use the encrypted messenger app that was pre-installed for more information. The line went dead as she hung up.

I opened the messenger application and pulled it up onto my screen. She had messaged me saying that she wanted to tell me before, but it was for my protection. We had a lengthy conversation as she gave me the details of my next move. She told me that I would be coming back into the US soon under my Canadian cover. I opened the Canadian passport and saw a US work Visa in the middle of the fold. She told me where I would be staying and that I would have a handler once I arrived. Flight information, cover story, car pickup, the works. She told me that she knew that I would be tempted to contact my family, but to resist that urge as I would be directly placing them in danger. I asked her if she could tell me what my family was up to these days since it had been nearly two years since I had spoken with them. They assumed that I was dead. She paused before letting me in on some current events. My father had passed away unexpectedly and suddenly while away for a work trip in Pennsylvania. That was rough on me as I knew my mother had lost two family members in the course of a couple of years. Me being one of them. All the while, I was alive. These feelings of guilt and grieving ripped through my soul as I envisioned the pain that my mother had to be feeling.

We talked through the evening and into the night as she told me all about her role in what she referred to as "The Foundation." It was a concerted global effort, run by an underground community that was centralized around freeing the innocent children that had been caught in the crosshairs of these wicked, radical, and ruthless humans. The network was extensive and reached nearly every corner of the world. It consisted of government workers, current and past military members, hackers, bankers, truck drivers, police officers; even social workers were in the fold. We had a unified front; an army of well-trained covert operatives that were encircling this pyramid of wretched demons. For the first time in quite a while, I didn't feel alone anymore. This group had resources that were extensive enough to move me from country to country, watch my back, and even murder people on my behalf. They had just orchestrated a calculated defensive strategy, killed two men hunting me down, gave me a new international identity, a vehicle, and a safehouse in a matter of a few hours. The goddamned CIA could barely pull that off, especially in a third world country.

I would be heading to the United States in forty-eight hours. I was to remain in the safehouse until that time came. I was ready to come home now. I had a new sense of unity with my guardians and comrades, and I was prepared to lock eyes with evil, stand up, and help to further cause. My mission back in the US would not be to hide and conceal myself as I was in Brazil, but rather to take on a new role in The Foundation. I wasn't a victim, nor was I to be tucked away in a safehouse under the radar. I was a weapon, and they knew it was time for me to contribute again.

## 11: Loopback

The first night in the safehouse was odd. I had overwhelming feelings of anxiety as I thought of my return to my home country. It was somewhat surreal knowing that I was taking on yet another identity and coming back so closely to my family, although I wouldn't be able to contact them. I was almost more content being in another country and far away, as I couldn't be tempted to drive past their homes or go near them. When I was here in Brazil, I was far away both physically and emotionally and that made it more manageable for me. However, I was excited to come home. I missed the small things like being able to throw toilet paper in the toilet and not into some small trash can beside the toilet. I was excited to be able to drive a motorcycle without the fear of falling into a meter-deep pothole or being robbed while walking down the street in broad daylight.

There was something bothering me deeply. I was perturbed as I felt like I was running away again. I was always running. Even though my new mission in the US would be far less passive than my tenure in Brazil. I had created a life here, met a wonderful woman, and had become emotionally invested in my work. I knew that there was always a point at which I had to walk away. I couldn't save everyone and had limited resources. If I were to go after every horrible predator that I came across, I would never sleep. You had to know when to shut it down and when to turn it back on. Leaving the light switch on all of the time was bad for me and everyone around me. But still, there were things that I had to close up here during my last forty-eight hours.

I remembered a particular finding that I had noted when reviewing the massive data sets on General Saad and his co-conspirators. There was one particular item that I had marked for later review, as it was close to home. If you can recall, General Saad was involved in the online marketplace scheme and was selling kids online to predators paying large sums of money. Well, one night Gamble and I went down a rabbit hole and wound up on the other side with some information that stuck with me. Gamble had advised me to move on as it was too close to my proximity. See, when hunting in the devil's lair, it is a rule of thumb that you don't hunt where you live. It's just a fucking rule as in doing so, you reveal your position to the enemy. However, my position was already revealed. My identity was foiled, and I was being hunted. What is the one thing that predators do not expect from their prey? To hunt them back…

When I was reviewing General Saad's intricate life, I found a target in Fortaleza, Brazil. This one was a case that I wasn't able to forget so easily. One of General Saad's clients that was a frequent purchaser of children disguised as eBay products was a regional politician and business investor. Gamble and I were able to track a purchase through his personal WhatsApp and stitch the messages together with the eBay purchase records. We set up a fake eBay website that looked identical to the real site and intercepted one of the messages from General Saad to him. We led him to the fake website and once he made his purchase, we had the IP address and relative geolocation of his domicile. Once we had that information, we put together a heat map of where the guy lived. We landed on the southeastern side of the city outskirts. There was a moderate size condominium and a fairly large house complex beside it. The home had large walls surrounding it and a concreate courtyard inside. Google Earth is a lovely thing indeed.

The home looked almost like Osama bin Laden's home in Pakistan. At least that is what the layout reminded me of. It looked like the perfect place for a piece of shit predator to live and commit his heinous acts. Once we had the lead on this guy, I took the liberty of sending him a nice piece of malware in the fake eBay purchase confirmation email and he opened it. It always boggled my mind of just how careless these people were, even though they were committing crimes that could land them in prison for life, or even the death sentence in some cases. Nevertheless, one night I was able to get a live feed into his home security system. I had access to his local area network and perused around, seeking more information on his daily life. It was this next part that burned his image into my mind. He had two daughters and a wife. The security cameras inside of his home picked up just about everything. He regularly came home after 1 or 2 in the morning completely inebriated drunk. He would wake up his entire house upon arrival. I would watch the kids scurry into their mother's room when his headlights pulled into the carport. That's never a good sign.

In one of the videos, he walked into the house around 2:30 a.m., beat his wife inside of the upstairs hallway until she was laying in the fetal position on the floor. Then, he proceeded to go to his eldest daughter's room. She looked to be around ten years old. The other one was maybe 5 or 6. They were so fearful of him that it made my hands sweat just thinking about the hell that this family went through regularly. I watched the video footage and the look on the eldest daughter's face when he closed her bedroom door behind him was a look that I had seen before. I had no idea how long he had been abusing his precious children and beating his wife, but I had a fair idea on how long he was involved in peddling children on the digital black market. It wasn't a one-time deal. He was a frequent customer of good old General Saad. The purest of evil are the ones that can do this to their own flesh and blood. It took a special kind of demon to be able to live with themselves after destroying the innocence of the ones that looked to them for protection. As I mentioned before, I wasn't hiding anymore. I was a weapon, and there were some things that I had to take care of before I left Brazil.

I sent a message to Gamble and waited a few minutes. I told him that I needed him to check the camera feeds in the politicians' house, external street cameras in the surrounding area, and his cell phone activity for the last couple of hours. Gamble started to type as I saw the ellipses panning the message screen. He would type and then stop, never sending a message back to me. I sent Gamble another message and told him that I would be taking this on with or without his help. However, I would appreciate the assistance greatly. He hesitated before replying, "ok, I got you"... He gave me a briefing on what was happening inside of the home, outside, and on his mobile devices. The wife was home sleeping, and the kids were staying at a family member's home outside of the city. They had gone away on a church retreat in the interior parts of the state and were not coming back until the weekend. The wife was at home sleeping on the sofa in the loft area outside of her children's rooms. The father had left the home about an hour ago, but Gamble wasn't sure where he had gone to.

My opportunity was now, and it was perfect. I looked down at my black backpack and opened the front pocket. There was my handgun. I had never killed anyone before. At least not directly. I had been a part of this phase of my work but had never pulled the trigger. I did have significant training in weaponry and had been using firearms since I was a young boy. I remember the first time I had shot a gun. I was six years old, and my father taught me to shoot a .45 caliber Colt 1911. It was my grandfather's service pistol from the army when he was in Okinawa. I remembered how scared I was when I pulled the trigger. My daddy held my arms straight and we aimed at an old chicken coop that was on our property. I squeezed the trigger while closing my eyes and head the first bang. My father whispered into my ear and told me to open my eyes on the next shot. This was only a few weeks after I had been assaulted by the man in the shopping mall bathroom, so I knew why my father made me open my eyes. He told me to focus, breath, feel the gun as a part of me and squeeze the trigger. Bang, and a another one…bang! I kept squeezing as the tears ran down my face, envisioning the man in front of me. After the magazine was empty, I ran inside to my mother. I remember how angry my mother was with my father that day. He sat outside and shot that gun nearly all day. I knew that the pain he felt was more than I would ever know. I knew that pain now. The pain of an adult that was not able to help a child being victimized, let alone his own child. I remembered my father's pain and thought of the mother of the two girls in that house of misery. She was lost and her children's innocence was being torn right in front of her. I could help, and I was not going to let another parent feel the way that my father felt.

I put on a black hooded sweatshirt, jeans, and a pair of boots. I had a nice pair of motorcycle riding gloves that fit my hands perfectly. I swung the backpack over my shoulder as I tucked the 9mm into the back of my jeans. I put the helmet on and walked down the stairwell leading down the safehouse. I looked back at the building as I pulled the motorcycle key out of my pocket. I rode into the night, down the barren Brazilian streets. It was a quiet night in that part of town as there was another festival happening by the beach. Most of the police were pulling security around the festival, so the police presence was minimal in other parts of the city that night. I rode through the streets calmly as I listened to the music that I had on the headphone earbuds underneath my helmet. I listened to a calm symphony from Chopin and Bach and practiced breathing exercises on the way to the politician's home.

As I approached the street where the man's home was, I killed the motorcycles engine about 200 yards away from the front gate. There was a guard stationed atop the inside of the shack overlooking the street below. I was peering over to the front entrance from behind a concrete wall. The area that I was in was poorly lit as the streetlights did not extend this far over. However, the front entrance was well-lit and had no traffic. I waited a few minutes after scouting the area and sent Gamble a message, letting him know that I was there. He replied, "I know you're there. I saw your headlight from the camera in front of his complex dummy. It's been a while since you've been out of the house, huh?" Gamble told me that the wife was on the phone with her sister and that he could hear the conversation through one of the cameras inside of the house. He said that she was crying and recanting her situation to her sister on her phone call. I waited there for the next thirty minutes without a single car or pedestrian passing by. It was nearly 3 in the morning at that time and this place was a literal ghost town. Gamble sent me another message and told me that the father had called his wife. He said that she was hysterical after a brief, but heated conversation and she appeared to be scrambling to pack a small suitcase. She was running around the house looking for something, but he wasn't sure what. She kept running outside into the carport and looking through their other car. "She must be looking for the car keys," Gamble said. She was trying to leave before he came back! "Shit man, he's on his way. 3 km out!"

My heart started to pound so loudly that I could feel it in my teeth. You know when you get so nervous that your testicles seem to crawl back into your body? It felt like someone had put an IV drip of diesel fuel into my veins as I pulled the 9 mm out of my waistband. I pushed my bike into an open alleyway and faced it down the narrow dirt road. It was only large enough for a motorcycle as it was used for pedestrian traffic. The getaway route was pre-planned by Gamble as it led to a nearby favela. If I made it into the favela, my worries were not with the police, but with the local gangs. I'd have to take my chances. At least I was armed this time. "2 minutes out," Gamble replied. I started my breathing exercises again and I inhaled through my nose deeply and exhaled through my mouth. I positioned myself on the same side of the road as the house and the entry gate, about forty feet down the street. I was behind the concrete wall corner that rounded their property. I could see just over the top of the wall and noticed a light on inside of the man's house. It suddenly turned off as I saw a faint reflection of a car's headlights illuminate the adjacent concrete wall on the other side of the street. It had to be him. I could see a car approaching my position as it swerved out of the lane and into the middle of the road. It had to be this drunk bastard. I readied myself. Breath man, I whispered as I racked the handgun back and put a round into the chamber. I could see him approaching the gate as he was about fifty yards away from the front entrance and one hundred or so yards away from me.

I started to walk with my left shoulder against the concrete wall, approaching his car as he waited for the gate guard to open the door from his perch atop the complex. I moved swiftly, staying in the shadows of the streetlights. I kept the helmet on as I didn't want to waste any time in my exit. I was about fifteen meters away as I saw his face inside of the car. He was lighting a cigarette and the light from the flame showed me that it was him. I had seen him so many times on camera and in photos, but now it was real. He was right there. I kept walking slowly as I saw the guard give a thumbs-up to him outside the tower window. I saw the blinking orange light on the gate door flashing as I heard the metal door beginning to slide across the opening rails. I was ten feet away from him, but he hadn't seen me yet. As he waited for the gate to open up, I came up alongside his driver's side. Everything slowed down. Time stood still in that moment. It was like a video in slow-motion, frame by frame. I could hear music playing loudly inside of his car. With his lit cigarette in his mouth, he caught an image of me and slowly turned his head to my position. By that time, I was already pointing my 9 mm at his temple, only about two feet away from him. I closed my eyes for a split second and heard my father's voice. Softly and calmly, he whispered in my ear, "open your eyes and squeeze, child." I opened my eyes and breathed in deeply before squeezing the first shot. Bang! The glass window shattered as the first round struck him in the side of the head. Bang, bang, bang; three more shots as he slumped over forward. I looked over my right shoulder as the gate opened up about halfway and saw his wife standing at the carport. She had stopped and was looking right at me. She wasn't running away. She wasn't trying to stop me. She wasn't screaming or crying. She was peaceful. She folded her arms and stood her ground as I took the life of this man who had tortured her and her beautiful little babies for years. The guard in the tower above slammed the door above closed and dropped to the floor in his tower. He had hit the button to close the gate door. As I stood there watching the gate close, the man's wife stood firm the entire time, staring at me in the eyes. She was unwavering and fearless.

The door closed as I ran back down the sidewalk. I entered the narrow corridor of the alleyway where I had stowed my motorcycle and got on. I started the bike and made my way down the alleyway without my headlights on until I came upon a clearing. As I made my way back to the safehouse with my mind wandering into the deep abyss, I didn't feel guilty. It was actually the exact opposite. I felt as though I had ridden the world of a parasite that was spreading through society. The sentiments of revenge wouldn't suffice to describe how I felt that night, but rather pure satisfaction and a driving sense of mission inside of me. I thought of all of the parents and loved ones that had been affected by this man and his lack of compassion for his fellow human beings and felt serene. I had thought about this moment many times over the course of my life and often wondered if I would be able to grapple with the tremendous feelings of guilt. However, there was no guilt in my soul, nor fear, only tranquility. I rode through the city's backstreets and felt as though I owned the night. I wanted to stay right there and bask in the moment, but I had to make my way back to the safehouse.

I came back to the safehouse and got on my computer. I sent Gamble a message, letting him know that it was done. Gamble never failed to surprise me. We had a sort of a friendship in which we were always trying to outdo one another. It was a game of chess that kept both of us moving in a common direction and a higher sense of purpose. He didn't let me down this time either. He sent me a screenshot of a news article from a top Romanian news outlet. Apparently, Interpol had been tipped off and executed a sting operation, uncovering an underground network of children being bought and sold on eBay. They had executed sixteen warrants over the course of the last twelve hours, rescued nearly 25 kidnapped children, made eleven arrests, and had nearly a dozen suspects on their international most wanted list. One of which being General Saad.

While I was taking care of a "local problem" in my own fashion here in Brazil, Gamble had orchestrated a multinational sting op and taken down a large nefarious and likely profitable network. I could only image the faces of the people at the top, knowing that their agents of death were either winding up dead, missing, or in prison for the rest of their natural-born lives. It was a monumental moment in our operation, and it was worthy of us taking a breath and giving ourselves a moment to realize what we were accomplishing together. We had not only gone on the offensive, but we had crystallized fear into the minds of our adversaries in a one-fell-swoop, coordinated, calculated, and intensely complex mission. I knew that Gamble had more significant ties that I had previously assumed. If we could pull something like this off, I wholeheartedly understood the depth of good in this world, and our collective commitment to the vanquishment of evil.

That night, I laid awake for hours thinking of the life that I had taken. From my military career, I had spoken with many guys that had taken a life before and they recanted their experiences to me as if it was permanently welded into their cerebral cortex. I remembered the moment that his eyes met mine and he knew that his time had come. When taking the life of a person that is filled with a lifetime of guilt, there is almost a sense of relief that you can see in their soul before you pull the trigger. It was almost as if he had been expecting the day to come for so long that he accepted what was inevitably going to happen. It was an odd experience as I still could not conjure any remorse, nor did I seek to. The only fear that I held was that I had opened a door inside of my own soul that I wouldn't be able to close. If I could snub out a degenerate so swiftly and without haste, would I continue to do the same? I had many questions that night, but I eventually slept peacefully with the thought of his family and the new life that they may be able to create together, putting their nightmare behind them.

The next morning, I tuned into the local news to see if it had made the headlines. As I flipped from one streaming news outlet to another, I thought about last night and the look on his face before I pulled the trigger. It was a surreal feeling, being the maestro of someone's last moments on this planet. I didn't care for it too much, although I knew

119

that what I had done was not only warranted, but long overdue. I couldn't get the thought out of my head and wondered if I should have handed it in a different way. Maybe I could have turned it over to law enforcement. Maybe I could have put together a story for the local news stations… Something, shit anything. Maybe I should have done this differently. I put those thoughts aside as I scoured the internet for articles, news feeds, blogs, videos, and any other information on the situation that I was part of last night. Nothing was circling through the ether about the murder of a well-known, respected and wealthy man right here in the city? It was highly unusual. I mean, murder is a common occurrence in Brazil. However, the usual gang on gang violence would even make headlines the following morning. The killing of a seemingly innocent civilian in front of his house didn't? It just didn't make any sense and I had a feeling deep in my heart as to why. You see, when something bad happens and there is no news of it to be found, that is so for a couple of reasons. Either the authorities do not want to disclose information because they have a lead on a suspect, or someone is covering it up to keep it out of the limelight. Either scenario was no good for me and I know that it was only a matter of time before someone stepped on my trail. In the real world, it's not like the movies. You don't have to leave dirty boot prints, tire tracks, or hair follicles to be sniffed out. Everything usually comes crashing down because someone is talking. Luckily for me, I had no connections with this gentleman prior to the past few days and the online reconnaissance that I had performed. Actually, if anything the traces would go back to Gamble as he had given me the intelligence on the target, and I was just the gun.

It was time for me to start moving. I had burned the bridges here in Brazil and I needed to go. I knew that to be true and I could feel the pot starting to boil. There were rules in this game, and I was breaking them all over the place as of late.

No killing: that's gone out the window.

Don't fall in love: Yea, too late on that.

Stay under the radar: Hardly…

At that point, I could see just how quickly one could become tangled into the web of treachery in this world and I was right in the middle of it. I had a compromised identity, staying in a safehouse, killed a man in front of his wife, and I was being exfiltrated from the country. Above all else, I had created and crystallized a romantic connection here and would be leaving her behind as well. I really couldn't think of anything that I was doing correctly at that point. When you're on the run, it's a big-time rule to never become attached to anyone or any place. I really could give a shit about Brazil, but I had someone that I felt close with after such a long time of lonesomeness and the thought of leaving bothered me more than the fact that I just took a man's life. I really cannot explain what that felt like but can only equate it to seeing the sun rise after a moonless night. When the night is so dark that you can't see your hand in front of your face, but then the sun starts to rise above the horizon. Giving you light, warming your skin, and illuminating your path to exit into safety. Out of all of the darkness, I had formed a bond with someone that I knew was truly on the side of righteousness. The only problem that I had was that she was staying here, and I was leaving.

## 12: Red-Eye

1745 hours the next day, I started to gather my stuff from the safehouse. I was executing my regimen to prepare for my departure. There is a list of things that one must accomplish before heading into international airports that regular civilians don't even contemplate. I completed all of the usual items like packing my bags, making sure I had the passport, wallet, proper clothing. However, I also had to ensure that if I were caught up, I could weasel my way out of a situation before being questioned too far. You see, when you are traveling with an assumed or fake identity, your paperwork is only part of the battle. The other aspects are what get people caught up. I had to go through my checklist meticulously and in a calculated way so that I could either explain, fight, or flee my way from anyone seeking to stop my passage.

I started to clear my electronic devices from any remnants of my life. I had a digital image of a computer saved on a USB drive that I loaded as my primary operating system. This image took the place of anything on my computer and was designed to demonstrate a boring life that I could explain if some nosey customs agent wanted me to turn on my computer. It had a bunch of fake financial reports with Canadian company logos on them, burner email accounts with my assumed Canadian identity, business proposals with my fake name signed at the bottom, and more. I took my phone and replaced the SIM card with a Canadian one that Rayssa had given me. It was fresh and void of any past activities, phone calls, messages, etc. My phone background was a dual picture of Niagara Falls from the Buffalo, NY side and the Canadian side so that if an airport agent looked at it, they would believe that I had been in both Canada and the United States before. I had fake text messages in my message queue over the last few days from spoofed Canadian and United States phone numbers. The messages were filled with tourist pictures of Brazil, anxious messages of homecoming, family photos from Canadian families, and fake work conversations from colleagues in the United States. I had a call log a mile long that showed frequent calls to and from Brazil, the US, and Canada. Hopefully an agent would never call one of the numbers. However, I had a game plan to call a US phone number in which Gamble would answer as a US national if I needed someone to vouch for me.

Everything was perfect and I had confidence that I wouldn't be stopped for any reason. You see, people that think covert identities need to be complicated. In the movies, you see special operations agents acting as apple farmers when they go undercover. It couldn't be further from the truth. In reality, when you change your identity, you need to make sure that you can hold a conversation about a particular subject for hours and days if needed. You need to have the ability to teach something new to someone who is an expert in that field. My training in counterintelligence taught me how to construct a covert identity on-the-fly if needed and this was the most important catalyst in creating a successful alternative identity. If you strayed too far away from that, you were putting yourself and others at risk of being discovered. My new identity as Mr. Michael Jalisto was simple. I wasn't married, didn't have a girlfriend, and I was in the computer programming field. I had come to Brazil twenty-five days ago to partake in the parties, music festivals, and I was an avid electronic music fan. I created fake PDF versions for an electronic music festival here in Fortaleza that took place just a week ago. I made sure that the QR codes went to a fake music festival website that I stood up as well. I was heading back to the United States to visit my cousin in Nevada. My cousin is a graphic designer and lives outside of Reno. I was flying into Las Vegas, renting a car, and driving to stay with him for a couple of weeks. I had a follow-on flight booked from Las Vegas to Ontario, Canada exactly two weeks from my arrival in Vegas. I carried proof of Canadian citizenship, my Canadian passport had seven prior US visit stamps of entry and departure, and I had proof of my job back in Canada. I even carried a fake work ID badge for a fake software development company in Canada. I created an online business presence for the fake company, false LinkedIn profiles of corporate executives, and a nice website for the company. My storyline was tighter than a steel drum and I knew it. I had done this before and knew exactly how to talk to people.

Traveling under a false identity is 50 percent preparation, 49 percent confidence, and 1 percent paperwork. People regularly travel on shitty fake passports without problems simply because they are prepared for conversations, and they are confident in their abilities.

My story was tight, but I needed a secondary plan. Going on a mission without a "plan B" was bad juju. There were no surefire promises when it comes to international air travel under a false identity, so I needed a fallback measure if things got dicey. I knew that the most probable situation would include either the authorities keeping me in Brazil sending me directly to Canada, or even worse; being discovered by someone other than the authorities. All scenarios were dangerous as we never knew the reach of the malicious actors and I could easily wind up as farming compost if I ran into the wrong person in my journey. I was a wanted man by some pretty nefarious and resourceful people, and you can never underestimate the power of the vast amount of money involved in this dark underground world. We constructed a fallback story that I was an undercover US DEA agent that was working in Brazil to track a global cartel network. For other people traveling under fake identities, a burner story like this would never work out. However, Gamble had managed to put some data in the DOJ's records that could validate my identity if shit hit the fan. Interpol and the US DOJ have a joint system that they use to identify their assets that are working on international projects. Gamble had created an identity for me that would checkout if they were to really dig into it. That story was pretty straightforward as if the authorities were to query me for information, I would not be obligated to share that with them due to national security reasons. However, if they searched for my identity, they would indeed come up with a picture of me, age, height, sex, biographical information, and other data that I could correlate on the validity of my persona.

It was 2100 hours, and my flight was to depart at midnight tonight. I was ready. When I was exiting the safehouse, I made sure to clean up behind me. No physical or digital traces of my stay were present. I had disassembled the pistol into about ten different pieces and thrown them in dumpsters around the city last night along with any remnants of my Brazilian identity. I threw a few computers hard drives into a sewer drain outside of the safehouse after I had purged the data and then thrown them in the microwave. Last night, I left the motorcycle in the street with the keys in the ignition. Brazil is an easy place to get rid of a vehicle as the only thing you need to do is to leave the keys in it overnight. Of course, the motorcycle was no longer there. Someone had already stolen it so if anyone had spotted the bike last night when I took out the world's greatest dad, they would find it somewhere in a Brazilian favela belonging to a criminal.

I went out into the street and hailed a taxi. It took a few minutes for one to pass by with their light on, but after a bit one came by. We didn't talk much on the way to the airport, and I took some time to focus and get myself leveled for the journey. As we drove through the city, I thought about all of the things that I had seen and done here. Both good times and bad, I appreciated the lessons that were welded to my spirit. I wanted to send a message to Rayssa and thank her, but I couldn't risk the communication on the new SIM card that I had. We approached the highway exit leading to the airport and I looked to the sky and watched a flight taking off heading north. I wondered if anyone on that plane was aware of the evil that this world held. Probably not, I thought. The majority of people are so consumed by their day-to-day lives that they don't take the time to think about the other side of this life. That made me comfortable knowing that so many people led a happy and simple existence. I wouldn't wish for anyone to experience the type of life that I was leading. There was no glamour in doing what I do. It was a lonely place for anyone, but it has to be done by someone.

The cab driver pulled up the airport terminal and I handed him forty Brazilian reals for the ride. It was only a fifteen real trip, but I told him to keep the change. He had a picture of his family on his dashboard. Two little kids, both boys and a wife. They looked happy and content with life. I smile at the man and get out of the car. I was traveling light. Just a backpack and a medium sized suitcase. One checked bag and one carry-on, I told the airport worker at the ticketing counter. She asked for my passport as I reached into my backpack to pull it out. I had one headphone in my ear playing some music as I smiled at her and handed over my passport. She began typing the information into the computer while periodically looking down at the passport. She looked up at me and paused for a couple of seconds before looking to her left at her coworker. She motioned over to one of her colleagues at a ticketing counter about fifteen feet to my right, calling him over. He was an older gentleman with gray hair and appeared to be a manager of some sort. I glanced over my left shoulder and noticed two military police officers walking through the terminal. One of them made eye contact with me as I turned my head back to the ticketing counter. I could hear the steps of the military police officers getting closer to my position as the attendant began talking with the gentleman that came over.

She was asking him how to manually enter the information into their system as if something was wrong with the passport. I was getting a bit nervous that the passport had something wrong with it. The older gentleman looked at me and asked me if I had any other form of identification. I said, "I have my ID card for my job but that's really it." He said, ok that will do. Can I please see that? I handed him my job ID card and they began to enter the information into the computer. I heard the two military police officers approaching to my right. I didn't want to turn around and look at them as I feared that would raise suspicions. I was looking at the ticketing counter attendant to my right and kept an eye on her for visual cues to the police officers behind my right shoulder. The attendant to my right smiled and waved to them, calling one of them by his first name. She looked excited and exited her work area to jog over to him and give him a hug. It looked like they were family or close friends by the way they embraced. They began to talk about their week and how happy he was to see her. I was in the clear and smiled at the group before looking back over to the ticketing counter. I asked the gentleman, "is everything ok"? He looked up at me and said, "yes, yes everything is fine. Our system is not working properly this week and we are having to manually enter all information instead of scanning passports like usual." The woman looked at me and apologized, saying that she was new on the job and didn't understand how to do this yet.

After a couple of minutes, they checked my suitcase and printed my tickets. "Terminal B, gate 11" she said. I thanked the ticketing workers and started to move to my next waypoint. I came up the escalator and followed the signs to the security checkpoint. There were only a few people in line ahead of me. I was hoping for a bigger crowd. More people going through security creates a sense of urgency for security workers. Less people going through gives them more time to scrutinize and inspect. There were a few families and couples, but it appeared as though I was the only solo traveler in the line. There were three open lines in the security area, so we were moving quickly. I approached the security worker and got my passport and ticket ready. As I walked up to the security station, I smiled at him and greeted him in Portuguese. "Boa noite, tudo bem"? That means, good evening, how are you? He looked up at me and said, "I'm fine" stoically. I noticed that he was listening to a local soccer game. It was between Fortaleza and Ceara. These two teams were bitter rivals and Fortaleza won by four goals. I assumed that he was not a fan of the Fortaleza soccer team by his deflated demeanor. I expressed my unhappiness for the ongoing game and told him that I was a fan of Ceara. I said that I was sick of Fortaleza winning and Ceara needed to start playing like a real soccer team. He smiled at me and said, "I have suffered as a Ceara fan for a long time and tonight's game is no different." We smiled and laughed at the fact Ceara was being beaten up again and he handed me my documents and told me to have a good evening. It's amazing what a little bit of observation and social engineering can do when you are fleeing a country on a fake identity.

I opened my backpack and took out my laptop and cell phone, placing them into the plastic bin on the conveyor belt. I started to remove my shoes as one of the security agents told me that I could keep them on. As I walked through the metal detector, I noticed a man standing against a wall about fifty feet to my left toward my gate. He was on the phone, and it seemed as though he was intentionally trying not to look in my direction. Sometimes it's easier to see people that are trying not to look at you rather than people who are observing you. Maybe it was nothing, but I kept my eye on him as I held my hands and arms in the shape of a T so that the security agent could briefly frisk me for contraband. I gathered my belongings from the bin and placed them into my backpack. I headed toward my gate and approached the man standing against the wall. He didn't look like a law enforcement agent by any means. Long hair, beard, and wore business casual attire. You can tell when someone is institutionalized in law enforcement or military, and he most certainly was not. We had about ten feet of distance between us as I passed by him, and I noticed that he was reading a magazine. I couldn't tell what the magazine was, but it had bright orange and green writing on the cover page. I approached a small shop and stopped at the magazine rack. I saw the same-colored magazine that the man was holding. I reached for it and read the cover. The magazine was about home decor and floral arrangements. While it's certainly not unheard of for a man to read such material, he didn't fit the typical description for this magazines' demographic. The real reason for my suspicion was that the magazine was in German language. Not Brazilian Portuguese, not English, shit not even Spanish. My antenna was up. I kept it moving and made my way to the gate.

Instead of stopping at gate eleven, heading for the US, I carried on and didn't look back over my shoulder. As I approached the next set of gates 15-25, I made my way to gate number 18. This flight was heading to Santiago, Chile. I sat down against the glass window in a seat and watched people in the airport passing by. Within a few minutes, I noticed the same guy walking down the middle of the terminal, looking side to side as if he were searching for someone. I lowered my head and pulled the brim of my hand down a bit and waited. After a minute or so, I slowly raised my head and noticed the guy sitting about twenty feet away at the next gate over. The screen on that gate showed the next flight heading to Bogotá, Colombia in about thirty minutes. Ok, so here's a guy that speaks German, or at least has an interest in German floral arrangements, who is heading from Brazil to Bogotá, Colombia. I've seen more suspicious things in my life but given the circumstances, I needed to figure some things out here.

I looked at my ticket back to the United States. The first flight into the US was heading from Fortaleza, Brazil to Las Vegas. It was beginning to board. I could see some of the passengers lining up at my real gate. I waited. They called zones 1, 2, 3, and finally 4. I was still sitting at gate eighteen and keeping an eye on the German florist sitting at the gate to Bogotá. I heard the airport staff member speaking over the communications system calling for the last passengers for the flight to Las Vegas. I still waited. I was ready to make a move. However, if I went straight to my gate for the Las Vegas flight, he would surely follow me. What if he had connections at the airport and they were going to take me as soon as I made my way to the gate. My gate was to my left. The remaining gates in the terminal were to my right. I got up from my seat and went right. I walked quickly down the terminal walkway. I turned my phone's camera on and held it in my hand as I walked, recording a short video of what was behind me. As I continued walking, I pressed play on the video and saw the man walking behind me about 25-30 feet.

I could see a men's bathroom approaching to my left in front of me. In the middle of the men's and women's bathrooms, there was a smaller bathroom that was suited for a family or handicapped persons. I went straight to the smaller family bathroom and opened the door. For the second time in my life, I was being followed into a public bathroom by a man seeking to do me harm. As I opened the bathroom door, I knew that I could simply lock the door behind me, and he would have no chance of getting in there. He wouldn't be able to cause a scene as someone would certainly spot him and call for help. I could yell for help as well. This time was different though. I knew someone was following me. I knew what languages he spoke and how poorly he concealed himself. I knew that he wasn't likely to be military and I was leading him into there with me, not the other way around. I wasn't the victim this time and I wanted him to follow me in there. I chose the bathroom that nobody else would enter as I was hoping for him to join me in there.

I opened the door to the small bathroom and made my way inside. I took a brief look around at my surroundings and went straight into my backpack as I set it down on the floor in front of the toilet. I grabbed my laptop charger cord. It was a thick cable, not like a cell phone charger. I quickly turned the sink on and splashed water all over the floor in front of the door. I eased my way back behind the door swing range so that when he opened it up, it would conceal my position. I waited, counting down from ten as I knew that he had to be about ten paces from the bathroom door. As I counted down, I saw the door handle begin to dip slowly as if someone were attempting to open the door without making much noise. Just to make sure it was him, I shouted "occupado, tem alguem aqui." That means, there is someone in here, the bathroom is occupied. If it were someone else, they would quickly cease attempting to open the door after hearing my voice. The handle continued to drop, and the door began to open up. I noticed his shoe moving forward as he quickly entered the bathroom. As I watched the door closing behind him, he was fixated on my backpack and running faucet. It distracted him for just enough time to let the door close.

As he began to turn his head to the right and in my direction, I wrapped the cord over his head and landed it directly on his neck. I put one hand over my other, crossing the cable and tightening it. I turned my back to his back and lifted his feet off the floor a few inches with the complete force of the cable around his windpipe. As his sneakers hit the floor, I could hear them squeaking against the wet tiles. He couldn't get enough traction on his shoes to move anywhere. The cable was wrapped so tightly around his neck that yelling was out of the question. He was kicking as I used the leverage of my back to keep him lifted off the ground. He was trying to hit me with his hands, but they were only landing on the sides of my thighs and a few in the side of my belly. I felt something sharp on my right elbow a few seconds before he stopped kicking. Something hit the ground and it sounded like metal. As his body went limp, I lifted him higher and wrapped the cable tighter just to make sure.

I looked down at the ground as I let his body down and noticed a decent sized knife lying beside his lifeless body. I knew that I didn't make a mistake. He wasn't in there to have a conversation about German floral arrangements with me. However, I had already won a battle for my life in a public restroom once before. The difference was that this time, I wasn't the victim. I locked the door and began to frisk him down. I grabbed his cell phone, wallet, and plane ticket. He had a ticket for Las Vegas as well. His seat number was only 5 or 6 rows away from the seat on my ticket. He didn't have much else on him except for a folded piece of paper with a couple of phone numbers on it. I took all of it and put it in my backpack. I cleaned myself up quickly and dragged his body over to the toilet area to make it appear as though he collapsed on the toilet. Maybe that would buy some more time for me. Before leaving the restroom, I opened the door about two inches and looked outside. It was pretty desolate. I couldn't see anyone outside of the restrooms. I took his knife and bent the inner lock of the door so that when I shut it, it would lock from the inside and even a key wouldn't open it. I poked my head out of the restroom, making sure that my route was clear and exited. I had my right hand in my pocket with his knife opened up as I clutched it. In case there were more assassins in there, I was ready to defend myself at all costs. I walked up to my gate to Las Vegas and presented the assassins ticket to the attendant. She smiled at me as the light on the barcode scanner turned green. I was boarding the airplane as a dead corpse in a bathroom less than 100 yards away.

Just in case his handlers were tracking his travel status, I wanted to buy myself a bit more time and maybe even respond to them using his cell phone. Maybe I could pull some useful information from them if they thought he was still alive. As I sat down in his seat, I opened my phone and pulled up my encrypted messenger app. I took a picture of the man's Brazilian passport, his US passport, plane ticket, and driver's license. He was carrying a German driver's license and passports for both Brazil and the United States. I sent the pictures off to Rayssa with a message reading, "please help, fix this. I am on the plane...but he isn't. The body will be found soon. I am on cameras in the airport." As the pilot came over the intercom system, the flight attendants began their traditional seatbelt presentation to the passengers. Rayssa sent me a message back saying, "all set, will take care of it. Safe travels." I knew that she had the resources to change ticket information and possibly even passenger manifests. She had people in high places and after all, this was Brazil...

I got settled in and asked the flight attendant for a few mini bottles of vodka before we took off. I drank one for me, one for him, and a third to calm my nerves. I laid my head back, put in my headphones, and pressed play on a new audiobook. The plane began to move down the runway faster and faster until the wheels lifted off the pavement. I was heading home.

## 13: White Noise

As we reached 32,000 feet, I began to run over the next phase of my plan. Reaching the airplane and taking off was only half of the battle. I still had no idea who or what was waiting for me on the other end of the journey. As the flight attendant came around with the concession cart, I began to take notice of some of the finer details surrounding my flight. It was a Boeing 787 Dreamliner. The capacity of this plane was around 250-300 people. When I joined the air force, I wanted to become a pilot originally, so I took an interest in learning about airplanes, so I knew a fair bit around modern planes. There were usually around fifteen staff members on international flights of this distance, not including the pilots. I also knew that since we were heading to the continental US from a South American country, there was a 1 in 3 chance that a US Marshall was onboard somewhere. Hollywood always says that you would never be able to determine who the US Marshal was, but spotting a Fed was second nature to most in my line of work. As I was entering the plane, I didn't notice anyone that fit the traditional description, but I was keeping an eye open for them.

My seat was just in front of the middle of the plane, over the right wing. This was the seat of my friend that I left in the bathroom back in the airport. My original seat was only three rows ahead of this seat. It was within perfect sight distance, so I knew that he had some information on where I was going to be seated. Maybe he even had a part in choosing my seat for me. Nevertheless, I was in his seat now and I was in control for the moment. However, I knew that it was only a matter of time before things would catch up to me. I had to place myself in his shoes and those of his handlers. I assumed that they would be expecting some form of communication from the

135

air. There was a young lady in the seat in front of me. She had just fallen asleep and left her purse hanging off the seat's right armrest. She and I were in the aisle seats, and I could see that her purse was open with her wallet visible. I checked to ensure that she was sleeping and glanced back toward the back of the plane, then to the front. I reached forward and took her wallet out. There was a Visa credit card in the front envelope pocket of the wallet. I took out the assassin's cell phone and connected to the in-flight internet service. There was a paid option for internet connection during the flight. I used her credit card to purchase an internet connection for the flight. I made sure that I registered the internet connection with her seat number, her name, and credit card info. I placed the credit card slowly back into the wallet and dropped it into her purse. She was none the wiser and was still sleeping. As the connection came up on his cell phone, notifications began to chime in. There were several emails, WhatsApp messages, Signal messages, and two missed phone calls from US phone numbers. Some of the messages seemed innocuous, but one of the senders on his Signal application seemed to be different. It was some kind of instruction that they had sent to him. It was a single message, sent just thirty minutes ago that read "Terminal 3, gate C. Upon arrival, draw to the main entry loading dock C twelve. Confirm for copy." This message could have meant many different things. It could have been an order to switch out with another asset, a command to bring me to a more secluded area, or something else completely. I would probably never know since dead men tell no tales, but I knew that this man's resources were deeper than I had originally assumed.

I had to assume two things; the first was that I was not on this plane alone and someone was with me, watching me, and tracking me. The second assumption that I knew was inevitable was that when this plane touched down, I was sure to be met by another adversary. Either way, I had about eight hours to formulate a plan and execute it. There was an in-flight map radar that showed our location. We were over the country of Colombia at that point and our heading was taking us toward the Gulf of Mexico. We had around eight hours left in the flight before landing in Las Vegas. Once we touched down there, the war was back on and I was unarmed and at a significant disadvantage as I knew nothing of any plans, other than the quick message sent to my assassin. I took his phone and investigated a bit further. I learned more about the way that he spoke and responded to his handlers. He spoke in short sentences. You could tell that he was not completely fluent in English as even his text message responses were short and had foreign undertones within them. After careful review, I sent a message back to his handler stating, "Copy, confirmed. Target acquired. Original route in progress..."

I waited for a response. What if the handler perceived that something was amiss? There was a chance that I would be discovered, and my plan would be foiled. However, if I didn't respond, they were sure to pick up on the fact that his lifeless body was somewhere in a public restroom at the airport. I had no choice.

I waited a few more minutes. Finally, a message came through. It was a single short phrase that just said "confirmed, carry on." I was relieved when I received that. I felt as though I had the upper hand. Even if that wasn't true, it was a moment of peace for me. When someone is under extreme pressure situations like this, small victories are paramount in keeping a positive mindset. A positive mindset gives one steady hands. Steady hands can sometimes spell victory. It was important and I carried that feeling with me while I made my next moves. I had to exercise extreme vigilance on these next chess moves as they were likely to spell my fate. I was entering the United States again and the resources of my adversaries were likely to be as strong or stronger there than in the Middle East or South America. Depending on just how far the corruption had penetrated into the ranks of the US personnel, my death could be a swift one when I stepped foot off that plane.

When you are miles above the Earth's surface in a passenger plane, you don't have many viable options for evasion. You have a pre-chartered destination, and you are heading there whether you like it or not. For most people on that airplane, which was their intention; to leave their departure city and arrive at their intended destination without delay. However, I had other plans and I needed to improvise. I purchased another temporary internet plan with the dummy credit card that I was given prior to leaving Brazil. I sent a message back to Rayssa asking her about the flight manifest. She responded and said, "you're on the plane, my Canadian friend." So, my Canadian identity (Michael Jalisto) was on the plane's manifest and was heading to Las Vegas as well, formally at least. That was good. That meant that there was still a chance that I could get off the plane and work my way into the US under that assumed identity. The bigger problem resided in the fact that some professional pipe hitters were likely waiting for me to land and once they found out that their assassin was lying in a pool of blood in a Brazilian airport bathroom, they would turn the heat up on me significantly. For all I knew, his body was probably being examined by local airport police back in Brazil already. My mind was running through potential scenarios and steps that I could take, none of which were good options. However, maybe I would be able to make something happen. An old mentor told me one time that if I ever found myself in a dire situation, I should use my skillset and not someone else's skillset. Use my proficiencies to my advantage as best as possible before turning down uncharted roads. My best and most useful skillset was far from Jack Reacher, and I got lucky back there in the airport. I needed to use my technical skills to buy me some more time.

I observed. Scanning my surroundings, looking at the situation from a technical perspective. I needed to gain control of the situation and I knew that there were only a few possibilities of doing so. I couldn't necessarily commandeer an airplane and overpower some innocent pilots. That would certainly not be the lowest profile methodology to get me out of this situation. But I knew that I needed to prevent this plane from landing at the intended destination at all costs. If I told you that the thought of taking over the captain's chair didn't cross my mind, I would be lying. It did enter my thoughts and left just as quickly. 200+ people on this airplane didn't deserve to share my burden, nor did they deserve to experiment with my piloting skills. That was out of the question.

I observed more and began taking an inventory of my surroundings. By this time, the passengers were sleeping. The lights in the cabin were turned off, dinner had been served, and the vast majority of passengers were asleep or watching a movie on their in-flight entertainment system. I could see the blue hue from the screens illuminating the faces of the passengers. As I looked downward, I noticed a USB and power port in between my seat and the middle seat next to me. Both seats next to me were empty. Maybe my would-be assassin liked to travel without anyone close to him. I began to take note of the electronics system that was present in my area. Power outlets, USB charging stations, in-flight entertainment system, credit card reader attached to airplane phone/gaming controller, and digital seat adjustment controls on my armrest. I looked downward at the USB and power outlet and noticed a small port for headphones as well. That meant that the outlet jacks were in some form connected to the in-flight entertainment system as well. I grabbed my backpack from under the seat in front of me. It was lying on the floor as I tipped it upward toward me. I opened up the front pocket and pulled out my favorite pen. This pen had a hidden transition switch that turned it from a regular ballpoint pen into a somewhat of a flathead screwdriver. It wasn't as functional as a traditional flathead driver, but it was a useful substitute, nevertheless. I pulled the cap off it and slowly lowered it down my right leg. I kept an eye out for any stewardesses walking the aisle or suspicious passengers looking at me. Everyone was relaxed and resting still.

I took the flat part of the screwdriver and inserted it into the edge of the faceplate on the charging port. I began to shimmy the front plate away from the bracket until there was enough space for me to push the wider part of the screwdriver into the gap. Eventually, I was able to get the entire screwdriver into the space and put a square spacer into the gap, propping it open about an inch and a half. I pushed down on the cover and bent it forward. Inside of the cavity, I could see data wires running down the seat leg. I recognized that there was a serial cable, AC power cable, and a traditional set of wires in a harness. I reviewed the serial cable and the wiring harness. The wiring harness included a set of twisted shielded pair wires that were certainly capable of data transport. They appeared to be reserved for maintenance as there was nothing connected to the terminating end except for a small RJ forty-five connector, just like a regular ethernet cable. I pulled on it to see if there was any slack in the line. It was tight, so I pulled a bit further. It began to pull upward to me. I noticed that as I pulled on the cable, I could feel it running up the leg of my seat. I had pulled it up about 10-12 inches at this point and it was at the level of my armrest. I had enough slack to plug it into my laptop…

I pulled my laptop out of my backpack and opened it up. I extended the ethernet cable a bit further and plugged the cable into my laptop's port. I saw green and orange lights begin to blink on my laptop port and after a few seconds, a prompt came up on my screen stating that a new network connection had been established. I began to perform some reconnaissance and ran a network discovery tool named Nmap to determine what else was using this wired connection. I saw a handful of about ten devices, most of them appeared to be other entertainment systems or relays. There was one in particular that caught my eye. It looked like some kind of a router or bridging device and had an IP address that matched traditional network routers. 192.168.1.1 was the address. I went to it immediately and found that it was indeed a router. Not a Wi-Fi router, but a different manufacturer that I didn't recognize. I came across a login screen and entered the username "admin" and password "admin" to no avail. I tried a few more combinations with no success before firing-up a program called "THC Hydra," a password brute-force tool that was designed to crack login information for just about every kind of login or authentication system you could imagine.

After about twenty minutes of this program running, I had a match. Username: administrator Password: InFlightConfig1. I logged in as this user and saw a configuration menu that I had recognized. I began to search through the configurations before finding routing information for an upstream device. The upstream device was on a different subnetwork and IP address schema. The upstream device had an IP address of 10.0.1.52. I used the router's onboard command line interface to connect to the 10.0.1.52 device using the Telnet protocol. The Telnet protocol is a rather antiquated access protocol that is no longer considered to be secure. I reached another authentication menu, only this time it was already logged in as an administrator account. The admin account that was in-use was called "root." I knew exactly what I had reached at this point.

As I logged in, a graphical user interface was presented, and it had several subcategories present. From left to right and top to bottom, the menu options read, "Elevator, Rudder, Aileron: Roll, Pitch, Yaw, Longitudinal, Lateral, Vertical, Directional. Within a matter of thirty minutes, I had located the digital control panel to change the trajectory of this flight. There were several other menu options that included landing gear options and cabin options alike. From this area, I would be able to change the aircraft's position in the sky, manipulate the landing gear, change the cabin pressure and O2 levels, and even raise the flaps and significantly slow down the plane.

I watched the digital map and radar on the screen on the back of the seat in front of me as we passed over Honduras, Guatemala, and eventually Southern Mexico. The flight had around six hours remaining when we were coming over central Mexico. It was time to put the next phase of my plan into direct action. If I waited too long to make my move, I may end up touching down in Mexico and that was a risky option since the far-reaching arms of the criminal syndicate would certainly be strong in Mexico as it was in Brazil. Stopping in any South American or Central American country was to be avoided at all costs since taking out the man in the airport restroom back in Brazil. Since there could be others awaiting my arrival in Las Vegas, the only choice that I had was to attempt to place the plane at an unscheduled destination that was not on our flight plan. Maybe then I could re-route myself and shake the tail that was on me. I was a painted target, and I knew my original route had been overtaken by my adversaries.

I waited a while longer and reviewed some of the options on the in-flight control system using my laptop. The stewardesses walked by me calmly from time to time, asking if passengers wanted something to drink. I stood up from my seat and started walking toward the restroom in front of my section. As I walked through the cabin, I took note of the people seated in the plane on both sides. I took an accounting of their personal appearances and demeanors. Most of them were calm and appeared to be simply traveling to their destinations. They were living their lives, reading books, looking at magazines, playing games on their phones, watching movies, or sleeping the night away. I noticed a young mother and her two children. One of them was a little boy, maybe 7 or 8 years old. I stopped walking and handed him a paper airplane that I had folded up. His mother looked over at me and smiled, thanking me for giving it to him. The young boy reached his hand out and received my gift. He and his siblings looked calm and relaxed. Their mother seemed calm as well. I had a momentary sense of envy that I had to shake. Their calmness was something that I longed for but could never locate. I was in a war right beside them and they had no idea what was transpiring around them. I'm not in the business of causing pain and suffering for innocent people, actually I am in the opposite business of that. My goal was to save as many innocent and oppressed people as possible. However, in order to do just that I needed to make some sacrifices and create my alternate route to safety so that I could continue my mission. There was too much on the line for me. There were too many people depending on my safe arrival and that was all in jeopardy.

I went into the restroom and splashed some water on my face and cleaned my hands. I was sweating a bit by this time as we were quickly approaching the end of the line for me. I could either make a decision now, or forever hold my peace and take on whomever would be awaiting my arrival. As I stared at myself in the mirror, I knew that what I was about to do would be putting my life in danger and the life of these passengers in danger as well. I looked into my own eyes and weighed my options one last time. It was the only viable plan at this point, so I made my decision and opened the door. On my way back to my seat I approached the mother and her three children. There was a bit of turbulence while I was in the bathroom, and I leaned over to the mother and told her that one of the stewardesses had told me that we were likely going to go through some heightened turbulence, and she told me to take my seat and ensure that I was strapped in. I told her that I am sure that it is nothing, but I wanted to let you and your children know so that you could put your seatbelts on as well. She smiled and thanked me, her youngest did the same. I gave him a fist bump and walked back to my seat.

The map showed that we were about 200 miles South of Cuidad Juárez, Mexico. I knew that the closest airport in the US would likely be Las Cruces, New Mexico. I pulled my computer back out and opened the screen. I was still connected into the in-flight router, and I authenticated into the next router in the line. I selected the aileron and placed my cursor over the "roll" right option. I set the roll to five degrees right, not too much. I hit enter. Immediately, I felt the plane pitch to the right just enough to dip slightly. I had control of the airplane...

I put the same movement into position, only to the left this time. 5 degrees aileron roll to the left, enter. Same movement, to the left. I waited a few seconds and saw the stewardess in the front of the plane pick up the wired telephone. She plugged her other ear with her finger with the phone up to her head. She listened intently to whomever was speaking to her. I placed my cursor over the same left aileron roll option and increased to twenty degrees. I hit enter again. The cup that was sitting on the tray table of the passenger in front of me slid across the surface before hitting the floor. The seatbelt sign turned on and flashed for about sixty seconds. I switched the cursor over the lateral axis elevator pitch. This was the configuration to take the plane higher or lower. This option was responsible for essentially raising the nose upward or downward, depending on selection. I chose to take the nose higher twenty-five degrees and hit enter. The plane began to climb. We climbed for around fifteen seconds before the pilot corrected the trajectory. I saw the configuration menu blinking and the autopilot switch was turned off. The pilots were taking full control over the airplane at this point.

I switched the elevator lateral axis control to negative forty-five degrees this time and clicked the enter key. The plane began to descend rapidly. We went from a clean and level horizontal flight path to a downward 45-degree angle in seconds. The passengers all began to buckle their seatbelts quickly and the seatbelt sign was flashing and making continued beeping noises. One of the pilots came over the intercom system and explained that there was some sort of issue occurring with the plane and they were taking over manual control. They informed us to sit tight as they corrected the issue. The faces of the passengers began to worry as the stewardesses all took their jump seats and buckled into their seatbelts. One of the flight attendants had her eyes closed tight as the pilot attempted to correct the trajectory of the flight. I made one more move to again adjust the aileron roll, this time forty-five degrees to the right. The plane went nearly sideways, and I noticed that my St. Christopher necklace medallion was dangling toward the window seat from my neck. The pilots took over the controls again and corrected the plane. Their correction of the plane's roll was rather rough, and the baggage above shook and crashed in the overhead compartments as he corrected the aircraft. I went back into the airplane Wi-Fi system and purposefully misconfigured the Wi-Fi router with incorrect settings. Then, I turned off the in-cabin Wi-Fi communications capabilities so that if there was another adversary onboard, they wouldn't be able to communicate to the ground to let them know what was going on. The Wi-Fi signal lights all turned off when I hit the switch to shut down the router. I waited about thirty seconds before the co-pilot came over the intercom system again and notified us that we would be needing to make an emergency landing due to aircraft safety protocols. The pilots didn't give much more information on that before the intercom system went silent again. I kept my eye out for anyone attempting to use their phones to communicate with the ground, I saw some people attempting to make a Wi-Fi connection and talking to one another about the lack of connection. I didn't notice anyone on the plane with a successful connection. That would have been a red flag if someone were to have an out of band communications device or satellite phone.

The airplane began to make a hasty descent as the pilots took us down to around 10,000 feet before coming over the intercom system again. The pilot made the announcement that we would be making an unscheduled emergency landing in Las Cruces, New Mexico. It was right where I had anticipated. We were officially off-course and preparing to land at a different airport. The passengers were calmed down a bit now, but the slightest turbulence bump sent some of the passengers into prayer and panic. I was the only one on the plane that knew we were in a safe aircraft. I grabbed my carry-on bag and moved over to my original seat, leaving the plane ticket of my assailant in the seatback pocket of his assigned seat. Everyone was so focused on looking out of the windows that they didn't notice me changing my seat. Even the flight attendants were consumed with speaking with one another and looking out of the emergency exit windows on the doors. I was assuming my Canadian identity and was ready to land this plane. I would soon need to work my way out of the Las Cruces airport as quickly as possible. Our plane was flying over desert sand as far as you could see. We dropped lower, down to 1000 feet, then 500, then 100 before the wheels squeaked on the runway at Las Cruces. The pilot slammed down on the brakes and put the engines in reverse. The runway that we landed on was certainly not the best to land such a large aircraft. I was back on the ground in the United States and was ready to choose my next path. However, I was not in the clear, by far. Landing on the ground was only half of the battle and I still needed to make my way to safety, and I didn't have any planned resources at this point. No covering fire, no escape route, no vehicle. It was on me to determine my exit strategy and find my route to my final destination. I was on my own again.

## 14: The Prospect

The seconds turned into minutes as we sat on the tarmac of the Lac Cruces runway. When a plane makes an emergency landing, it is not the typical deboarding process that you are accustomed to in normal flight operations, especially when coming from an international location outside of the US We sat there for nearly an hour, while I used my time as wisely as possible. I didn't turn on the cell phone of my friendly assailant just in case they were tracking the location of his mobile device. I knew that we were hours ahead of schedule so I figured that I would have some time before the alarms started to sound and they were looking for the plane. I fired up my cell phone and connected to a mobile VPN. The first thing that I did was go to a flight tracker website and enter the flight number of my plane to determine what someone would see when and if they were tracking the flight. The flight status was still showing "in-transit," and on the way to Vegas but I'm sure that suspicions would be raised if we were here for too much longer. If the plane wasn't moving on the flight tracker map, there would most likely be some commotion from the people that were seeking me out.

I sat back and scrolled through my mind, replaying the highlight reels that comprised my last few months of life. Things played out and then over and over again in my mind. The time continuum seemed to mesh events together in a non-linear and cyclical fashion. All of the reconnaissance, turning into physical actions, going on the offensive, defending myself, and finally evading capture. It was all so surreal, and I had a momentary thought that this may all be a bad dream. I remembered simpler times before I was intertwined in the harsh reality of my existence. One would assume that anyone would be uncomfortable living a life of evasion such as this.

However, it was part of me and had been since I was a child. I knew nothing else but to defend myself and seek to protect others. I had grown into a purposeful reality that far surpassed any job or role that I could imagine myself fulfilling. I scanned the faces of the passengers on the plane and recognized that they were not the slightest bit aware of my presence. To them, I was another passenger. A passenger with normal life issues; bills to pay, seeking a job promotion, relationship problems, buying a new car, taking vacations. None of these were items on my list of worries or aspirations. My sole purpose was to survive and serve a higher purpose, but not in a cliché sort of way. I was fighting for those without a voice. I was running for the forgotten children. The ones left behind. The ones that were lost. When you enter this vein of society, you quickly recognize the brutality of man and true oppression. Until I entered into this realm, I was living in another dimension. However, imagining myself living in the safe space of life was not an option for me.

I held my single carry-on bag close to my chest on my lap. I sat patiently, waiting for the pilot and crew to release us from the plane so that I could chart my next course. The pilot came over the intercom system and relayed a message to the passengers. He started by apologizing for the unexpected issues with the aircraft and that they would be investigating what exactly had happened up there and that each passenger would be compensated for the horrible situation that had taken place. He said that we would not be taking off from Las Cruces tonight as this was a temporary air stop for us and aircraft maintenance would not be available to even look at the plane until late the following day. The stewardess came over the intercom with more instructions. She said that we would be deboarding the plane and would process customs clearance here in Las Cruces. Then, we would have the option to depart the airport after customs clearance or wait in the terminal for separate smaller planes to take us

149

tour destination in the morning or afternoon the following day, as there were no more flights heading out of Las Cruces for the evening. The passengers groaned a bit. Some of the passengers were just relieved that we were on the ground. It was nearly 2 a.m. by this time and I could see a desolate flight line beside us, with no aircraft or crew filling the runways or taxiways.

I readied my ticket, Canadian passport, and any other documentation that I may need. I had already flushed my assailant's plane ticket down the toilet and put his passport inside of one of the life preservers bags under his seat. I figured that someone would be looking for that at some point, but it would buy me enough time. The stewardess came over the intercom again and began the deboarding process. The passengers began to gather their belongings and walk toward the aircraft exit. They had placed a portable stairway off the plane exit and passengers were descending to the tarmac below. As I walked through the cabin, I kept my eye on the passengers to my left and to my right. I walked off the plane and nodded at the captain as he was standing in the doorway of the cockpit. He had a look on his face and seemed to be inspecting the passengers visually as we exited. I could tell that the pilot knew something had been manipulating the aircraft, but he wasn't certain if it was due to mechanical malfunctions or someone toying with the controls. He just had a suspicious look on his face, and he knew that something wasn't right.

I followed the line of passengers across the pavement and into a single terminal door. There were no passengers waiting in the terminal and only two airport workers that I could see. There was a single canine police officer standing by across from our departure gate and he had a German shepherd. I took my phone out and sent Rayssa my geo coordinates, longitudinal and latitudinal to ensure that she knew where I had detoured to. As I followed the crowd, I looked down at my phone and saw a new message from her. She sent an image to my cell phone; I clicked download and waited for the image to load while walking through the terminal. The picture pulled up on the screen and it showed a single image of some kind of a drawing. It was a stencil drawing of a skull with wings stretching backward. The skull was outfitted with what appeared to be an old school motorcycle helmet. I wasn't sure what it was, so I took some time to think as I continued walking through the terminal. I was walking behind a group of people that were talking about the situation on the plane, complaining that they were going to take legal action against the airline. Some of them were just thankful to be on the ground again.

I remember one little boy that was telling his father how much fun it was, and he wanted to do it again. That made me smile a bit as I continued following the line of passengers down the terminal walkway. As we approached the security checkpoint and makeshift customs and immigration center, I started to become more anxious. I was wearing a long-sleeved shirt over a T-shirt and a hat. I took off my hat and long-sleeve shirt and inconspicuously tossed them into a trash can as I walked closer toward the security checkpoint. One of the tenants of evasion tradecraft is to wear layers. It is easier to shed layers than put clothes on.

We approached the security center and the airport staff had 4 or 5 lines formed up to process passengers. It was chaotic and we could tell that this airport wasn't equipped to deal with the volume of passengers. I watched the security staff begin to process the people in front of me as the large line began to split into various directions, leading to numbered stations. As I approached closer to the checkpoint, I noticed a security official standing off to the left of one of the stations, station number 3. His station was closed, which I thought was odd. As I observed more intently, I saw that he was wearing the same uniform as the other agents. Black pants, long-sleeved white shirt, black shoes, forward ball cap. However, his right sleeve was rolled up and I noticed a tattoo on his forearm. I looked closer as he panned his eyes across the crowd of people approaching the checkpoint. I took interest in his tattoo and noted the structure of the tattoo was similar to the picture that was sent to me. Skull with wings, motorcycle helmet. His tattoo had a knife blade clinched between the teeth of the skull though. It was slightly different, but nevertheless this had to be a sign. We locked eyes as I neared the front of the line. I gave him a slight nod and he turned the light on in his guard station. He calmly gave me a wave over to him and told the airport agent that his station was ready to go. As I walked toward him, he rolled down his sleeve and buttoned his cuff.

I came up to the station and gave him a greeting. He was a stoic guy and all business. His facial expression remained the same as when he asked me for my passport and trip documentation. I handed over my Canadian passport and my flight itinerary. I was nervous that the tattoo may have been a rare coincidence and I would be apprehended here in Las Cruces. He picked up the phone inside of the guard station while looking over my documentation. He turned to the side and looked down at my documents, every few seconds looking back at me. He kept saying, "ok, yes. Canadian. Ok....yes, I will. Copy that, ten minutes ETA." He hung up the phone and grabbed a pen and a notepad from the corner of his desk and began to write. As he wrote something down on the paper, I looked around me to see if there was anything suspicious in my periphery. Everything looked clear so far and I looked back at the agent, asking him if everything was all right. He looked at me and nodded with the same stone look on his face. He had dark eyes, almost black and had a solid build. I could tell that he was in the military at one point in his life by the way he kept himself. He put my passport on his desk and slammed a visitation stamp on one of the pages before sliding it across the counter to me. I opened it up and noticed a folded paper note between the last page and the back cover. I didn't open it just then. He looked at me and told me to enjoy Las Cruces before I thanked him and turned away.

As I walked away from the security checkpoint area, I took the note out of the passport and unfolded it while walking toward a stairwell, adjacent to the escalators and elevator. The note had a few lines of writing on it. A phone number with a 575 area code, local to Las Cruces, license plate number, "black Jeep Grand Cherokee," and the first name of a man, "Tommy." I memorized the information and tucked the note into my back pocket while I continued walking toward the exit stairwell. I turned my phone camera on and walked with the phone in my hand to my side, taking a burst of pictures behind me while continuing to point my eyes in front of me. As I walked down the stairs, I looked at the pictures and didn't see anyone in the pictures that appeared to be following me or too close. Everyone else was taking the escalator or elevator. As I exited the escalator, I kept moving toward the exit doors on the northwest corner of the terminal's pickup area outside until I finally came out of the doors. The warm New Mexico air hit me, and it was the first smell of the United States that I had in quite a long time. I closed my eyes for a moment and breathed it in. It smelled like the desert. There is a different smell in desert climates than that of wooded areas or lush forests that is difficult to explain, but I remembered that distinct difference. Coming from Brazil, the smell of being back in the United States was a warm welcome to my senses.

I saw some car lights approaching from the distance. I could see a vehicle wrapping around the terminal road. I could tell that it was some kind of truck or SUV as it neared closer. It had deep blue LED headlights and fog lights below. I could hear the low rumble of the tires and knew that they had to be relatively rugged tires, based on the acoustic reverberation humming inside of the terminal pickup point. As the vehicle approached closer, I noticed that it was a Jeep. It was a Jeep Grand Cherokee, black, same license plate as in the note. The windows were heavily tinted, and I couldn't see inside of the vehicle. It stopped before it reached my position and turned off the headlights. I couldn't see through the windshield much either. I noticed the burning ember of a cigarette being smoked by someone in the front passenger seat. The passenger cracked the window open as a low cloud of smoke lifted from the top of the vehicle. I saw the hand of someone in the backseat pop out of the back passenger side pop out of the window and wave me over to the vehicle. I approached slowly and cautiously, looking around me as I walked closer. What did I have to lose at this point? If they were going to kill me, I was dead anyway. If I went the other direction, there were sure to be others waiting for me around the corner. I had no choice but to continue my approach to the vehicle.

I arrived at the passenger side of the vehicle, standing about ten feet away still, waiting for the passenger in the backseat to say something or give some kind of acknowledgment. The front passenger unrolled the window and I noticed he had jet-black hair, slicked back in a ponytail. His face was weathered from the sun, and he appeared to be Native American. I could tell he wasn't any sort of paramilitary operator or law enforcement. As he looked at me, I said "what's your name?" He looked at me and responded, "Tommy....Need a ride to Vegas?" I didn't trust him, and he didn't trust me. I could see that his hands were on his lap but couldn't see what he was holding. By the way that his arms were resting on his lap, it appeared as though he was holding something. I looked him over and scanned my eyes across the vehicle before making my way to the driver's side rear door. As I pulled on the door handle and opened the door, I gazed into the vehicle and saw three occupants. The driver was a young woman with red hair, the front passenger, and a man in the backseat. The man in the backseat was the only one looking at me and he was wearing tactical style clothing. Desert sand cargo pants, military style boots, and a black short sleeve button-up shirt. The man in the backseat said, "get in, we have to go right now." I didn't hesitate and entered the vehicle. I placed my bag in the middle seat, in between the man and me. He instructed me to put it behind me in the cargo area of the Jeep. I obliged as the driver began to move the vehicle through the terminal pickup area.

I engaged in conversation with the man in the back as the woman driving had a few words with Tommy. I asked the man in the back who they were as he looked away from, he and stared out of his window. I began to ask more questions about where we were heading, who sent them, and how they knew I was here. I got a chime from Rayssa on my phone, it was another text message. She relayed the same phone number that the airport agent with the tattoo gave to me. I pulled out the note to double check the number and read it off as I looked at my phone. Tommy reached back with his hand open and asked for the note. I placed the note into his hand and noticed a similar tattoo from that of the man at the security checkpoint. Skull with wings, motorcycle helmet, and this time there was a Native American type of headdress with feathers atop the helmet. I asked Tommy who he was and why they were helping me. He turned back to me and began to explain. His voice was low and had the sound of a man that had seen the world. Tommy told me that him and his driver were part of the Hells Angels, New Mexico chapter. The guy in the backseat was a prospect and played the role of security detail for them. Tommy said that their chapter was an ally of my group and our cause, and they were responsible for getting me safely from point

A to point B, and that was it. He gave me the rules. Never get out of the vehicle unless instructed to do so, no phone calls until given permission, and I was to only follow instructions from him or the driver. He said that prospects had to earn that right and I was in the custody of the Hells Angels at this point.

The drive to Las Vegas from Las Cruces would take us more than ten hours, so we had some time to kill. I watched the night sky as we drove down the highways, thinking about how I would make my way once I arrived in Las Vegas. It would be easier to blend in there as the population of tourists offered all types of concealment among the diverse population. I dozed off for an hour or two before awakening to the Jeep pulling into a gas station off a highway leading through the desert. I could hear the crushed stone and gravel under the tires crunching as we pulled up to the gas pumps. There were two bikers standing next to their bikes in front of the gas station. They looked over at our vehicle as one of the men approached us. Tommy didn't appear nervous at all, but the prospect in the back pulled a .45 caliber pistol from his door pocket and pulled the slide back, loading a round into the chamber. The biker approached Tommy's window as Tommy unrolled his window. The biker and Tommy smiled at one another, and the biker began to pump our gas. It was unreal. Tommy had enough respect among the biker community that we had protection waiting at predetermined spots along our route. This wasn't a biker gang escort; it more closely resembled a planned military covert convoy. I was impressed with their planning and coordination. As the biker put the gas nozzle back in the pump station, we went on our way and back onto the highway.

Tommy explained the situation to me in more finite detail. He said that they had been a part of this mission for decades now, going back to the early 1960s. He told me that the Hells Angels had been fighting against child sec traffickers alongside John F. Kennedy and some discreet members of his entourage and family. I never imagined a Hells Angels leader would be imparting knowledge on me that JFK was somehow involved in an unsanctioned, unofficial, and covert operation against child sex predators. I wondered if that was one of the reasons he was shot. I knew that I would never know the true answer to that question, but maybe it had something to do with the eventual massacre of him and his brother, among others in their circle. Tommy told me that I was part of a very extensive, powerful, and all-reaching network across the United States. It consisted of members of Congress, military officials, police officers, Mexican cartel sicarios, Hollywood actors, and even 1 percent bikers like himself. Throughout this past year, I had begun to acknowledge the vast expanse of resources that were guiding me, and I knew that it was more grandiose than I had originally assumed. I just never imagined the reach of the network to be so vast and organized.

We were about eight and a half hours into our drive when Tommy began to give me more information about the people I would be meeting in Vegas. They weren't bikers like him and his crew, but he didn't explain where they came from or what they did. I noticed that he did speak of them with great reverence and that was significant coming from a man that so many other men appeared to respect and fear. Whoever I was going to meet was a level above Tommy and his crew. The man in the backseat handed me a manila envelope and told me to open it up. I pulled back the metal prongs that held it closed and looked inside. More documents and identification awaited me inside of the envelope. A New Mexico driver's license, a car keychain with two separate keys; one looked like a house key and the other had some sort of a bank emblem on it as if it was a safety deposit box or something. There were a few business cards inside, alongside a note with some print on it. I couldn't see exactly was the typing said as the inside of the Jeep was dark, but it looked like a bulleted list of instructions of some kind. There was a small clear plastic case inside as well. It contained about five cell phone SIM cards, each of them had a different logo of separate cellular providers on them. There was a credit card and a 3-4-inch-thick stack of 100-dollar bills with a bank band around them. It must have been twenty to twenty-five thousand dollars. Tommy reached back and handed me a gold medallion, attached to a gold chain. It wasn't a necklace but was more of a pendant. It was a ten-dollar gold coin from the year 1917 and was weld-crafted onto a short gold chain. Tommy said that was my real ID card and if I ever needed to prove who I was, that I should brandish that.

The man in the back handed me was a two-foot-long hard black plastic case. It was a rugged case that resembled some sort of weapon transport case. I put it on my lap and popped the two side latches and opened it up. Inside, there was a black 9mm Glock 19X pistol. Aside from that, there was a disassembled rifle. It was completely taken apart, but there was a receiver, folding lightweight stock, barrel, and a slim tactical scope inside. The man opened up my backpack and reached behind us in the cargo area, grabbing box after box of ammunition. While he packed one ammo box into my backpack on the car floor, his other hand was readying another box to follow behind it. He placed around ten boxes of ammo in my bag. Tommy leaned back and said, "if you need more ammo, just remember that you are in Las Vegas. Ammunition is more common than water out here." We neared the city, and I could see the Vegas lights projecting into the sky from miles away. The city illuminated the desert as we made our way toward it. As the highway lights began to light up the inside of the Jeep, my heart started to pump faster and faster, as I had that old familiar feeling as if I was entering yet another battle zone. The man in the backseat grabbed a small handheld radio from the seat pocket in front of him and turned it on. He carefully dialed it into a channel and began speaking into it. "ETA ten mikes, subject in-transit, heading on bearing north, 3, Romeo, Delta, Delta, Zulu, Bravo; confirm receipt; over." "Mike's is shorthand for "minutes" in military lingo, so I knew that we were getting close to some kind of stopping or pivot point. The way that he used the phonetic alphabet was familiar to be as a military man. I recognized that my original assumption was likely correct, and this man had spent some time in the service. His demeanor was familiar. As we went underneath an overpass, the streetlights became stronger and brighter. The man in the backseat looked behind him to see if anyone was following us. They knew that I was being hunted as well as I did. As the lights from Vegas street signs grew stronger, the man in the backseat reached into the inside of his black jacket, pulling Colt 1911 .45 ACP pistol from his side holster. In the moment that he pulled his weapon to ensure that he was ready for any incumbent threats, I noticed the glimmer of the city lights against his belt buckle. It was a large oval-shaped buckle. Silver with some type of golden emblem across the front of it.

I squinted my eyes to get a closer look at his attire. Black leather military style boots, tactical khaki cargo pants, and a black jacket. It looked like he had some sort of vest underneath his jacket, but I couldn't confirm. His belt buckle drew my attention again as the lights from the city intensified. I noticed the emblem in greater detail this time. A large Texas longhorn shined in the light. The Texas longhorn emblem was gold, surrounded by a chrome or silver colored oval... "Cowboy?" I asked him. As he pulled tapped his extra magazine against his door's armrest, he looked over at me with a stoic glare that I had seen before. "You know me son?" he responded.

159

"Afghanistan...The interrogation facility. The helicopter landing pad. I remember you." He looked at me and nodded slightly. "I met a lot of people over there, son. What were you doing there if you don't mind me asking.?" I explained what my role was and what I was doing. I told him that I was involved in the black Mercedes clusterfuck and that I was fortunate enough to meet some good people during that situation and they had helped me to evade and escape. He didn't seem too surprised to see me, actually. It was almost as if he knew. However, his demeanor made me realize that he was a busy man as my presence did not seem to faze him. He was a focused individual then, and he was just as focused now. How our paths crossed this time was a mystery to me. Tommy looked back at us and said that "Mr. Gardner" was in charge of my safety once we hit the ground in Vegas. He would be accompanying me for the foreseeable future until I was in a position to move independently.

A man's voice came over Mr. Gardner's radio again. "Heading 6, 4, ten, niner, Charlie, Whiskey, Alpha, Kilo, Gulf, November, confirm receipt; over." Mr. Gardner replied, "Confirmed, ETA 5 Mike's, prep the LZ. Mr. Gardner holstered his sidearm inside of his jacket and reached behind him. He gave me a black ballistic vest and told me to put it on. He handed me a black zip-up jacket and told me to put it over the vest. I hurried up and put the gear on hastily. He reached back into the Jeep's third row and pulled out an AR-15, equipped with a night scope, pistol grip, and flashlight apparatus attached to the bottom of the front rail. It looked similar to the M-4 rifle setup that the Navy SEAL teams carried in the Middle East. The version that Mr. Gardner had in the Jeep was black instead of desert tan color. As we moved closer to the destination, Tommy told the driver to cut the headlights off. As we got closer, I saw a small parking lot approaching. The driver had cut off the headlights but left the fog lights at low power to give just enough illumination for us to see where we were going. We pulled into the parking lot as the driver turned slightly to the east, where I noticed a small dirt road at the back of the parking lot. The building to my right appeared to be some sort of a warehouse. There was a sign on the front of the building, but I couldn't make it out as it was extremely dark in the lot. Mr. Garner handed me another weapon from the back as well. It was a Draco. Draco's are a short version of the AK-47 and fire a 7.62 by thirty-nine round. He handed me four magazines. Two of them were duct taped together inversely so that I could flip it over once one of them was empty. I had fired AK-47's many times in the past, so I was familiar with this setup. This was much shorter and lighter than the AK-47 but was comfortable for me.

The driver led us down a dirt road for a few minutes before coming to a clearing. There were two men there on four-wheeler ATV's. Beside them, there was another off-road ATV. As we stopped the Jeep, I noticed that the other ATV was a two-seater dune buggy type vehicle. It was low to the ground and had big knobby tires on it, some serious flood lights on the top roll cage, windshield, and a nice dashboard setup that was dimly lit. Tommy got out of the car unarmed and approached the two men on the ATV's. He had his hands to his side as he walked toward the two men. Mr. Gardner had his rifle propped on Tommy's seatback and had his sights on the two men on the ATV's. The two men both were both visibly armed as well. The one man on the ATV in the back had a rifle sitting on his lap at the low ready position. The other man on the front four-wheeler had a rifle slung on his back. Both of the men appeared to be wearing night vision goggles that were on top of their heads and flipped upward. Tommy engaged in conversation with the front man as we waited. After a few minutes, Tommy looked back at the Jeep and signaled for Mr. Gardner and me to approach. Mr. Gardner pulled the latch on his door and put one foot outside of the vehicle. The driver told Mr. Gardner, "Good luck, you're on your

own for now. If you need us, you know where to find us."
Mr. Gardner told me, "Get your shit, let's roll."

I exited the car with my backpack, rifle slung around my
shoulder, and my pistol tucked in the back of my pants.
We approached the two men and Tommy as Tommy gave
me the keys for the ATV. Mr. Gardner requested that I
give him the keys. I would be riding shotgun. I thanked
Tommy for his help in getting me cleared from the airport
and he shook my hand. He looked over at Mr. Gardner
and told him, "You know what this means. His life is on
you for now. He's high value for the cause and we need
him to carry out our mission. Take care of him and let me
know if you need the club for support. We'll keep the dogs
off you as long as possible, but you need to get him to the
safehouse. Go now, and if you see anything that spooks
you, take care of it. We got your backs, and you know
that." Mr. Gardner told the two men on the four wheelers
to lead and that we would follow. They nodded at him. The
two men appeared to be Mexican or of some Hispanic
descent. I couldn't tell where they were from exactly, but
their accents were most definitely Spanish. Mr. Gardner
started up the engine of the buggy as the two men tore off
onto another dirt road leading into the desert. Mr. Gardner
throttled down the buggy as I looked behind us at Tommy
and his driver heading in the opposite direction.

We were on our way to our next location. At this time, I
knew the extensive nature of the network that I was a part
of now. Hells Angels, airport security workers, Special
Forces, military, civilians, Latino renegades, Brazilian
officials, and many others were contributing to the cause.
Moreover, these people were responsible for ensuring my
safe passage through multiple countries and now through
the Nevada desert. It was a wild experience that
continued to gain steam. I knew that I was surrounded by
more than a small militia. This was a group that was well
equipped to handle and combat the evil that was seeking

my demise. I knew that my journey had just begun and that I was a member of a fraternal organization that had no boundaries, no racial barriers, geographical limitations, and certainly no lack of formalization or funding. I felt like I had a chance in this mess for the first time in a while. The dust from the road trailed behind the buggy as we continued into the night, and I was overcome with a sensation of community and a newfound sentiment of morale. I wasn't alone and I was reinvigorated for the mission phases that awaited me.

## 16: Men in Red

Brutality had become the norm. Citizen on citizen violence, corrupt politicians, child exploitation rings, drug cartels, sicarios, hitmen, and underground fraternities that were fighting against plagues of humanity. As we rode through the desert that night, I was overwhelmed with my vision of the world. I envied those people that sat home and watched CNN, waiting for the next world crisis while eating their popcorn. The truth was the world had no idea of what the actual dark underbelly of society actually looked like up-close. We had become a culture that was sheltered from the truth. However, abundance of shelter breeds places for evil to operate, relatively unhidden. At this point, almost nothing surprised me. The only surprise that I had by this time was the realization that all of this evil, this separate world was right under the noses of the general public. In a previous life, I had no idea. Naive, ignorant, and walking through life; I had been blind to the truths that were held in the shadows. Albeit quite a bit to stomach, the truth was better than comfort in ignorance in my opinion. Mr. Gardener, a.k.a. "Cowboy" and I rushed across the desert trails, occasionally leading through some heavy greenery, trees, and small bush trails. It was mostly rocky, flat, and sandy. The buggy's shocks bounced as we rolled through the desert that night.

Eventually, we led to this ranch in the middle of nowhere. It was desolate around the place and a single dim yellow floodlight illuminated the front walkway, leading into the ranch's garage. It was a fairly large garage from the looks of it. As we approached the home, the two guys on the four wheelers flashed their lights at the garage doors. We came to a slow crawl for a couple of seconds before the garage doors slid open and apart from one another. A man opened the doors and waved us inside, checking our trail and looking around the ranch's compound to ensure that we were alone. The two four wheelers went inside first, then our buggy. Mr. Gardner put his right hand on his sidearm as we entered the garage. It was dark inside. Only a light in the back corner was on when we pulled inside. It looked like there was some sort of a little office in the back corner and a man sat at a chair inside. I couldn't see his face but there was someone inside of there. The man that let us inside closed the garage doors behind us and folded a large metal bar over two lock joints on the door, placing a locking pin through them and securing the entryway from unwanted visitors. The two men from the four wheelers began chatting with the man inside in Spanish. It wasn't a Mexican dialect from what I could hear. It sounded like Spanish but had different slang than in the Mexican Spanish language that I was a familiar with. Mr. Gardner and I engaged in light conversation as he pulled his bag and weapon from the back of the buggy. He dusted off his pants and wiped down his rifle with a black bandanna he pulled from one of the cargo pockets. I asked him if he had seen me that day on the helicopter landing pad in Afghanistan. He paused briefly before whispering to me, "I don't want to hear about what you saw that day, understand me? You just keep it moving alongside me." I picked up his queue that he may not know these people all too well and I shouldn't divulge or trust them. Our situation seemed temporary.

As we unloaded the buggy, the other men unstrapped their packs from their ATV's bungee cords on the back racks. The man that let us in complimented me on the rifle that Cowboy gave me. I smiled at him as if I was familiar with the firearm. In reality, I had no familiarity with this particular weapon system. To really feel comfortable with a firearm, I needed to fire it, train with it, and know exactly how to break it down and put it all back together. This rifle was fresh to me. The man from the back office stood up, as I saw his silhouette painted on the wall behind him. He reached over and put some things on the desk before stepping out of the room. He was a slender guy, maybe 6 feet tall, slim build, around sixty years old give or take. He had long jet-black hair, a scar on the left side of his face that ran from mid-forehead to his jawline. You could tell that wound was old as the scar tissue had become one with his personality. He spoke to us, and I recognized that he was certainly Native American. He was a kind man and greeted us warmly, but with respect as if he revered us. He looked at Cowboy and asked him, "is this him?" Cowboy responded in his southern Georgia accent, "live and in the flesh sir, that's our midnight rider." He looked over at me and chuckled as he asked me, "now you're playing real world cowboys and Indians, only we're on the same side, hah!." The way that Mr. Gardner said it and how the Native American man smiled afterward at him told me that these two knew each other quite well, almost as if they had seen battle together. A warrior can always see when two men have bled together. It's something that you can't explain. It just is…

The man told me his name, "Nantan Lupan." He was an Apache from the Lipan Apache Tribe. They were from modern Texas and had a big-league reputation. Their archrivals at one point were the feared Comanche. The Comanche were brutal. Rapists, murderer, nomadic, and took no prisoners. I asked him what his name meant, and he responded, "Nantan Lupan means Chief of Wolves where I come from. Some say it means Gray Wolf, which at my age may be more suitable." Nantan introduced me to the three men inside as well. The two that escorted us were his sons. The man inside was a close friend of his. Nantan welcomed me to "their tribe." He told me that I was very important to their mission, and they knew that I would make it there. I was surprised and inquired as to why. Nantan replied, "You have many friends. Some of them are here today, others are far from us. We have all been watching your work. You have been able to accomplish some things recently that we have been yearning to achieve for some time now. I replied, "the Brazilian?," thinking that he was talking about the snuffing of that Brazilian on my way out of South America. Nantan replied, "Not him. He was just for fun. Great job on that by the way. However, you managed to dig a bit deeper than that. Do you think that you would have all of this heat on you for that scumbag? Mr. Gardner chimed in, "Do you think that we could have executed an international extraction on you for you taking out that meaningless piece of shit?" I guess not, I replied. Nantan looked around the room at his tribe and then back at me. "General Saad has an important lady in his life, doesn't he?" Why yes, he does, I said.

Nantan told me that they have been looking for this mystery woman for years now. She is at the top of this and had been a ghost. Without her identity, they had been constantly chipping away at her underlings for over a decade. I had apparently stumbled across the queen of the hive. Nantan said, "Helena Clark, Intelligence Director for the United States Department of Justice--child exploitation predator leader. It has a nice ring to it, doesn't it.?" Nantan and his men told me that they had been tracking a high-level US government official since late 2010 but could never get close. They said that every time they felt as though they were closing in on the head of the operation, people wound up "very dead, very fast." Nantan's brother, uncle, and many friends had already perished in the wake of this evil string of covert personnel. This was obviously personal to him, and I had bought them a ticket to the show. Nantan went into detail about the extent of their operations. They had been tracking a small elite group, known as "The Red Hoods." The Red Hoods were a small group of high-ranking members of this cryptic society and were directly and solely responsible for the financial and logistical operations involved in international child sex trafficking. It was a bombshell conspiracy theory and if true, would involve extremely prevalent and wealthy people. Mr. Gardner pulled a laptop from his backpack and opened it up atop a large stack of wooden pallets. He pulled up a website showing an event calendar for a well-known casino resort in Las Vegas and scrolled down the list until he arrived at an event that showed "registration closed." He clicked the link as it led to an external web page. The title of the event was "Annual private banker's conference--April 18th ." Nantan explained that every year, these figureheads descended to Las Vegas. They came from all over the globe to meet with their malicious co-conspirators and review planning operations for the largest and most sadistic child sexual exploitation ring that the world had ever seen. Naturally, the attendee list was always private. However, Nantan told us how he and his men had been investigating this annual conference the past four years. Each and every time, the event took place at the same location. The attendee identities were unknown. They would arrive in blacked-out cars, surrounded by inconspicuous bodyguards, and would stay for a maximum of forty-eight hours before heading to several private planes at a local private airport.

I inquired as to why Nantan and his crew had dubbed them "The Red Hoods." Nantan's connections with local and national Native American tribes had apparently been a valuable resource over the years. The previous year, Nantan was able to insert a covert agent into the property during the event. The Red Hoods met on the top floor of the hotel resort. The entire top floor was designed and reserved only for the elite of the elite. Not even billionaire high rollers were able to occupy that floor. Some past presidents of the US had stayed there over the years, but not all presidents were able to use the space. It was very selective, highly secure, and reserved for what seemed to be a small list of people. The covert agent from last year's event was able to make their way to the top floor in disguise as emergency elevator mechanics. They had scaled through the south wing elevator shaft from four floors below and were able to get some photos of what was occurring inside of the penthouse. Mr. Gardner plugged in a flash drive into the computer and pulled up a photo roll. They showed around a dozen people inside the suite, dressed in deep crimson red robes, adorned with red hoods. The participants mingled inside of the event with their faces concealed by the red hoods. There was one person, draped in a black robe. Gold lined the collar of the hood, and I could make out the outline of the subject's body. Clearly visible breasts protruded underneath the black robe, and she walked around the room, handing small, polished metal cases to each of the attendees. It looked like some type of a cult or religious ceremony. I asked Nantan what was inside of these metal cases. They appear almost as old-fashioned chrome cigarette cases, but none of the participants were smoking or opening the cases in the photos. Nantan told me that his covert agent was able to hear some of the conversations happening inside of the suite that day. Conversations regarding billions of dollars, international multi-billion-dollar companies, and code names for what seemed to be prominent figures. The agent told Nantan that he was certain that he heard a conversation mentioning congressional funding for their operations.

Nantan told me that after the event, he and his tribe had experienced massive backlash. He said that the war truly started after that event and that is when his crew was forced to go underground. "There were many executions trying to find us. There are not many of us left now. We underestimated the reach and power of them, and we paid dearly." Apparently, Nantan and his people had information on some of these identities and when they attempted to conduct secondary operations, they began to feel the full wrath of this evil group. I wondered what

169

the next moves were. Nantan and his men were in hiding at this point but were apparently fully invested in this operation. Nantan asked me if I would like to see something interesting, and I agreed. Nantan told me that the keys to taking this operation down were complicated. "Complicated missions require complicated measures," he said. Today was April 12th, so I knew that their plan involved this upcoming meeting in some form. Nantan told me that they had brought me here for a specific reason. He said that the path that led me here was no mistake and that I was an integral part in the ultimate chess move. Nantan asked me if I knew who Evgeny Vladimirov was. Evgency Vladimirov was a once famous world-class chess master. Vladimirov was well-known for his complex and tactical routes to capture the queen and puzzle his opponents in swift fashion, using minimal moves on the board. Nantan told me that in order to take the queen, I had been selected as the one person that could get us inside information and place a tag on the targets of our underground hunters. My mission orders were clear. I was to use my skills to successfully infiltrate the meeting, gather as much intelligence as possible, unravel the identities of the group members, and then we would hunt them all down. One by one, Nantan, Mr. Gardner, and our allies would find these people and deliver swift and smooth justice to them. We were determined to deliver the deathblow to this sinister syndicate and put all the others following them on notice.

I had worried that we were at a disadvantage though. The hunting of Nantan's group worried me and I couldn't help but feel the sense of a negative premonition around us. I wondered if Helena and her counterparts had a bead on us already. I wondered how we would know that and if we were all preparing to walk into a full-on ambush. Nantan and Mr. Gardner looked at one another before he closed his computer. Nantan's eldest son picked up an LED flashlight from the pack on the front of his ATV and

170

clicked it on, then off. Nantan looked over at him and Cowboy before asking me to come with them. "Where are we heading?" --I asked them. Mr. Gardner responded, "you want to see our ace in the hole, don't you."?" Nantan took the lead and Mr. Gardner grabbed the flashlight from his son. His younger son pulled his pistol out of the back of his belt and followed them, waving me in behind him. "Come on now, you'll appreciate this one," Mr. Gardner said as he smirked. Nantan looked at him and his son and chuckled as he continued forward toward the back of the garage. We walked into the doorway of the small office that Nantan was working inside of when we entered the garage. There wasn't much inside of there. A small desk, an old metal swivel chair with a brown leather seat, tiny trashcan, and a metal filing cabinet to the left of the desk against the wall. Nantan pointed to the filing cabinet as he looked at his son, giving him a slight nod. His son pulled the filing cabinet out from the wall, sliding it against the floor. As we backed up, Natan's son pulled the cabinet even further away. We could barely fit inside of the small office, so we had to back up as he pulled the cabinet to its new position in the room. Mr. Gardner clicked on the flashlight and Natan's son put his hand on the floor where the cabinet was positioned before. He pulled up on a metal latch and opened up a door in the floor. Natan's son waved me over and told me to look inside. Mr. Gardner pointed the LED flashlight down into the hatch as I peered inside. I saw a man at the bottom of the hatch, about six feet down. There was a small metal ladder leading into the hatch. The man was naked and laying in the fetal position on the floor. His arms and legs were shackled together with metal chains. The chains were attached to a large metal hook in the floor of the space. He had a black fabric covering his eyes and duct tape over his mouth. "Who is this?" --I asked Nantan. He didn't say anything immediately. I looked over at Mr. Gardner and asked the same. Nantan looked at me and showed me his mobile phone. It was a picture of a news article with a man on the front page. The article was titled, "Virginia Congressman Michael Rangiri--Missing for over 4 weeks." Nantan put his finger to his lips and instructed me to keep quiet and do not react. They had a fucking congressman inside of a dark hole inside of a garage in the middle of the Nevada desert? Nantan's son unfolded a note from his right breast pocket and put it on the table in front of me. I looked down at it and it contained a gallery of text message screenshots. The name of the sender was Bryson Ribeiro. Bryson Ribeiro was a congressman. I heard that name before. I believe that he visited Afghanistan when I was over there actually. I read the text messages and knew exactly why he was where he was now. Line after line of Ribeiro ordering the hit of one of Nantan's men. Who Ribeiro was talking to in these text messages was more important to me. I asked Nantan who the person on the receiving end of this conversation was. Nantan told me that the hit went out on his crew because of Ribeiro and people were dead within a day. "It was calculated and organized, the way that they did it. It was brutal." Ribeiro had ordered the assassins to make it look like a drug trafficking hit. The bodies of three of Nantan's men were found strung up to a bridge in El Paso, Texas. They were mutilated and showed signs of significant torture, before they opened them up from neck to waist. Nantan's crew had gotten close, maybe too close to these people. For a sitting member of Congress to order a hit on Nantan and his people, it was a sign that the heat was on them. These things are usually handed by people well down the ladder, and this was a symbol of the proximity.

The older man that opened the garage for us walked into the office. He was carrying a toolkit and a flashlight with him, along with what appeared to be an audio recorder of some sort. The man descended into the hole where the congressman laid. He went down the small black metal ladder and reached the bottom, signaling us to close the hatch. Nantan's son closed the hatch door and pushed the desk across the top as we exited the room. "What are you guys doing with him?" Nantan said, "well, he's no good to us dead yet. He has been a wealth of information since his check-in at our accommodating hotel here. We intend to milk this cow for all its' worth." These guys were the real deal. I mean, you had to have some serious cajónes to kidnap and torture a corrupt congressman. The US Secret Service was most certainly looking for him, along with the FBI and every other state law enforcement agency in the area. These guys didn't care anymore. They were invested 100 percent and were motivated to take this all of the way.

As we sat down in the garage, we began to look over what Nantan's crew had, intelligence-wise. Mappings of potential targets, full hit lists with verified targets, compromised assets or snitches that were now working for us, activity logs of suspects, home addresses, work addresses, phone numbers, email addresses, social security numbers, credit card numbers, credit card transactions, banking info, global cell phone logs, photos, video files, audio transcripts of their meetings, publications, news and journal articles, you name it; we fucking had it. I got to work on my fair share, using everything that they had up until this point. I requested the names and addresses of all of the suspects that may be attending the conference, and all of the confirmed identities of those who were verified and known to be working with the syndicate. I set up a makeshift workstation on top of a box inside of the garage and spread the intelligence files out on the floor around me. Mr. Gardner gave us all the security protocol if we had to leave the facility in a hurry. Regardless, there was a lot of work to get done in a short period of time if we wanted to mount a successful operation by the eighteenth of the month. The more information that we could gather on positive target identifications, the better we would be able to mark our targets with certainty and unfold their operations. Something big was going down at this meeting, and we knew that we had one shot to get them into the open. Our mission wasn't to merely kill these people. If that were the case, we would have already placed hitters out there and the hunt would be in full effect. This was different and personal to all of us. We had a unique opportunity to unravel their operations, reveal their funding and logistical operations, and locate the buzzing network of child exploitation that they were running. We may even be able to lift some of these kids from their clutches if we played our cards right.

The night went on as we worked together. Collaborating intelligence, marking subjects, and connecting the dots of our findings. My work in South America and Afghanistan came into play. I held some valuable pieces to the puzzle and when placed together with all of this, it made sense to me. General Saad's ring of wealthy financiers, yacht clubs that were transit safehouses for moving children, opera houses right in New York City that had underground lairs dedicated to holding child auctions, Swiss bankers that gave child traffickers funding and even credit to strengthen their network, and much more. The corruption that plagued our institutions was so vast and had so much depth that you wouldn't even believe it if it were in a Hollywood movie. In fact, Hollywood was apparently one of the worst offenders. We had intelligence, tracing back to some of the most successful Hollywood moguls and A-list celebrities. Their crimes ran backward in time to that of Vaudeville cinematography in late 1900s France. These were all used as fast-track railways in the child exploitation realm. We knew that the head of one of the United States' largest mainstream media news outlets had close ties with General Saad and his US-based counterparts as well. The shear amount of people that were in some way related to child sexual predation was stunning. Government, banking, hospitality, transportation, entertainment; even the intelligence community itself had assets. Occasionally, you hear news about some air force officer getting caught with kid porn, but that is most certainly not the tip of the spear. It is a barely noticeable freckle on the face of this massive illicit and evil operation. One person stood out to us as particularly suspicious, but not high in the ranks. He was a wealthy finance mogul that had a rather quiet existence, aside being spotted by paparazzi with past US presidents, famous actors, and British royalty on occasion. The worst part was that these people were very organized. This was a well-oiled machine and they had powerful people, significant funding, and they used the same tradecraft as narco traffickers and intelligence agencies to conceal themselves.

I followed the intelligence paths to one key individual. This man was apparently very close with the congressman. The other was an unknown subject. The man associated with Congressman Rangiri and appeared to be highly technical. His identity wasn't hard to find, however there were certain signs that this person may have a false flag identity. When I was performing some open-source intelligence gathering on him, it seemed to always lead to paths unknown. When seeking his family ties, the trails ran cold and usually led to very obscure parts of the internet, or even into the dark web. I traced this man in some online forums. For a few hours, I studied the way that he talked and how he typed. His English was good, but not flawless. I noticed certain words were spelled differently. One stood out to me in particular. He typed "colours" instead of "colors." Subtleties in his language led me to believe that he was of English descent or at least spent time in Great Britain or England at some point in his life. I found his online moniker associated with several technical forums on the dark web as well. One trail led into others and eventually, I located an interesting dark web forum on hacking for hire. It was a cyber-attacker mercenary site where malicious hackers could be hired to perform certain jobs. He wasn't there to get hired though. It appeared as though he was running the forum and was managing several groups of Russian, North Korean, and Chinese cyber-threat actor groups. Mostly bank hit jobs and ransomware from the looks of it, but I could tell that he was skilled and trained in cyber-warfare as well. His language and skills had the hallmarks of something that I was familiar with and that I knew well. I sought his past work and found some articles that he had posted inside of the forums, showing cyber extortion in Romania, ransomware attacks in Palestine, and hacktivist activities in Berlin. It was wild and I would not have expected someone of this caliber to be associated with the criminal underground that Congressman Rangiri ran with.

I remembered my training. We were taught to throw false flags when concealing ourselves online. It was always more than just using proxy servers to hide our IP addresses, burner cellphones, and using untraceable operating systems that self-destruct when unplugged. We were taught to use language in certain ways that would constantly throw off our adversaries. When we were concealing our online identities, using undertones and accents of a different language could buy you just enough separation to ensure that those hunting you would take another path. I commonly used these techniques in changing my online language tones to mimic that of other countries. I generally used Russian Cyrillic keyboard emulators to portray my identity as that of a Russian comrade. However, I knew someone that was a master in using British English to throw off adversaries. It was unmistakable and showed the marks of someone that I knew very well. Perry had used this tactic before right in front of me when we worked a case together in Afghanistan. He was mimicking an Indian man living in

London so that we could catch the leader of an ISIS sleeper cell in Rome, Italy. I knew that this must be him.

I turned over to Nantan's son and asked him where Nantan was. I closed my laptop and woke Mr. Gardener up as he lay on the floor with his head on his backpack. "I need to talk to you and Nantan quickly." We walked to the back of the garage as I led us through the back door. Nantan was inside of a smaller room lying on the floor atop a sleeping bag. He was getting some rest when I swung the door open. He rose from the floor and asked me what I had found. I gave him the online moniker of the alleged British hacker and asked him how Congressman Rangiri wound up in this garage. He came in closer to me and asked me to repeat the name of the online handle again. I told him once again, as he looked over at Mr. Gardner. Nantan said, "The congressman was given to us as a gift by an unknown person inside of this arena. We have no idea who this person is or what they want. But whoever they are, they helped us several times over the past months and basically delivered the congressman to our front door. Whoever this person is, he or she has helped to put us into a position of leverage." I responded to Nantan and told him that I knew who this person was. "Can we trust him?"--said Mr. Gardner. "You already know him," I replied. "Son of a bitch. No shit...That's your friend, huh? The one from Afghanistan? Ha-ha...small world indeed"--said Mr. Gardner.

We had an asset on the inside. I knew now why they took him out of Afghanistan so quickly. Back then, I had not the slightest suspicion that Perry was so deep into this circle, but now I understood. He was feeding Nantan intelligence and was up-close and personal inside of the ring. If anyone were to lead us to the men in red, it was Perry. A thought came across my mind...A phrase. An old sequence. "Russia stole my little brother and best friend. WW2 made many movies and three is my lucky number"

7

89

121

9573

I had the acronymic code that I memorized for the satellite phone from Major Pickens in Afghanistan. "Give me a satellite phone, now!" I said as I looked around the room. Mr. Gardner opened his pack and pulled out a sat phone and unfolded the antenna above the hand unit. I punched in the numbers. 7..89..121...9573 and hit "call." A short beep ensued before the line was ringing. It rang three times, then 4, then 5, and six. It rang until the line rang out. I put the phone down on the table beside us and thought for a minute. The phone began to buzz on the table. The incoming call was marked as "restricted." I grabbed the satellite phone and pressed the green button and raised it to my ear. I heard static and some background noise, but no voice. I uttered a single word, the name of the online moniker that I suspected was Perry. I waited…. After a few seconds, I heard some tones coming back on the line.

- Long beep
- Single beep
- Long beep
- Long beep
- Single beep
- Three single beeps

Morse code…It was morse code for "yes." Perry was confirming that he was inside of the seventh circle of hell. His bravery astounded me and suddenly, I knew that we had everything that we needed to take them down. It was only a matter of time now before we cut our way out of the belly of the beast and spilled its blood on the golden halls that they once walked with impunity.

## 17: Tradecraft Operations

That night, we relocated to a safe house about twenty miles from the initial site. We went deeper into the desert terrain to an outpost. It was an old mining facility on a Native American reservation and Nantan's connections secured the area for us to get to work. We went underground and set up our gear. They had a full facility under the earth. We took an old wooden staircase down one of the mine shafts until we reached an old, abandoned miner's staging area. There was a cove inside that Nantan's crew had retrofitted with all types of gear. We had an internet connection rigged to a hidden satellite above the mining facility. The connection was surprisingly strong for where we were. They had run cables down the mine shaft walls into our work area. There were people coming in and out as the night went on. Bringing in supplies, food, water, ammo, rifles, explosives, and anything else we needed.

I decided to catch some sleep. I had been awake for nearly 2 full days and my mind was foggy. I couldn't work if I didn't get some rest and I knew that I needed to stop and recharge. Mr. Gardner showed me a separate area that I could go rest in. It was small, but had a hammock slung and a small light inside. There was a wooden door that was outfitted with a metal slide lock. As I put my gear on the ground beside the hammock, I pulled the door's slide lock only to find that it was jammed. I had a sudden flash memory of the bathroom stall of my youth. The one with the broken lock. I had this thing, you see. Whenever I went into a room, I checked the locks. If the locks were not functioning properly, an overwhelming feeling of anxiety would come over me. However, I didn't feel any fear or anxiety at this moment. It was a liberating sense that I had. Instead of dwelling on the broken lock, I put the

180

thought aside and put one leg into the hammock, then swinging my body inside and laying back. I was free. For the first time in a long time, I had a sense of peace about me. I wasn't on the defensive side of the field now. We were the hunters, and we were the ones to be feared, not the contrary. As I closed my eyes, the rush subsided. All of the miles traveled and the situations that unfolded had led me here. I was with my tribe, and we were putting on our warpaint. I closed my eyes and drifted into a slumber, letting my worries fall away from my body and mind, knowing that we held a strategic advantage on the battlefield.

I wasn't sure how long I was out for, but I awoke to one of Nantan's men tapping my chest with his hand. It was quiet still and everything seemed calm. I asked him what time it was. He said that it was 1400 hours. I figured that I had slept for about 8 or 9 hours. That was the most sleep that I had gotten in quite a long time actually. I emerged from my quarters and joined a few of Nantan's men boiling coffee. We sat on the dirt floor and brewed a pot of freshly-ground coffee over the fire. The smell of the roasted coffee grounds was decadent. The aroma mixed with the familiar drumbeat of my comrades working was home to me. I felt as though I was right where I wanted and needed to be. After a few minutes, I came over to a large, brushed steel table. It was over 10 feet long and there were three other people sitting there working on their computers. One of them looked over at me, as I opened my laptop and said "Welcome to our command center. Want to get in on the action with us?" I was excited. It had been a long time since I worked alongside anyone else. I had been working alone for quite some time now and the thought of collaborating with other people was invigorating to me. That familiar ambition came back to me, and I joined in on their operations. I reviewed what they were doing and who they were targeting. They had a large list of targets up on their screens, but a few of them were marked as key players. I asked them what the task order was. They showed me how they were tracking a few guys out of Beijing that had close ties with US Customs and Border Control officers. I asked what the significance was. They told me that they had gotten lucky and stumbled upon some guys in the US Customs and Immigration that were collaborating with Chinese spies. "What would Beijing want with the US Customs and Immigration department."?" I found that the web of deceit ran further and deeper than just child trafficking. Nantan's guys had significant intelligence on an internal rouge operation within the US Customs department that was aiding Chinese spies with some pretty astounding shit. They were moving fentanyl together, to the tune of over 30 million dollars' worth per week, running guns from the US to China, and selling US manufacturing trade secrets to Chinese spies.

The whole situation was fucked. I asked them what this had to do with anything that we were working on. The guys explained that their mission was wider than mine and involved a number of different objectives. Their purpose was to root out corruption at any level and by any means necessary. They never knew when a lead would help to assist another objective that they had or that I was working on, so they kept everything in the same arena. One of the guys at the table with me was former CIA. The other two were hackers that had apparently found a higher purpose. All of them were equally skilled in their tradecraft. The first guy was a solid programmer and created sophisticated exploits. He was so skilled at making computer vulnerability exploit packages that the North Korean government had once offered him over 20 million dollars to work for them for three days. He had denied the opportunity, but it was a lot of money, nevertheless. The second man was very young, maybe 20 years old. He was a social engineer aficionado. His skills were not behind the keyboard, well not exactly at least. He was highly adept at making people bend to his will, regardless of the situation. The other two guys told me to watch out for him or else he would convince me to make dinner for him and wipe his ass. The third person was the quiet one. Ex-CIA, 40-45 years old, and had a serious grudge. He was the kind of ex-employee that you do not want to be on their bad side by any means. He was the real deal. His past experiences included taking down foreign governments, rocking nation-state cyber attackers to their core, and putting foreign rouge dictators on their heels so that the US government could impose their will. He didn't speak much, but he was the alpha in the operation, and everyone knew it.

The group brought me to school on the way that the financial aspects work within these groups. I had always wondered; couldn't we just follow the money? The short answer to that was obviously yes, to a degree. However, these people had produced some creative methodologies to fund their operations and receive payments. It was something that astounded me, really. Art, of all things...art? Apparently, the dark criminal underground that comprised the child sex trafficking world was also made up of fine art mavens and wine connoisseurs. It made sense and was quite brilliant. You see, how can someone actually exchange millions, if not tens of millions, or hundreds of millions of dollars without being flagged by any one of the agencies that keep an eye on money movement? Well, it seems as though fine art was at the top of that list. You can't just exactly send someone a million dollars via PayPal for illicit activities or products. However, if bad guy one wants to buy something from bad girl one, then bad girl one can sell them a relatively worthless painting for millions and call it a modern-day Rembrandt. Art dealers and brokers within this space were complicit as well. You ever notice why fine art dealers and the community that surrounds them is generally strange? Now you know. The same goes for fine wine. A handful of elite people in Napa, California that owned their own vineyards while simultaneously being some of the biggest brokers and consumers of this illicit trade was staggering as well. This tactic also made sense. You plant some shit grapes, squeeze one hundred bottles of wine per year, and sell them to deep-pocketed bidders. It was a true money game, and it had the exact opposite stench to that of great wine and fine art.

We went deeper into the layers. The money washing, the exchanges using cryptocurrencies, even rare novelty automobiles were involved. This started to draw lines of parallel between suspects and trade. They sought out "private bidders" at art auctions and galleries and incognito wine aficionados that rolled in high-roller circles. From there, they were able to weed out the demons and tag their ears. Nantan's group had flawless execution, for the most part. But they were lacking some deep technical expertise and that is where I come into play. One of the biggest problems that we had wasn't finding these people, but actually building cases on some of them at the top. Nantan's group had enough intelligence to deal a significant blow to them and eradicate a large portion of them if they chose to do so. There were a couple of resident problems with that though. The first issue was that if Nantan's crew were to launch a genocide against the malicious actors, then the trails would lead cold quickly. The roots would shrivel up and the snake's head would grow back at some point. Not only this but wiping out entire swathes of child predators would turn the rest of them on to our tactics, leaving the children in captivity astray. The second catalyst for quick and swift strike prohibition was that the media would cover it up as acts of terrorism. 21-gun salutes, bagpipes for the fallen, and ceremonious eulogies for the pieces of shit that were taken out. That was simply unacceptable. We needed a multi-pronged and sustainable assault. While we were all dreamers, we were all realistic as well in knowing that we would not be able to tackle this problem globally in one-fell-swoop. We needed assurance that our sources, methods, and tactics would be concealed to some degree and that we could continue our mission indefinitely until the problem was eradicated. Only then could we continue our mission if we fell. We needed to create a continuous force that was formidable to the future of this empire.

I went to work on several key subjects and began downloading the bytes of data that we had on them. I had what I needed to get things rolling past the checkpoints that Nantan's crew had brought this to. I had some of the cellphone numbers of members that were suspected to be attendees at the shithead conference, but the crew didn't have their full digital hooks into them. They were top of the list targets, high value ones that we needed so that we could map out the quick action force. I had used some pretty slick smartphone malware once upon a time in my past and it came to mind. The Pegasus program was a malicious payload that allowed me to take full unadulterated control over smartphones. I had socked away a hidden file dump online where I could retrieve the packages if I needed them again. I went out to a private Google file drive and logged in with a burner account. The files were still there, in all of their glory. I downloaded them onto the laptop that I was using. Of course, I was running a burner operating system with Kali Linux on a removable thumb drive. It was the only way to surf the internet airwaves, in my opinion. If we got compromised, simply pull the drive and the data is wiped. Nantan's crew had a huge metal drum with a lid on it. It was a 55-gallon steel drum. I asked what was in it. One of the guys told me that it was hydrochloric acid and that if the location were ever compromised, they could start tossing hard drives into the drum and the acid would nearly immediately compromise the hard drives. It was easier and cheaper than a degaussing machine, I guess.

Once I had the Pegasus malware ready to go, I set up a download watering hole site on a shared online drive that anyone could get to, given that they knew the hyperlink. I readied a cell phone emulator and began to craft a nice phishing text message for my victim. I set it up so that the recipient would believe that they were receiving a video file for download. These fuckers loved videos. That was their weak spot, of course. I had two phone numbers of these people. They had been in contact with one another for some time now and Nantan's guys had traced multiple phone calls between them. Apparently Nantan had people inside of some of the major telecom providers and cell phone companies that were willing to help. I took the phone number of the first subject, as he was the person that usually called or sent text messages to the other and spoofed his phone number in the cell phone emulator. Then, I sent a message from his spoofed cell number to my target. The message had a nice pedo tagline and a video link. It was a short message, but effective, nevertheless.

On the other side of things, Nantan's contact at the telecom provider company was now routing calls and texts to our emulator number. That meant that if my target responded to the sender, it wouldn't actually go to him. Rather, it would come to our underground call center, right here in the middle of the desert. I sent the message and the video download link, monitoring the download on the web side to determine whether anyone was reaching it or downloading. We waited. 5 minutes, ten minutes, then thirty, then an hour. I got up to walk around and familiarize myself with the surroundings a bit further. It smelled exactly how you would imagine an underground spy shack to smell, like shit. It was musty, dusty, and not very presentable to anyone of any class. Luckily, we weren't those people, so it was perfect for us. There was a long hallway corridor leading down to the south end of the bunker. There were small lights hanging from the ceiling and it reminded me of an old book on Vietnamese tunnel systems that I had read when I was young. I peered down the tunnel as a hand tapped me on the shoulder. It was the CIA guy. "Come over here, take a look at what we got," he said as he turned down the walkway back to our workstation.

I arrived back at the laptop and sat down. They showed me a short conversation that they were having with the target. He was excited to download the video but said that nothing was happening when he opened it. The team acted quickly when I was away and once, he downloaded Pegasus, they uploaded a real video that they had lifted from some dark site. It was a video of a recorded murder apparently. A kid…

I asked them why they went so overboard. The CIA spook replied, "look here. This was after we sent him the real video." The target was obviously excited by the content and was asking for more of it. He wanted the source so that he could peruse a collection of these types of videos, rather than settling for just one of them. They gave him the source and off he went. I looked over at the command console of the Pegasus software and saw everything. I had the steering wheel of his mobile phone at this point. Click, turn on camera. Click, turn on microphone. Click, download all call logs. Click, download text messages. Click, download photos and videos. Click, install other ghost applications and modules. Click, we got this motherfucker.

We watched him as one of the guys began to back trace his picture through some search engines. LinkedIn pages, Facebook, Instagram, Twitter, looking for hits and matches on his ugly mugshot. They searched until they had a potential match. Former White House staff…Nice touch. He was a logistics guy, not too high up in the political sphere of influence and he had just enough notoriety to get him connected with powerful people. He was perfect for us. See, we didn't want anyone too high profile. When you are attaching to a mule like this, less famous is best as they do not have the same levels of caution or privacy training. Famous people are more difficult as they tend to keep an eye out and look over their shoulders more often. He was our diamond in the rough and we began full exploitation. We waited for him to type and retrieve all of his login credentials for bank accounts, private email servers, social media, hidden messaging apps, and even his own private collection of evidence that we had on him. For some of these people, we intended to remain in the shadows. However, when you are close to the nucleus, it's time to jump off the carrier wagon and wield your longsword. This guy was the epitome of a bribery subject. We had enough data on him to completely ruin his life, and we began that process.

First step, cut off communications with the outside world. All messaging channels locked down, no outbound calls or messages to anyone but us. Locked email accounts, locked social media accounts, cancelled his home phone landline, and cut the onboard communication subscription for his car. Locked his Apple accounts and deleted his access to nearly every service that he could use to communicate. Then, we sent him a message. It was a screenshot of him on one side of the viewing pane with what he was watching on the other side. Across, we placed a message for him. "Don't do anything. If you contact anyone, shut off your phone, or leave your house, we will release all of your devious content to the media immediately. If that does not work, we have agents within fifty yards of you that are eager to meet you." They weren't lying about that part either. These people had local police officers on their payroll in just about every major city in the United States. Apparently, cops were taking it upon themselves to thwart evil as well. They had an off-duty cop sitting at a gas station air pump in his car within viewing distance from the target's home. We sent another message to him. "Black Ford Explorer, Exxon station." We watched on his smartphone camera as he looked out of the window and sat back down in his chair. We had this guy dead to rights with nowhere to turn.

At about this time, Nantan came over to check the mission. He never looked excited, only determined and watching the next moves. The CIA spook took over the mission from there and began to work on the target. He was an expert at the social engineering aspects of clandestine ops, so I was out of my league here. I can get them in the digital front door, but I was happy to turn over the operation after that. They played the game with him, let him calm down. I watched as they talked to him as if they were pitiful and he began to respond with remorse. It went on for about thirty minutes or so and then they raised the level of intensity, as he was calm and docile by that point. The CIA guy put the ultimatum down on the table for him. It wasn't what I had expected. You know, the names and identities of those involved. No, it was completely the opposite. We didn't ask him for information. The only thing that we did was instruct him to continue living his life, as normal. Were there strings attached? Maybe a few, but we weren't asking him to roll the entire circle over. We knew that they had protections in place to sniff out rats within their circle. The best thing that we could do is leave him alone, observe him, and keep the card in our back pocket. We knew that he was inside of the tight knit circle but could not locate his rank among the group. As I said, he wasn't overly wealthy, didn't have a flashy lifestyle, and had the appearance of a normal person. The shit heads inside of his circle were always more watchful of their people that had extravagant lifestyles since they were more likely to be compromised at some point. It's a simple numbers game. More attention, more risk. This guy, on the other hand, must be a trusted asset within the circle of evil. We were going to use him as our tunnel rat within the depths of the labyrinth.

We tracked him for the next few days, in conjunction with working other viable avenues. He carried on with his normal activities, nothing out of the ordinary. We had hooks into his cellphone, mobile networks, and vehicle. We saw where he went and who he spoke with. Life for him was normal and boring, to be quite honest. We waited for something to happen; anything exciting. Hour after hour, we watched him and listened. It was about 2 p.m. EST and we picked up an incoming phone call. However, it wasn't coming from the cellphone that we had a live connection on. We picked up a buzzing noise coming from near his cellphone. We could hear some radio signal static on the receiver that we had next to the desk. It was receiving audio feedback from another cellphone, but we didn't have a connection to it. He had another phone and we needed access. The buzzing and static were intermittent, almost as if not a phone call, but messages or silenced notifications. We had a program that we embedded into his laptop, which was within proximity of the buzzing noises. The technique that we leveraged to hack into the rouge phone via Bluetooth was called "BlueSnarfing." This is when you utilize a Bluetooth receiver module, such as on a laptop, to pick up nearby Bluetooth broadcast signals and your way into whichever device is transmitting. This is a proximity attack that is generally only possible if you are within short-range of the target device. However, we had access to the target's laptop that was within spitting distance from the unknown cellphone.

We ran the program and waited. As it cycled through its processes, I grew anxious. I knew that these types of hacks were not only difficult, but sometimes nearly impossible to accomplish, especially when performing it at a distance. We were always looking for new challenges and we had modified the Bluetooth hacking modules so that they would leverage a brute-force technique that intelligence agencies use to cycle through smartphone PIN codes. Less than a minute later, we had a match on the Bluetooth connection code, and we were getting signals from the device. Luckily for us, the vendor of the cell phone was Huawei, a Chinese manufacturer and they apparently loaded their cellphones with a simplistic Bluetooth connection code. It was four digits, in reverse sequence: 9876! The rouge cell phone was an older model, not running on any type of 5G or 4G network. Most likely a flip phone as the signal was using an older cellphone protocol. We began to ingest the data packets inbound and outbound on the device. The buzzing noise that we were hearing were indeed text messages, old school SMS. It looked like the sender was using some sort of online program to send the codes as the sender number was a short-code, and not a traditional 10-digit phone number as if it were coming from another cellphone. The guys were in the process of deciphering the incoming text messages and were coming back with decoded messages. They looked like some sort of instruction sets. Seemingly random letters, occasional duplicates, but with no apparent sequence or patterns yet. It was some sort of cipher… The code read, "F S T O M L E DP OV EEL OEN LIR NCAT."

When dealing with ciphertext, you need a key to understand the messages. This goes all of the way back to the ancient Greeks. The Caesar Box was one of the earliest known ciphers actually. It was created around 100 BC and used by Julius Caesar to send secrets to his field generals. I knew that there were similarities to the Greek empire and the hierarchy of this circle, so we decided to begin there. To decode a Caesar code, one must count the number of characters in the code. In this case, we had twenty-five individual characters. After the first step, then you must determine how many rows you can divide the letters into equally. The square root of twenty-five is 5, so we broke the code out into five equal rows of five letters each.

- FSTOM
- LEEDP
- OVEEL
- OENLI
- RNCAT

Once we had the blocks of five broken down, we could then read down the first line, then the second, third, fourth and fifth to get the message in clear text. "Floor Seventeen: Code Lamplit." One thing that I had learned in this game is to never put it past the egotistical maniacs to use one of the most antiquated ciphertexts in history. It was simple, rudimentary, yet effective in many cases. We began to receive more information, not anything incriminating but we were receiving instructions on their annual meeting. It was coming together, and we had a line into our target. We then monitored our target as he used his laptop to double encrypt the incoming messages and send them out to his constituents. He was using a far more advanced methodology to encrypt the messages and deploy them to the attendees. He was using a steganographic method to embed messages into JPEG photos and send them as "advertisements." It was actually quite genius. He would embed secret messages into pictures so that only the recipient would think to decode them using a pre-shared key code. Our target used an email address that looked like a spam advertisement to their emails. The emails from our target were likely landing in the spam folders of the recipients and they would open them and place the JPEG into a decoder tool and retrieve the messages. This method was being used so that if any investigation ever took place, the investigators would pass right by the recipients spam folders and messages that appeared to be from advertisements. It was quite slick, but we saw it all happening in real-time. Message after message, we watched and took notes. We counted over 30 unique recipients until our target stopped sending. His list was completed, and he gave the instructions to the attendees. Where to meet, which floor, what time, the code phrases for entry, the code phrases for immediate termination of the meeting, information on who in the local police department would be providing security. He was even sending information on which blackjack table was "friendly" to their evil group.

I saw this mission as an immediate and irrefutable success. However, Nantan and the CIA guy didn't seem as pleased as I was. They were cautious and had a sentiment that things were aligned too neatly. I overheard Nantan talking in a tone as if he had seen something like this before. "It's too easy. Keep an eye on this guy, ok," Nantan said to us before walking down the narrow hall to the adjacent room in the bunker. We kept observing our target over the next few hours and worked on additional leads. Only time would tell if we were on the trail or being led astray. Either way, we were moving towards the target and finalizing the tactical aspects of the mission.

## 18: Incoming

I never believed that courage was something with which you were born. I always thought that it was learned. However, I never saw myself as courageous or brave. I always was afraid inside of me; it's what propelled me through my life thus far. My fear and I were like soulmates. I always heard stories of brave men, courageous people but I couldn't see myself in that light. The kids that we were fighting for were brave. To me, bravery and courage are traits that someone can only hold when they are outgunned, outnumbered, or overpowered. Yet, they still pick their head up and spit in the faces of their enemies. That to me is courage and these children had it. I guess you could say that I had a moment of courage back in that restroom when I was a kid. Surely outnumbered, definitely overpowered, but my mind stayed crisp. The ultimate test of a human is performed when they are under significant pressure. The pressure of certain death and how resilient and resourceful a person can be in those situations was simply amazing. Children were always the most courageous to me, as they were frail and weaker than these predators, yet they were resilient and resourceful; some until the very end. These are the thoughts that kept me moving through my life. I wasn't brave, but I had a moment of courage one time in my life.

As I sat in the bunker on my cot that night, these thoughts swirled through my mind like a hurricane ripping through the Caribbean. The waves of thought were fifty feet high, and the winds were strong and cold. I sat there for hours, just thinking, strategizing about the mission at hand and how we would continue to have the upper hand. Nantan came into the doorway of the small room that I was occupying and was holding a satellite phone in his hand. I looked up at him and he took a long puff of his hand-rolled cigarette and held the phone out to me. "I think you need to make a phone call." Call who? I was caught off-guard a bit, but Nantan said it in a tone that implied me calling someone that I knew, someone that I personally had a relationship with. I knew that I needed to call Perry as Nantan had suspicions about the upcoming operation. See, if we fucked this up, that was it and we were done. On the other hand, if we did this right, then we may be able to cause irreparable damage to their psychopathic syndicate. The stakes were high enough for us to potentially compromise everything. If we did not have complete assurance and confidence in our intelligence, the mission could not go on.

7-89-121-9573, I dialed the number on Nantan's sat phone…

It rang for ten seconds, then twenty, until finally the line clicked. I spoke slowly on the line and heard a voice come back. The volume was very low, but I knew my friend's voice. He was alone on this call. We were talking on an insecure line, so we had to be careful and not use too many specifics. Nantan called one of his guys into the room and they set up an Iridium satellite comms encryption module so that we could speak freely with one another. Once we had the line encrypted, I let Perry know that we had a secure line. He let out a long breath as if he felt a sense of relief come over him, as did I. It had been a tumultuous run for us since we left Afghanistan. I knew what I had been through, but I had no idea the depth as to what Perry had been traversing this whole time. Perry filled me in on his movements since we split. I had been surrounded by a network of protectors, while Perry had been inside of their operation alone this whole time. He had gained their implicit trust and I could tell that he had regrets in how he had done so. I wondered what he had to witness in order to be trusted by these monsters. Perry was tough though and was always about the mission. He had been working this group for a long time and Afghanistan was the queue that he took to dive into the deep end with this.

Down to business now. It was time to map this out. After Perry and I got caught up, I put him on speakerphone, and we went to the drawing board together with Nantan's team. Perry gave us insights into three different rings operating on the US-Mexican border, one in Upstate NY, and a major distribution hub in Houston, Texas. Three targets in addition to specifics about the convention taking place here in Nevada. The gameplan specifics were not clear to us just yet, but we knew that this had to be a forceful strike. The mission needed a nickname, but we would cover that later on. The US-Mexican border group was controlled by the Mexican narcos, and they had help from some corrupt US Border Patrol agents and Mexican Federal policemen. This group was in charge of moving kids from Mexico into the US and vice versa. They went both ways. The cell out of Houston was in charge of international distribution outbound from the United States. Apparently, kidnapped kids from the US were almost never kept inside of the country due to the risk and high-profile nature. They had a rule to ship them out within forty-eight hours. If they couldn't ship them out, we knew what happened to them. Houston shipped from their ports to all around the world. Perry said that they used commercial trade routes that routed through the Gulf of Mexico, across the Caribbean and over to West Africa. Usually, they would dock in Somalia and use the local traffickers to move them across land into the Middle East or Asia. The Upstate NY operation apparently used Canada as a mount point for moving kids north. They had a major route coming through Syracuse and Buffalo, rolling through the Canadian border on the St. Lawrence River, then up to Nova Scotia. From there, they would ship out to Norway and then finally to Russia. Once they hit Russia, they were gone forever. It was an industrial approach to the most horrific trade in human history and we had the maps.

I could hear the drums beating inside of my head. The sound of a primitive warrior percussion rhythm was pounding. Bang, bang, bang, BANG. It got louder as the thought of the operation took ahold of me, it was like a drug for me, and that drumbeat had been there with me all of my life. Perry explained their movements and the locations of the safehouses in Houston, Buffalo, and Mexico. The CIA spook scratched notes behind us onto a small red flip notebook. After he filled a page, he would rip it off and hand it to the man next to him. One by one, he ripped the pages, handing the next page to the next guy beside him. They peeled off and took each page back to the command center to get things prepared. After Perry had given us all of the information that he had, the CIA guy and Nantan walked back to the command center together as I remained on the line with Perry. He has a somber tone to his voice. I knew Perry well and I had never heard his demeanor in this fashion. He was optimistic and energetic, but I could sense that he had accepted whatever fate was in store for him. He was burrowed into the belly of the beast, and he knew that this was bigger than him, it was bigger than me, this was bigger than all of us. We understood that. We had both come so far together on this mission, but it always felt as though we had miles to go yet. It's like running a race that has no finish line. However, we also understood that we could change things right here and right now. This wasn't about sending a message or knocking them back on their heels. We had the tools to bulldoze them from their pedestal in a way that nobody had before. All of the law enforcement, government operations, military missions, state and federal police operations couldn't hold a candle to what we had in our hands. We knew that if we turned all of this information over to the authorities at this point, it would reach the corrupt tentacles of their group and they would simply crawl back into their conk shell and switch tactics.

Perry gave us the locations of the massive distribution hubs, the identities of hundreds of top players, trade routes, government officials that were involved, and the exact information on the meeting for the top dogs. It was the Mecca that we so yearned for, and Perry helped us to find the last keystone. We traded a few more words, but I knew that he wasn't going to be joining us physically. I didn't try to convince him otherwise.

Perry gave me some words that have stayed in my mind, in the exact place in which they entered that day. He said, "This is what we were created for, and you know that, Scott. Over seven billion people roam this Earth every day, with only a small fraction of us that are willing to throw away all normality to pursue a higher purpose. This isn't a war for oil or gold. This is the only war for our future. The children that we are saving will carry the torch, just like you and me. They will always remember the ones that saved them and will always have the memories of the tortures that they endured. They are the only ones in which the fire burns bright enough inside of them to carry this on and win. People say that after these kids are rescued, they are shells of their former selves. I don't believe that, and neither do you. We know the truth and we know the things these kids are capable of. Something has been stolen from these children, as it was stolen from you, but someone has also been given to them. Courage. We may not be able to fully eradicate this disease, but maybe they will. If not them, then their children will, and their grandchildren until one day, this evil walks no more. Until then, let's light the fucking path for them." Perry told me not to call this sat phone number after we got off the call. He said that the line was going dead today after we were done.

There was one last thing that Perry left us with before we ended the call. He had set up a GPS tracker on his position so that we knew where he was headed to. He told us to follow the tracker with a program that he had sent to us. He wrote the software himself so that nobody else would be able to follow his beacon. It was a steady satellite tracker, so there was no need for triangulation of a cell number or waiting until it hit a Wi-Fi signal. It was online all of the time as long as it was intact. We loaded the program that Perry had file dropped to us and brought it up on the screen. We could see a bright green circle on the map. He was within a hundred miles of our position. 2 miles from downtown Las Vegas was his exact spot. He must have been in a house or apartment building somewhere there, as there was no noise of crowds on the call with him. His green circled position stayed steady right there. I ended the call with Perry and began to think deeply about our brotherhood. One of Nantan's men tapped me on the shoulder and I turned and looked at him. He told me to "get my mind right, don't waste what he just gave to you." He was right. I couldn't wallow in self-pity or fear now. It wasn't the time to do any of that. I would have time for emotions later. Right now, it was about making the most of the time that we had and the new resources we had just been gifted. We began the mapping and intelligence gathering process. We got into the street cameras for the Houston area, around the distribution points that we had on the map. We had a full visual of a large warehouse at a shipping yard. There were two facilities that we had targeted. One was in Galveston Bay and the adjacent Trinity Bay. The live video and aerial imagery showed long rows of shipping containers and parked vessels. There were people loading green, black, and red shipping containers on top of one another. Perry had told us to keep an eye out for gray containers. There were no gray or white containers to be seen at that point. Only green, black and red.

The next target was in Buffalo. We had some connections in the Northeast that were in the area. We sent them to the border patrol stations at Niagara to get a visual confirmation on some things that Perry had tipped us off on. He instructed us to seek out the customs guard station that had a ring on the side of it, only visible with ultraviolet light. That evening, our asset went to the guard stations through an adjacent field and brought a UV flashlight. He had a distraction set up at the border with one of his allies in a vehicle blasting music through the checkpoint. We were on a call with the guy in the field and could hear the music blaring. It was actually hilarious that the music they chose was Jonny Cash's "Ring of Fire." As the guards descended on the car, our guy painted the guard shacks with the UV flashlight. Out of the six guard stations, the fifth station showed a small diameter ring just above the side door. It was about six inches in diameter and was bright as the moon on a clear night. Guard station five was the route in and out of the US for Canada trafficking. Checkmate.

The final zone was Mexico. You would think that Mexico would be a bit more difficult of a target to paint since it was outside of the US jurisdiction. Lest we forget that corruption runs deep down south and money talks. We had a big crew in Mexico already, so this was an easier one for us to coordinate. Just South of McAllen, Texas there was a Mexican town called Reynosa. These two towns shared an international border and there was a private airstrip in a field 1 km east of Reynosa that Perry gave us the drop on. We had a team of five Mexican assets setup inside of the Reynosa city central. They positioned themselves into the highest building that Reynosa had and busted out the binoculars and pointed them east to the airfield's location. They could see heavy activity. We asked them to report what they were observing, and we got silence back on the call. The guy on the call stuttered for a minute and said, "I think we found what we are looking for papi." There were children being loaded, five to fifteen at a time, onto small private jets and prop-driven cargo planes. Small enough to avoid unnecessary attention and protected by armed narco traffickers. There were even two uniformed Mexican local policemen helping to load them.

Over the next three days, we sprawled assets over Buffalo, Reynosa, and the Houston/Galveston areas. Cumulatively, we were running command and control for nearly 30 ground assets across these locations, and they were gathering deep intel on the routes and safehouses that served the three hubs. The ground assets were able to locate and pinpoint over 15 safehouses, transit zones, and holding areas that they used to move the children around prior to shipping them internationally. Within these three days, our ground observers and assets estimated that these three points combined moved nearly 1,000 children per week, if not more than that. At that rate, these operations could be responsible for nearly a half a million kids each year. These are not small numbers by any stretch of the imagination. In fact, we had just located the busiest choke points for the international child sex trafficking trade in the Western Hemisphere. We had human assets in each location, and we were preparing for a coordinated attack on the points, but we had to tread lightly. One slip could spell the end of the mission and we could be back to ground zero. Our ground assets reported back that they noticed a shipment of empty shipping containers coming into the port of Galveston. Red, black, and green Maersk type containers came in via semi-trucks, as usual. However, a flat-deck shipping container brought in 30 or 40 dark gray shipping containers to the port. What was odd is that there were workers loading the red, black and green containers but the dark gray containers were placed in a separate loading area, and nobody was loading them. They were brought inside of an old shipping hangar with heavy equipment. Then, the drawback doors for the facility were closed. We had the ground observers work at night to watch the hangar. That evening at nightfall, they reported back movement inside of the hangar. "Lights up, one of the guys said over the comms line." There were lights on inside of the hangar as our observers could see an amber hue radiating from inside of the hangar. "What's going on there"--one of Nantan's men asked. "Don't know, some activity ramping up here, hang tight. Keep the line quiet. I'm getting closer." Our guy walked across the top of a metal catwalk and onto some old scaffolding alongside the waterfront walls to the hanger. He found an open shaft at the roof of the hanger and went inside. We could hear his breath as he appeared to strain in gaining access to the hangar. "Holy shit," he muttered under his breath. "Hundreds of them." We looked at each other around the command center. "More than hundreds. Can't count. Coming out now," he whispered into the microphone. We waited for him to clear out of the building and get back to a safe vantage point.

As our ground asset in Galveston's port got back to safety, he cleared his throat and said, "do you read me clearly?" Yes, we do, loud and clear. What is your observation? Hundreds of them. Fucking hundreds of them, maybe more. I don't know how many. They are coming up through the floor of the hangar. Triple-file lines, up a stairway beneath the floors. They are putting them into gray cargo containers. This would explain the lack of shipments inbound to fill them. No trucks, no vans, no evidence. They were moving through an underground network, like the rat bastards that they were. Hundreds of kids must mean that this is THE major distribution location as none of us had ever seen numbers like this before in one location. Our adversaries had become so brazen that they were moving the equivalent of a typical American town full of children on a monthly basis. They were operating with complete impunity and immunity.

The Buffalo location was different though. Even though we had located the marked guard station, where were the victims? Perry told us that Buffalo was used for only high value victims. High value victims? What does that even mean? Nantan spoke up and told us which types of children are considered to be high value. They weren't high value because of their value in the sexual exploitation networks. They were high value for their organs and blood types. Apparently, there exist wealthy people around the world that pay a premium for the organs and blood of rare children. Buffalo was where the RH negative blood type kids passed through, in addition to children that had strong genetic code in their DNA and were viable candidates for organ donation to the children of wealthy and powerful people around the world. It couldn't get any more sinister than this in my opinion. Perry told us that shipments through this checkpoint were much less frequent, as the children were rare. Once a month, they were bringing through a caravan of cars and trucks with actors that appeared to be the children's families. He said that the caravans usually came through within the same day and always traveled in blue Toyota SUVs. They always went to the marked guard shack so that the guard would let them through.

We had the intelligence that we needed now. The routes, tactics, and personnel involved were all being observed. It was April 14th at this time and only forty-eight hours from the meeting of the minds in Vegas. We knew that we needed to move quickly. We expanded our footprint in the three locations and had assets flown out to each of the locations. While Nantan had a large expansive network of ground assets, seemingly all over the world, there were a select few individuals that he called "part time help." The part time help was reserved for emergencies and high value missions only. Former army Rangers, navy SEALs, hired hitmen, and men "who make bad things happen and make people go away." They were reserved for the most important times, and this called for bringing them all into service. We had pipe hitters on the way to each of the locations and two of Nantan's longtime advisers coming to join our group here in Nevada. I knew that it was time to solidify the battle plan and chart the tactical aspects of the operation. We were operating on a different level now. It wasn't as clandestine as before and we were building a shock force to run this network into the fucking ground.

## 19: Contributions

In every person's life conquest, there are defining moments that tell the tale of who we are and who we were. Whether those moments shine a positive light or a gloomy shadow on our names is up to us to decide. Throughout the journey, I learned what the world really looked like. I was a big fan of science fiction movies, and the Matrix series was my favorite. There were striking similarities to the Matrix and the world that I now operated in. People can go through life, living on the surface, and existing in a predetermined simulated world. School, college, student debt, corporate America, work until your 65, retire, and die when you are 73 ½ years old. Play it safe and leave this world quietly. Or we could decide whether or not we wanted to be truly free from the forced reality of ignorance that so many consume and live. We were the group that chose the red pill. We were the ones that chose to not only see the truth, but to create our own truths. When there is no resistance, innocent people have always suffered. This has been written throughout history. Nazi Germany, Stalin's Russia, Mao's China, and many more of these cases around the world. The resistance was the break in the levy and was sometimes the only thing standing in the way of complete domination from evil sociopaths, narcissists, and psychopaths. We were that resistance, and we would continue to stand right in the middle of the tank's path until their treads wore down to smooth metal. Feelings and emotions were separate from operations and in order to pull this off, the task at hand was all operations. We had a large network throughout the world, and we needed to call on the loyalists to mobilize and complete the operation. We needed all hands on-deck, and we didn't have to beg for that to occur. We all called on our separate yet connected units. Nantan's network was massive and well-funded. They pooled the majority of international resources and even a solid percentage within the US. I focused on gathering cyber resources to do the dirty work on the wire.

The two individuals that Nantan called in had arrived on-site with us. As they walked down the metal stairway, the CIA fella greeted them as if they knew each other. They didn't smile at all, nor did they acknowledge the other people in the room. They were wearing tactical military green pants and black long-sleeved shirts. I could tell by their gait that they were not military though. They were polished in a different way and were absolutely covered in tattoos. One of them had a large, serrated knife tattooed on the left side of his neck. They went straight into the command room and began setting the table with materials that they had brought with them. They each carried medium-sized black roller suitcases and a black backpack. They put their cases on the ground and unzipped them, flipping the lid over. The other guys and I watched them as they began to unpack their cases. One of the cases contained a disassembled rifle, long silencer and a considerable amount of ammunition. The other case belonging to the gentleman with the neck tattoo didn't contain a rifle though. It was packed full of plastic explosives, charging systems, and remote detonators. The front part of the case had three metal containers carrying various types of hazardous liquids. Two of them were marked with red tape and the third had a bright green X marked on it. I backed up as I saw the volume of explosives that this man had in the case. He looked up at me and asked Nantan where he could mix some liquids as we were in an enclosed area. We were standing next to enough explosives to wipe out 5 city blocks. Nantan signaled the man to follow him. Nantan took him into the area that had the upward ventilation shaft. The man lit a cigarette and watched as the smoke raised quickly up through the ventilation system and away from our work zone. "This will be fine," the man said as Nantan walked back over to us. As the other man finished unloading his case, he separated everything out on the table in an organized fashion. There was a tactical assault rifle, extra magazines, two handguns, and silencers for all of them. Aside from this, he pulled out three claymore mines from his backpack.

Nantan's crew and I sat at the mission table and began to map out our strike zones. Mexico, Galveston, Buffalo, and Las Vegas. We had four different areas of operations (AoR) that we needed to coordinate. Nantan worked to get resources ready in each location. We were readying assets in each location. At this phase of the operations planning, we had surmounted seventeen people in Mexico, eight in Buffalo, thirty for Galveston, and just six people for Las Vegas. In total, the mission had over sixty ground assets across the four locations. Each location was assigned a squad leader, appointed directly by us. We made sure that the squad leaders at each location had the full scope of the mission in their briefings as we sat with them on a virtual conference call. We talked logistics about the larger mission with them together, then broke out into smaller sub-groups. Each team was assigned a mission team within our facility and a communications channel directly for them. There existed four separate war rooms in our bunker, one for each mission. The communications channels that we leveraged were completely encrypted and each of the locations were using separate encryption keys so that if one channel were to be compromised, the others could still remain independently protected. Each mission also had a cyber asset assigned here at our headquarters. Nantan put one of his men on each of the mission zones. Mexico, Galveston, and Buffalo were all assigned to his people. However, Las Vegas was left without. I wondered why we had not solidified the resource to care for the Las Vegas operations yet.

The soldiers at these locations were not weekend warriors. They were truly dangerous motherfuckers. These were the types of people that the military didn't want. They were the forgotten sons of the world. These were the types that you would call when you wanted to assassinate top tier hitmen. They were real "break glass" types, and all of them knew exactly what they were doing. It was interesting to see the reach and magnitude of our resources. Just like our adversaries, we were coordinated, calculated, and determined. I don't believe that our enemies had fathomed our power until this mission. Before this, we struck in the shadows and always walked back into the forest. However, this day was different, and we were ready to shock our enemies in a way that no military, police force, or paramilitary operation had ever done before. The mission directors for each zone had a live video feed on each one of the staging areas in Mexico, Buffalo and Galveston. We had the three location's video feeds on the TV monitor in our mission control room. I could see several people on the video's gearing up. They had professional equipment too. Night vision goggle sets, rifles, explosives, communications gear, body armor, and everything in between. We watch them getting things ready for their local missions.

Nantan stood next to me, and we talked for some time. "Look at this. Everything seems to be coming together, doesn't it? The power of our cause is strong and has touched each one of these men in some way throughout their lives.," Nantan said. I asked him what he meant by that. He said that all of the people that were getting ready for the strikes were once victims in some way. He laughed and said, "you think that we're paying them to be a part of this."?" I shrugged my shoulders. He responded, "son, these people want this as much as you, me, and everyone in this bunker. They are willing to give their lives for this, and some will. They have accepted that, just as you and I have. We are willing to die for this. I will always be willing to give myself for this cause, just as you always were and always will be. This mission that we are about to embark on is not meant to put a dent in this disease. It is meant to bring them to their knees, make them beg for mercy, and create such a slow death that the messages will ripple across their community for one hundred years. We will do it again, and again, and AGAIN as long as it takes. This mission that we serve will go on without us. We are lighting the everlasting candle in the tunnel of darkness for so many that are victimized by this evil. They will always know their way and be able to see the flicker of the candle through the tunnel. This time, we're turning the fucking floodlights on for them." Fuck yes...The hair on my neck and arms stood at attention and I looked across our facility and the TV monitors, seeing everyone working together. I had never seen anything like this before. An entire network of volunteers, unpaid, and completely free; working in unison with one another to bring down the evilest empire that existed. I immediately recognized why this man was revered by so many. Alone, we were victims but together we were a formidable and tactical force.

Nantan called the CIA guy, the two stoic hitters, and me into the back room. He looked at us as we stood in a line facing him and said, "This is precisely the crew that I want for Las Vegas, and I couldn't think of a more capable pod of people that I trust. I know that you will succeed. This is the most important mission, and you all know that. We must be calculated in how we operate here. Our ultimate goal is to bring this operation down from the top. I noted that the mission plans stated six people for Las Vegas. However, we had Nantan, CIA guy, and the two hitters. That made five of us in total. "Nantan, who's number 6?," I asked. Nantan looked at me and said, "without Perry, this operation isn't possible my friend." Perry was our canary in the coal mine in this operation and was already embedded with the enemy. He was our Trojan horse and was the key to our success. Nantan had been planning with Perry for quite some time on this operation and they had formulated a plan together. Perry was to be at the conference coming up and would be inside of the inner circle. As I said before, he had garnered the trust and confidence of our adversaries in a way that none of us were ever capable of before. Perry was going to be the ace up our sleeve and would get us access to the meeting by any means possible. We needed to be in the exact location before they were. Perry was going to help make that happen for us. Since Perry had been attached to these people, he was providing counterintelligence and cyber protection for them. That meant that Perry had access to meeting locations prior to their encounters. He was in charge of ensuring that the digital spaces were clear and void of espionage capabilities. Also, Perry was used to provide assurance that the physical spaces were not outfitted with listening or video devices that could potentially compromise these people. This time, Perry would be doing the exact opposite of that and would be granting us full, live, unadulterated access to the meeting space. Perry was in charge of giving us eyes and ears. Then, once we had full visual and audio, we were going to execute the mission.

It was an important facet of this mission that Las Vegas was the last stone turned, after Mexico, Buffalo, and Galveston. It was paramount that the leaders in Vegas had no communications with any of their counterparts in the three other locations as well. The final strike was on the meeting in Vegas, timing was everything. Mexico was first, Buffalo second, Galveston 4th, and then…welcome to Sin City. Over the course of the day prior to the strikes, we worked tirelessly to stack the deck in our favor. For Mexico, we called in some resources from the opposing Mexican cartels and tipped them off that there was a big deal going down in Reynosa. Our resources convinced them that their rival cartel was going to be moving a large shipment of cocaine and fentanyl from Reynosa to Texas on the day of our strike plans. However, we offset the location to about two miles from the airfield. We did this to ensure that the local police would be distracted by their presence and if we ran into a gun battle against the actual cartel moving these kids, we could multiply our local force from 17 to 100, with the help of the rival cartel sicarios. We had them on standby for our orders.

In Buffalo, the eight assets that we had on the ground were a mix of American and Canadians. There was one woman on the team that was leading the ground operations. Nantan told me that she was a close friend of his. She was definitely Native American. She had long jet-black hair wrapped in a braided ponytail down to her lower back with a long curved-blade dagger in a sheath strapped against the outside of her thigh. He told me that she was from the Iroquois tribe that once controlled most of the northeastern United States. As I looked closer at the ground operators that were assigned as leaders, I noticed that they all resembled tribe members. In fact, all of them had the same long curved-blade daggers strapped to their thighs. They were leading together, and I had imagined that they had been sent there.

The Buffalo mission plan was relatively straightforward. 3 assets would be mounted on the Canadian side of the border around 2 km from the crossing station. Three would be on the US side, a few hundred yards away from the crossing station, and two would be responsible for descending on the corrupt agent that was manning the guard station. For Galveston, now this was a bit more complex than the others. Galveston was the stake through the heart of this operation and if we executed properly, we would cause the earthquake that we so desired. Galveston was to be performed by land, sea, and air. We would be sending drones in first. Rather high altitude for small drones as well, nearing 2,000 feet above. We would perform intelligence, surveillance, and reconnaissance above the hangar and surrounding areas. Then, a strike force would make their way into the facility from the two side entrances and the roof. Once inside, they would then open the hangar doors to allow the rest of the crew to enter. If things went badly, the teams were to rendezvous on the portside gateway to the facility.

Over the course of that day, I worked to get things ready from a digital perspective. I had hooks into security camera systems within the city of Reynosa, traffic cameras at the Buffalo checkpoints, port security video feeds from Galveston, and lots of open cameras on the Vegas strip. Since we had identified most of the major players through Perry, we began mounting an operation from the financial side as well. It was our intention to strike with not only physical violence, but also monetarily. Our network was filled with resourceful people in sleeper cells that were awaiting further instructions. We had a few assets within the major banks of the United States, and we had a strong relationship with personnel in the bank of the Grand Cayman Islands for those members moving money in and out of the country. Needless to say, we had our financial hit list ready and handed it over to our finance operators. The goal was clear and simple. On the day of the strike, we were going to be draining the accounts of the major players and the house accounts. In total, we estimated that we could be looking at 450 million US dollars. That is quite a bit of cash, but this industry was much wealthier than that. We knew that they had their assets in other investments as well. Government bonds and real property were on our list for later plundering.

Moving 450 million dollars is not an easy task though. Our plan needed just a little bit of extra help. Through the help of some interesting hackers out of Russia, we purchased access to the IRS financial crimes alerting system. That meant that when we moved the 450 million out of the accounts and immediately purchased crypto currencies, those transactions would be flagged as suspicious somewhere along the line. Those flags get sent into the IRS for review and if the IRS validates the flag, then it would go to the FBI's financial crimes division. If we could jump the IRS step and prolong that process, by the time the issues were reported to the FBI, the money would be washed through at least five different crypto markets and distributed to individual crypto wallets $9,999 dollars at a time. We wrote an automated program to take care of those smaller transactions and it wouldn't take more than an hour or two to complete.

Phase 3 was the destined to be the death blow. We call this the Chernobyl effect. This phase included publicity and the media. When you coordinate such an operation, it would be a crying shame if it didn't make front page news all around the world. We wanted the radiation of these events to spread around the world for decades. Our goal was to root out the rats hiding under the floorboards and make it nearly impossible for them to move with impunity. The lasting effects of our operation must include significant financial disruptions, otherwise they would likely reorganize and surface again. We preemptively contacted resources within a news organization that focuses on whistleblowers. One of Nantan's crewmembers set up a conversation between a few of us and the people running some of the biggest stories in international corruption. We didn't give any form of information on who we were or what we were about to do. Nor did we let them know where our location was. To them, this could be some sort of a hoax. We told them that we had definitive proof that we had uncovered a network of high-ranking US officials, military members, top level executives, and business moguls that were running a massive underground child exploitation and slavery ring. Our faces were concealed with masks and glasses on the video call with them. They asked us many questions, but we promised them that they would have all of the information that they needed very soon. They were skeptical, but nevertheless gave us their undivided attention.

After the call was finished, I realized that we were ready. Well, we were as ready as we were ever going to be. Our ground assets were in staging areas in Mexico, Buffalo, and Galveston. Perry was relatively off the radar, but I was sure that he was preparing for the Las Vegas strike as well. We had our financial assets ready within the banks, cryptocurrency wallets prepared for the funds transfers, and a few trustworthy whistleblower journalists awaiting our information once we were ready. The bunker was calm, and everyone was relaxing. We had all been to battle before, so this was a familiar sentiment to all of us. The day before a mission is always slow. Time just slows down when you are aware of what awaits you the next day. Every so often, you get that rolling feeling in your gut like the first time you fell in love. It is more than butterflies though. Nauseous doesn't do the feeling justice either. It's just something that warriors feel before battle. I could help myself but to image if the ancient Roman gladiators felt similarly before they walked through the halls of the Colosseum. In our case, there were no chants from the crowd.

The only sounds that we heard were the cries of the children. The desperation of their souls, yearning to be released from the entrapment that was overwhelming them. We knew what we were about to attempt, but the children didn't know that anyone was coming for them. I wished that we could have reached out to let them know we were coming. I wished that we could have communicated with them. To tell them to hold on another day, just one more day and not to give up hope. There were people out here that didn't accept them as a statistic. There were people in this bunker and around the world in our network that were not satisfied in leaving these things with law enforcement or some corrupt justice department. We were here, ready and willing to die for them. I wish they could have heard us that day.

Hold on.

## 20: Retribution

20:00 Hours: The sound of duffle bags shuffling across the dust-covered concrete of the bunker woke me up. I opened my eyes and looked across the facility to see a couple of the guys packing up. The two hitters were sitting down on a wooden bench that was aside the main door leading to the stairwell. Their bags were packed and ready to go already. They were geared up, wearing all black tactical pants, body armor and mechanics gloves. Nantan was pouring a new batch of coffee for us. His men opened their computer screens and flipped a map over the table. The battle plans had been precoordinated in the days before, so this was more than a rehearsal. The TV screen lit up in the command area with the live feeds of our operators in Mexico, Buffalo, and Galveston. There was a separate computer monitor that had been setup off to the right on a separate table. The screen was blank, but the monitor was powered up. Just a blue screen painted the monitor, like it was ready for another video feed.

I heard the snapping of Velcro as the crews from our ground operations secured their gear and body armor. I had my eye on the Galveston crew and the leader was going around the room and talking to each one of her people. I could tell that she was a natural-born killer by her demeanor. She was comfortable in battle. A lot of these people were. I knew my place in this operation. I was providing digital close-range support from a digital perspective. I could shoot, and if it came down to it I would. However, people are placed where they provide the most value. My position was close range, but my job was to ensure that we had everything that we needed to secure the Vegas operation and carry out our mission.

Nantan gave me control of the operation, and he entrusted me to fulfill that obligation.

0030 Hours: Nantan, the CIA spook, the two hitters and I walked up the metal staircase to the top of the bunker. Nantan's two killers took the lead immediately as soon as we reached the top. They walked outside of the doors without hesitation, no fear, and they walked with a purpose to the blacked-out Mercedes Benz Sprinter van. They slid the doors open and made way for us to get inside. The van had everything that I needed. It was a rolling command center, equipped with anything that a hacker could imagine. Radio frequency devices, an electromagnetic pulse generator, high-gain antenna systems, monitors, lock pick sets, satellite comms, and everything in between. The floor of the van was modular as well. We opened the latch in the middle of the van and the guys put their heavy weaponry in there. There was a SAW machine gun already inside, accompanied by a few thousand rounds of ammunition. Duct tape, rope, zip ties, and a large medical kit were strapped to the netting on the right side. Nantan took the driver's seat and called me to ride shotgun. The three others sat in the back of the van, and we rolled out. The van was loaded up with enough gear to take out a small paramilitary force. I couldn't help thinking, would we really need all of this shit? I hoped not, but we were prepared for war.

As we made our way to the city, I looked out of the window and saw the lights of the Vegas strip illuminating the sky. This was our walk through the halls of the Colosseum. It was a quiet one, no chanting. They say that when death is close to you, you can feel it. I could not help but notice that my senses were more alive than I had felt in quite some time. My heartbeat was steady, not too fast. My hands did not shake or tremor. I was anxious, and ready to confront whatever came to me. The fear was gone and no longer a part of my being. The CIA guy

217

tapped me on the shoulder from the back of the van. He showed me a small laptop monitor that had a blurry video feed. It was someone walking with some type of a pinhole camera attached to the front of their body. It was about head-level so it must have been attached to a pair of glasses or a hat. "Is that Perry?" I asked. He nodded. "Perry's online guys, we got a feed" he replied to the group. Nantan looked into the rearview mirror and gave a half smile.

0430 Hours: We pulled up to the casino parking lot as Nantan took us up the ramp into a parking garage that was being renovated. There were no cameras on this side of the casino, but it had a great vantage point on the front side of the resort. I could see the large tower where all of the resort guests were staying. A few floors were relatively dark. I counted from the ground floor up to seventeen as my eyes scanned the building from the bottom up. Floor seventeen was dimly lit, barely visible light coming from inside as the curtains were closed. I could see the outline of light coming from inside of the room over the edges of the curtains. Floor 17 had two large windows that spanned the entire floor. It was some type of a penthouse suite to presidential quarters. These were usually reserved for special VIP guests only. The floor was certainly occupied and there was activity there. As we rounded the next corner up the parking garage ramps, we saw the top floor of the garage coming near. Nantan drove the van to the top and parked aside a closed stairwell entry door. He put the van into reverse and tucked us inside three large dumpsters that were just slightly higher than the top of the van. We had good concealment.

Nantan's men pulled a tan duffle bag from underneath one of the seats and opened it up. It had some uniforms inside of it as they handed them to one another. They tossed one to Nantan as the two hitters put them over their clothes. They were replicas of hotel maintenance

218

jumpsuits. Navy blue with gold logos on the breast pockets. They donned the hats to accompany the uniforms as well. I could still see a slight outline of their body armor underneath the uniforms, but you would have to be looking for that to notice. The two hitters and Nantan would be going inside. Mr. CIA and I would be rendering our services from within the van. He would be in charge of overseeing operations in Galveston, Mexico, and Buffalo. I was the close-range support for Vegas. It was important that he and I were directly next to each other as timing was everything from here on out. If we fucked up the timing on this, the entire mission was at risk of failure. Nantan would be going inside first and gaining access to the maintenance elevator with some social engineering. The two hitters would follow closely behind him to provide coverage if needed. They didn't have the softest personalities, so Nantan would need to use his skills in politics and wordsmithing to ensure that they gained entry. All three of them had audio connection live feeds back to the van and to the bunker command center. We had fallback support at the bunker, and they would dictate the protocol if we or anyone else were to be compromised.

The crews in the port of Galveston, Mexico, and Buffalo were ready and in-position. We waited for Perry's signal. I could see his video feed more clearly now as he appeared to be entering an elevator and heading up to the seventeenth floor. As the elevator ascended, he looked down at his hands and dropped a metal key slowly down his leg and pushed it with his foot underneath the edge of the elevator wall. As the elevator stopped on the seventeenth floor, he inserted a duplicate key into a lock beside the seventeenth floor button and turned the key. The elevator beeped a few times and the doors slid open. As Perry exited the elevator, he ensured that he scanned right and left with his head a couple times slowly to give us a visual of the floor. He turned left and walked to the suite's door and knocked. "Lamplit" he said softly, as the door opened up. We counted one man at the door, armed. Another was on the left-hand side. Both were wearing black suits without ties. They were clearly providing security. Perry was inside of the room and began to check the room for any signs of digital spy gear or radio frequency interference. His bug detector was a dummy unit. If he were using a real bug detector, it would have been sending alarms from the video feed mounted on his body. It was quiet but blinking green as he scanned the room. He unhooked the phone unit from the room and cut the incoming Wi-Fi router off by removing the ethernet connection from the back of it. He went into the bathroom and began to scan the area for bugs as well. We watched as he took out a small black box with adhesive strips on the back of it and placed it underneath the sink area. I knew what it was.

I had used these before in Afghanistan with him. It was a cellular signal jammer that was remotely activated when you wanted to knock out cell phone communications and GPS tracking in a certain area. It had a radius of about 200 meters or so and was very effective when engaged. Perry had also set up a small out of band video and audio recording unit on the bar that overlooked the common area of the penthouse. He wanted to ensure that we had the video and audio evidence that we needed for later.

0630 Hours: As we watched between Perry's video feed and the other locations staging areas, I noticed one of the guards inside of the casino penthouse heading to the door. He opened it up and there were three men and a lady at the door. Helena Clark stood behind the three men. She was unmistakable. Her evil gaze as she parted the waters of men like Moses cutting the sea and walking through the door. "Time to fucking move" Nantan said. "Scott, you stay right here with Clark, understand me."?" So, the CIA guy had a name apparently. I didn't peg him as a Clark to be honest. "If shit goes sideways, we need you both to salvage as much of this operation as humanly possible. Clark, you know which safehouses to bounce through if needed." Nantan and his two hitters stepped out of the van. His two men carried one case each and a toolkit. Nantan was empty handed, except for his curved-blade knife that he carried underneath the uniform. I could see the video feeds of the ground operators leaving their staging areas and heading out. After all of this planning, it was all finally happening. We had a live radio feed to Nantan and his two men as I instructed them on which routes to take in getting into the casino areas with less traffic. I was keeping them to the maintenance routes through the basement of the resort areas. The two men always stayed at least 100 yards behind Nantan in case he had to do some talking. It was best that he cleared the way first.

Perry's video feed was still live as by this time, at least ten more people had entered the penthouse and sat down in the common area. They were eating horderves and getting settled in. The room was large and had a circular sofa surrounding almost a podium-like raised carpeted area in the middle. Everyone was seated as Perry stayed back and pretended to be productive on his laptop. Helena took the middle stand and greeted the group. She began to discuss their operations and some of the "successes" of the year. They were treating this as if it were some types of a fucked up corporate retreat. She paid particular attention to an older gentleman sitting on the end of the sofa. Clark and I took a closer look at him and realized who he was. One of the biggest diamond traders in the world. He was notoriously wealthy and had a firm grip on 50 percent of the diamond trade throughout North America, South America, and Africa. These were the types of people sitting around the campfire that day. The conversations between the group continued as they talked specifics. Details, methods, identities, financials, and everything else. I listened to their conversations and cavalier demeanors as if they were selling plastic goods. These were humans. These were children that they had commoditized, tortured, and sold. Lives, not commercial goods. Lives of children and they felt nothing. They talked about the Galveston operation and drop spots through Mexico. They continued to talk more about other locations that we had no information on prior. East Asia, the Emirates, and even in the capitol of the US, Washington DC They flaunted their corrupt political partners on both sides of the aisle in DC, and even referred to them by their full names. It was insane. We were witnessing the largest collection of condemning evidence that we had ever encountered. They went on for nearly 45 minutes like this.

Nantan came over the radio. "We are in close. We made it through, no problem." I was relieved that he had made it into the resort and past the security. Now, it was my job to coordinate the next moves. I had to tell Nantan when it was time for them to knock on the door to that room after Perry gave me the signal. At that very moment, we would give the green light to engage targets on the ground in Galveston, Mexico, and Buffalo. Perry would activate the cell signal jammer inside of the penthouse so that communications in and out would be futile. If any of our enemies on the ground in Galveston, Mexico, or Buffalo attempted to contact the leaders, there would be no chance of a signal reaching them. In battle, if you can remove communications capabilities, then success is an expected outcome.

"You ready for this?" Clark asked me. "I've been waiting for this moment for my whole life" I said back to him. We both laughed and focused back on the mission. Perry was moving from the back of the room closer to the door. He stepped into the bathroom and looked in the mirror and smiled back at me through his video feed. I gave Nantan the green light and at the same moment, Perry reached into his pocket and pressed a switch on the cell signal jammer. I heard the audio from Nantan's radio connection back to the van. 3 knocks on the door as he said "Lamplit." I heard the door unlock and a man inside shouting loudly. One gunshot rang out, unsilenced. Then, a series of 10-15 shots went off. The 10-15 shots were silenced, so I had a feeling that they came from Nantan or his hitters. I heard the meeting attendees yelling inside, "call for help, call for help!" There was a lot of commotion in the room as I listened intently over the radio. Perry's video feed had gone out after he hit the cell jammer switch as it was using a cellular signal to transmit back to us. One of Nantan's two men spoke over the radio to us. "Nantan's hit bad. Guards are out of commission, room is secured. Close the fucking door." Nantan was hit, but he was alive.

Clark gave the green light for Galveston, Mexico, and Buffalo. Galveston was first up as we watched the video feed live. Our ground assets descended on the shipping hangar. They entered from the side entrances and went into the narrow corridors of the hangar's perimeter. The screen to the left showed Buffalo. Some of the crew had detained three Toyota SUVs about one mile before the crossing station. The blue Toyota SUVs were carrying high value children. The other men scrambled to the side of the guard station that was facing a wooded area. One of the men tossed a glass tube inside of the station's window and I could hear the glass break on the floor. The corrupt and complicit guard inside was meeting his fate by way of a noxious chemical gas. We watched the video as the guard slowly choked to death, alone inside of that small border shack. Mexico began to unravel as well. The team had intercepted a caravan of vehicles heading for the airstrip in Reynosa. The crew did not know how many kids were in the vehicles, but they said that there were three small buses that looked to be full. The team took out the pilot and the two crew members that were waiting at the airstrip. There were three other planes there waiting for their "cargo," so the team turned them over to the cartel's sicarios. We had paid them well to take these scumbags back to their farms and do with them what they please. Cartel sicarios were notorious for making people suffer.

The Galveston operation was in full swing. All of the team members had made it into the building safely. They made their way into the core of the building, taking down a few guards that were scattered throughout the hangar. They came into the central section of the building and met some resistance. I heard the crew leader shout a command to her personnel "Light em' up!." We saw flashes coming from the barrels of our team inside of the hangar. It went on for a good 3 or 4 minutes until everything was quiet. We were watching the carnage take place as our crew on the ground massacred the threats inside of the hangar. There were bodies of men everywhere inside of the central point of the facility. AK-47's lay beside most of the enemy troops, some had pistols. There were three of them that were still alive, but not for long as the female lead went through the facility and scalped each one of them. She tucked the scalps of her enemies into pant cargo pockets and walked through, stepping over the lifeless bodies. The night vision goggle live feed was steady now as she and her men went into the tunnel system below the hangar. We saw hundreds of eyes glowing of children crouched on the floor, some laying down with their heads down. We could hear the cries of fear and relief as they realized who these people were standing in front of them. The team began to carry out a few of the children that were too afraid to move. The rest of the children followed the team up the stairs and into the hangar. The line of them seemed to never end, it was flowing like a river. One of the men on the team was taking count as they moved them from underground to above. "50, 60, 70, 80, 90." Clark and I looked at each other and talked over the radio to Nantan. "We've got almost 100 from Galveston already and they're still coming up. One killed in action from our team. Everyone else is ok, a couple wounded." We listened back on the live feed from Galveston. "130, Jesus Christ 150, I lost count. They are piling out of here. We got over three hundred for sure." We went back to the radio and told Nantan "We've got 300 or more there."

Our crew in Galveston began to move the mass of children out of the hangar and into a staging facility onboard a Norwegian ship at the docks. We had set up an offshore operation for them to remain there until the news stations could capture the story and make all of this too public to obfuscate. It was a sovereign ship that was dedicated to an international amnesty program. They moved them down the dark corridors of the shipping yard and onto the ship ramp. The female team leader was in the front of the line carrying two children, one in each arm to the ship ramp. Once they had all of the children in there, they gave us the all clear." The ship began to disembark as we watched our ground team boarding small Zodiac boats and heading down the coast.

Perry, Nantan, and the two killers were inside of the Vegas penthouse and had secured the area. Perry had ensured that the entire meeting inside the penthouse was recorded with damning evidence to put this circle into the dirt. Helena Clark was lying face down and zip tied at the hands. The other members sat on the floor awaiting the orders of our team inside the penthouse. As Clark and I watched the video feed from inside of the penthouse, we heard the closed channel of our police radio scanner begin to chirp. Our central command center back at the bunker pressed through our radio connection. "You guys have fucking company coming your way fast. Convoy heading toward you. ETA 3 minutes, maybe less." "Where are they coming in from?" I shouted back to them. "Everywhere! Get the fuck out of there. We are picking up at least 10 SUV's with significant heat signatures inside heading from the east. We've got armed casino security rolling in from outside of the resort right now as well. Go! Abort mission, get the fuck out of there!"

We relayed the message over the radio to Nantan and gave him a route out of the building. "Second fire exit, go out the door, take a left down the hall. It's a private penthouse emergency egress system. Head down three floors to level 14 then cut over to the maintenance elevator and drop to the basement. We will pick you up there." Nantan paused for a few seconds. I could hear his breath slow down and become focused, then he spoke. "Perry, take that nasty bitch back to the bunker. She's got what we need to blow this system out for the next thirty years." Perry paused inside of the room and tried to get a few words out before Nantan cut him off. "Now, you know what we need to do. This is far from over. Get her down to the basement." Perry's camera panned across the room to Helena. He ran over to her and placed a black cloth sack over her head and tied it off at the neckline before picking her up off the ground by her zip tied arm. Perry headed to the penthouse door, cracked it open and took a look down the hallway. He ripped the door open and pushed Helena outside first, then pulled her to the left down the hall. We now had direct comms with Perry as Clark led him through the building to the fourteenth floor. One of Nantan's men set claymore mines in the hallway outside of the penthouse while the other rigged the room with C-4 plastic explosives laid at the base of the room all the way around the baseboards. Nantan got up and dragged himself over to the large glass window and shot through it with his rifle. He set up a bipod on his scoped rifle and hung it out the window, using it as a vantage point. One man was facing the door with his SAW machine gun, one was handling the explosive charge in his hand with a rifle in his other, and Nantan was ready to rain hell from above. Everything was quiet.

Clark hopped into the driver's seat of the van. "Ready Scott? Let's go get Perry huh?" He stepped on the gas and floored us into reverse. I was listening over the radio at Nantan. I could hear a bit of commotion coming from outside of the room some distance away. I heard tires screeching across the pavement as we barreled down the offramps of the parking garage, dropping floors quickly. I saw the caravan of black SUV's coming inbound from the east side of the building, directly in view from the smashed penthouse glass windows. I could see the penthouse curtains flapping in the wind above and could see a long barrel hanging from the edge of the penthouse window. The SUVs came in single file in front of the building. The sounds from outside of the penthouse over the radio got louder and closer.

I watched as Nantan's rifle fired the first shot downward at the lead SUV. I could hear the smash of the glass on the vehicle's windshield. Then, all hell broke loose. The first claymore mine erupted over the radio in the halls of the penthouse entry point. "BOOM," then another one a few seconds later. It was hailing bullets from the seventeenth floor downward at the SUV's as the men piled out of their vehicles looking for cover. I could see them hitting the ground quickly as Nantan painted them from above like a goddamned archangel. The SAW machine gunner began to fire inside of the room toward the door as the men began to ram the door from the outside. It was complete mayhem. The firing was so loud and was coming from all directions. We got to the bottom floor of the parking garage as Clark spun the van around and reversed us down the maintenance ramp into the basement. Perry was coming in over the radio. "Shit, I'm almost there. I can hear them. They are closing in on me." Clark floored the van in reverse all of the way through the basement floor. I could see the loading dock nearing behind us. That was the meeting point.

"Scott, get the fuck up here and drive. I'm getting out!" What the fuck? Where are you going? "Perry's not going to make it. They are going to take him out. We have to get him out of there with Helena." Shit! I jumped into the front seat as Clark swung his door open wide. He put his hat on backward and slung his rifle across his chest, tightening the Velcro on his ballistic vest. He looked back at me and gave me a smile before charging toward the loading dock door and into the dark maintenance hallway. I watched as he disappeared into the distance, passing by another shadow coming in my direction. It was Perry, with Helena in front of him. I could see the shadow of Clark running into the building still as he dropped down to one knee and began firing. Muzzle flashes came back at Clark, and he returned fire into the maintenance hallway. I could see 4 or 5 different muzzles flashing as they shot toward Clark. Perry stumbled as he crossed over the loading dock and he and Helena both dropped down the 4-foot embankment and hit the ground. Perry swung open the rear doors and tossed Helena inside and slammed it shut. He came around to the passenger side and got in. Before his doors could close, I slammed on the accelerator.

I watched in the distance as Clark was overtaken by the group inside of the maintenance hallway. Nantan and his men were still firing over the radio as we raced up the ramp and outside of the garage. I could hear the moans of Nantan and his men as they were being hit with rounds. Short thumps after a shot were fired. I could tell that they were all hit badly. Their breaths were fast. That meant that they were likely hit in the chest or lungs. The shots rang out close to their position. I could hear the voices of the men overtaking their position. They got closer as Nantan, and his men began to run low on ammo. I sped across the campus of the casino and could see fire and police lights coming in from the Eastern side. Perry and I stared up into the seventeenth floor window at the flashing of rounds

228

penetrating the room from all sides. The radio became quiet, and the firing slowed down. I heard the door open up to the room and men shouting inside. We watched and listened as they converged on our team's position inside of the penthouse. As I turned the van away from the casino, Perry and I watched the seventeenth floor as it became a ball of fire. Three consecutive rapid explosions rocked the building so hard that it shook my hands on the wheel. The entire seventeenth floor erupted as the windows of the surrounding floors blew out from the concussive blast. They were gone, but our mission never included all of us coming back alive. We had exactly what we needed to take this to the next level.

Between Mexico, Buffalo, and Galveston, we had 450 rescued children combined. The independent news organizations immediately sent the live feeds of our operation, barring any sensitive radio comms between our teams. They had footage of every high-level official inside of that penthouse detailing their crimes. We had a ship in Galveston harbor that would be the biggest media story of the century. There were dead bodies of child traffickers in Mexico, Texas, and Buffalo. An entire floor of the Las Vegas casino was a smoke bomb, and we had the ringleader in our custody. Our plans from here were unknown, but we knew that we had the keystone in gaining the upper hand. The 450 million dollars was mostly recovered and exfiltrated from the bank accounts of them and laundered into cryptocurrencies. After the money was washed, we built a non-profit clandestine organization, dedicated to providing material support and resources to the ones without a voice. We took down the largest underground child exploitation ring that night and became more well-funded than most fortune businesses. We had volunteers from 120 countries pouring in to contribute to our cause and whistleblowers coming out of the woods from deep within private and public organizations around the world. Our hacker community grew to 400 strong and we had surmounted an international militia that would support our future operations. That night, we became the hunters, and we were just getting started.

# Author Bio

Tyler Scott Ward is a veteran of the United States Air Force and former US intelligence agency contractor. He is the owner of the cybersecurity firm "Credence Solutions Group, LLC." and founder of the non-profit organization "The Night-Light Foundation" that is dedicated to combating child exploitation and crimes against children.

Tyler is an "ethical hacker" by trade and information security veteran that has served hundreds of private companies, government agencies and the United States military.

www.ingramcontent.com/pod-product-compliance
Lightning Source LLC
La Vergne TN
LVHW051227050326
832903LV00028B/2271